He went around the tree to see Kobie still in her cat form. She spun toward him and even from this distance, he could see she was unhappy about something. He barely got to sit when she bound over and knocked him onto his back and held him there with one large, firm paw. He frowned. She couldn't be this pissed that he'd stopped her from attacking his friend. "Hey…"

"Blair, you had two phone calls." Daisie came bounding over. "Mom read who called for me. I think Kelsey is a pretty name and," she held out the phone, "Layna too."

Shit. He turned and looked up at the she-cat giving him a hard look. She gave a low yowl at him and then released him and walked into the trees. He blew out a breath and glanced to see Calum leaning against a tree with his arm around a woman with long black hair. "Thanks, Daisie." He held out his hand for the phone and sat up. Out of the corner of his eye, he saw Kobie come back and almost wished it was the cat returning, the look she gave him was not friendly. He did not know why she was mad—okay, getting calls from two women in the past hour made him look like some kind of playboy, but there were explanations. Getting up, he looked over to see Calum's amused look. *Shit.* He'd missed a step or something somewhere.

<u>Writing As: J. Risk</u>

REALMS BOOKS:

THE ALTEREALM SERIES
1 *The Huntress*
2 *The Seer*
3 *The Empath*
4 *The Witch*
5 *The Chronos*
6 *The Warrior*
7 *The Telepath*
8 *The Healer*
9 *The Kinetic*

THE SOLRELM SERIES
Coming soon:

Concealed

GEMINI LEAGUE
Coming soon

Dark Moon

COURAGE

Animal Senses Series Book 4

Jacqueline Paige

Chapter One

Blair inhaled deeply, assessing all the scents that surrounded him. Slowing down, he approached the cliff's edge and sat. He checked the air again, he found nothing that shouldn't be there. Slumping, he huffed out a breath and slid forward until he was almost hanging over the edge.

He'd been at Bruce's for two weeks now and he wasn't feeling more settled with the turmoil rolling inside of him. Kelsey was mated to Gage. He'd known for years it was coming—*everyone* knew it was going to happen, but that didn't make the pain lessen. He watched some birds take flight in the bush below. Scenting the wind, he checked to see if they flew because of an intruder or not. Satisfied it was nothing important, he looked out across the land.

The last two weeks were meant to be a fix for his broken heart, a distraction, with tasks to occupy his mind and moods that kept bouncing from mopey to furious without warning. It wasn't working on any level. Usually, he enjoyed the change of scenery when visiting Bruce's—it was overpopulated with female shifters of his kind. He hadn't even been able to muster the excitement to flirt with the women. That made him more annoyed than anything. Was he going to be this pitiful always, or was this only a temporary rut he was in? He didn't know, needed to figure it out, but couldn't find the focus to work through it.

He was acting like a pathetic, lovesick—puppy, kitten, or whatever the appropriate equivalent would be. Glancing behind him, he knew he should continue checking the perimeter, but he needed a few more moments of his pity party before he got back to it.

That Tomas asshole had cranked up his game, and all the clans were on high alert. It felt like the Alliance was one step behind lately, and they needed to figure out how that was happening. Females were disappearing from all over. Bruce needed all the help he could get with the many women that lived here. He would not fail—again. Blair shook his head to try and prevent the next thought but was too late. Kelsey and the future Queen of the Alliance, Rayne, were abducted on *his* watch—Straightening up, he decided to get moving. He couldn't go and think about that. His blood pressure sky-rocketed when he did. A run usually helped to clear his head, but he couldn't go too far while he was helping Bruce watch over the clan.

Of course, the one thing that *nothing* helped to erase was the image of Kelsey in the middle of a thunderstorm, soaked and oblivious as she stood in front of Gage in his cat form, and accepted him as her mate. That moment had broken something inside of Blair. He'd been in love with Kelsey for at least five years, could be longer. He wasn't sure the exact moment it had happened—just one day it hit him. He'd spent the day in a fog trying to figure out how to tell her. He never got the chance. The next day he found out that the reason Gage was the jerk he was toward Kelsey, was because she was his mate, and he was trying not to claim her because she was too young. Nothing in his life had been the same since that day. *Nothing.*

Blair glanced to the East and checked for movement. Being here was supposed to be his new start, a cleanse. He chuffed at himself, *stop answering the phone when she calls, and you might stand a chance, idiot.* He looked in the other direction. How could he ignore the call when it was Kelsey? He'd even told Gage he was trying not to answer all the time, but it was Kelsey, and he was just a man. Dropping his chin, he looked at the large white paws on the ground in front of him—okay; he was mostly a man.

Turning, he took off full speed down the incline. When he finished this sweep, maybe Bruce would let him tear apart that old tractor and try to get it running. Mechanics, he understood—it was life that was a puzzle for him. Gage's old man, Ed, who was his Alpha, had taught him everything he knew about mechanics, big equipment, and repairs alongside Gage, Jake, and Gary. For that, he would always be grateful. That alone was also the reason he hadn't acted on the idea of going back to his birth clan. He owed Ed for giving him a purpose in life. His mother, before she passed away, had sent him to the Lockman clan. He was only two, so he remembered nothing about her but had to trust in the decision. According to Ed, he had some relatives living in his original clan, yet he had discouraged him from reaching out to them. In Blair's mind, if they hadn't contacted him, there must be a reason— or they just didn't care. Of course, someday he might need to know more. Now, was not that time, he couldn't handle any more intense issues in his brain.

Blair always considered himself easy-going or had until his first shift. That day he discovered he was a lethal weapon. He enjoyed the feeling, and it took all his restraint to not attack, maim or kill everything in his path when he was in cat form. If he was being truthful, as a man he often struggled to contain the rage inside of him. There had to be a reason, but he couldn't figure out why. Fury and rage were the only words he could find to describe what he felt and his need to control was insane at times as well. All the more reason to stay with this clan. Ed was a strong Alpha and if Blair's cat ever got out of hand, Ed's son, Gage, was damn good at using his dominant tone to control him.

Grabbing his jeans, Blair pulled them on and zipped them up quickly. Habit had him checking his phone immediately after that. *Six missed calls.* He clenched his jaw and stared at the screen; did he want to look? If any of them were from Kelsey, he'd have to call her back. "Sorry, Sweetie." He stuffed the phone back in his pocket and picked up his boots and shirt.

As he came out of the tree-line, he saw Ketu walking out on the other side of the lane. Ketu shook his head and pulled his shirt over his head. "Nothing out of place."

Blair flipped his shirt over his shoulder. "That's a good thing." It was—despite his need for blood and finding something to take out his frustration on.

Ketu nodded, then brushed his black hair back out of his face. "Bruce said there was trouble at a clan three hours west of us a few days ago."

Blair rubbed his hand over his short hair. "Yeah, I told Devin I'd happily go lend a hand."

Ketu stopped, putting his hand out so Blair would stop. "What are you running from?" He lifted his hand then dropped it again, "we usually have a blast when you're here—" he motioned up and down in front of him, "You're in Blair's body, but man, you are not our Blair."

Blair couldn't help smirk at that. He shrugged, "just working through a few things."

Ketu snorted, "work fast, dude, Layna is moping about like a heartbroken teenager and it's depressing."

Blair started walking hoping that would end the discussion. Layna was Ketu's sister, and she was a sweet woman, for that reason alone, he'd put space between them the moment he'd arrived. As if she knew he was thinking about her, she came out of the barn as they went across the yard. She paused and smiled at him. He gave her a brief movement of his head that he hoped came across as friendly and not offensive. He stopped when he noticed something. In all the years he'd been coming here, he had never put it together. Layna had the same build as Kelsey, her hair was a darker red, but the sprinkled freckles that covered her—*shit*—now he felt like a bastard.

He'd been using sexy little Layna as a substitute all these years. Hell, she even called him the two times her cycle had hit. *Fuck.*

After cursing a few more times inside his head, he turned to go talk to her. Out of the corner of his eye, he saw Bruce come out onto the porch of the house. Bruce leaned on the railing and jerked his chin, calling him over.

Bruce was a big burly man, the kids here called him Teddy Bruce. He may appear to be easygoing, but Blair knew there was a reason Ed trusted him to watch over the clan members here. The scars on the man's face were a testament to how not a teddy-bear-like he could be.

Blair glanced to see Layna noticed as well, and then she turned to go back in the barn. He'd fix that situation later; he decided as he went over to stand below the porch.

"You or Ketu pick up anything?" Bruce spoke softly, as always. Although he'd heard the man use a much louder voice, he preferred the soft version.

"It's clear." Blair shrugged. "I'll check up the road when I run into town later." He glanced over at the tractor.

"Sounds good." Bruce straightened up, "Gage called and told me to tell you to answer your goddamned phone."

Frowning, Blair pulled it out of his pocket. He quickly brought up the call log, five of the six calls were from Gage. The sixth was from Jake. He frowned. "I'll call him now." He waited for Bruce to give him a nod and turn to go back into the house. Hitting send, Blair put the phone to his ear.

"About fucking time. Where the hell have you been?" Gage's tone was harsh.

"Checking the boundaries. What's going on?" Tucking his hand in his pocket, he turned and looked back to the lane that led toward the cliff.

"A complete shitshow," Gage growled. "Coop's hurt and was in the hospital..."

Blair jolted like someone had just slapped him. "What?" Their kind didn't go to hospitals, they had a shifter doctor on call but risking going to a hospital was rare.

"Old fool tried to do something he should have had help

with…"

"Is it serious? Does Ed need me back there?" He would go back. He didn't want to, but it was Coop, so of course, he'd be there.

"Busted tibia, a stand gave out and crushed his leg. Nona and Shaelan say he can't even think about a shift for a month, maybe more."

He didn't know who either of those people was, but it was still the worst thing to happen to a shifter, being injured so badly you couldn't shift. "Fuck." Blair rubbed his hand through his hair.

"He refused to stay in the hospital, so Mom has him put up in the guestroom."

Blair nodded as if Gage could see him.

"Kelsey and I will be home tomorrow—so," he paused for a moment, "we'll be okay in the shop."

"Okay." Blair didn't want to breathe a sigh of relief into the phone, so he moved the phone from his mouth for a second. It was too soon to see Kelsey—*way* too soon. In fact, he didn't know how he'd ever face her again.

"The reason I've been trying to reach you is there's a whole other fucking mess."

Blair frowned, "with what?"

"Devin and Rayne are staying here to try to get this clan back on track…"

Blair still couldn't believe what Gage had told him last week, the sickness of the shit that clan had been doing and suffered through all these years still blew his mind.

"…we now have clans all over this continent with relatives of members that vanished," Gage sighed loudly, "the Alliance has designated a team to look into clans that were with the Alliance when it was formed, but haven't been seen in a while," he mumbled something under his breath, "but here is just a big emotional clusterfuck."

Blair cringed, knowing how well Kelsey would handle all that. For a brief second, he was glad he was a tiger and not a panther. "What do you need from me?"

"Dev's dad asked me to give you a call. The Alliance is ass-deep in so much right now they're running out of bodies to call in. We have all security amped up in all clans, so we can't pull any of those—just in case Tomas tries again."

Blair's whole body tensed at the very mention of the Tomas organization. "Makes sense, don't pull anyone from clan security. Just tell me where you need me—" he shrugged, "or what our King requires of me." It would do him good to have a definitive task to keep himself busy. Any task.

"We need someone to escort nine members of a clan from the border to," he paused and swore, "fuck, I can't even remember the details." He made a soft growling sound, "I don't think I've slept since we got on this damn mountain..."

"Send me the details later. Just tell me where I'm going and when to be there." Blair looked over at his truck, he could be packed up and pulling out in ten minutes.

"I'll get Dev to email you the finer points, but Blair?"

Blair lifted his chin at the tone. "Yeah?"

"I don't know what happened to the rest of the clan, but those nine are the last of it as far as we know."

A chill went down Blair's spine. "I'll get them where they're going safely."

"I know you will. We were going to send Cal with you, but he doesn't want his mate involved in anything like that right now and it's too soon for them to be separated…"

Blair's eyebrows shot up, "Cal's what?"

"Shit—so much has happened, I think we skipped over that." He cleared his throat. "Yeah, Cal found his mate in this village, and let me tell you, I would not mess with her. Vicious little thing." Gage chuckled.

"Holy hell. I can't believe Calum is mated."

"I'll tell you all the details later, and they're quite something."

Blair smirked at Gage's tone, "I look forward to it." He sobered, "I can be ready to head out in ten. Send me the details of where I'm going and make sure Devin has my number and all that."

"I knew we could count on you." Gage's tone was serious again.

Blair bit his tongue, literally, so he wouldn't ask how Kelsey was.

"Shit, I have to go. Marilyn just stomped by with the fork in her hand—I'll get Dev to send you that now." Gage hung up abruptly.

Blair held his phone out and looked at it. He didn't know who Marilyn was or why Gage sounded panicked over her having a fork, but he would definitely be asking him about it the next time they talked. He looked at the phone for a few more seconds, then hit send beside Jake's name. Stubborn old ass Coop was the last thought he had before Jake yelled into the phone over the sound of equipment in the background.

Chapter Two

Kobie paced away and stared at the ground, trying to gather her thoughts before she spoke. Turning, she looked back at Fischer. She'd grown up with him in her life from as far back as she could remember. He was her brother's best friend and unfortunately a one-form, other than that, he was an amazing guy. There had been a few times in her brief life she'd considered making a play for him, he had this boy-next-door cuteness going on with his sandy hair always hanging over his eyes. Kobie was too loyal to the clan to do that and other than his cuteness, she wasn't emotionally attached to him. She blew out a breath and placed her hands on her hips. "I don't know, Fish."

Crossing his arms over his chest, he gave her a sympathetic look. "Look, your brother made me promise that if anything ever happened to call that number and get you out of here," he heaved a visible sigh, "your dad agreed." He moved closer to her but seemed to know not to touch her right now. "I spoke to the Prince of this Alliance and he's a very blunt, straightforward man."

Kobie cleared her throat so she wouldn't give in to the tears that threatened to fill her eyes. *The prince, holy crap.* "I know the Alliance is trustworthy," she turned and looked out across the field, "but crossing the border and leaving here…"

Fischer grasped her shoulder and turned her, so she was looking at him. "There is *nothing* here for you now." He jerked his chin toward the house. "Dad and I can't keep you guys safe." He shook his head. "It's just a matter of time before they think to look here, and we can't go up against them." He frowned, "I still don't know how they didn't track you over here already."

She did but wasn't sharing how and besides, she knew this area better than anyone. Nodding, she stepped a more comfortable distance from him. Reaching up, she pulled the elastic from her hair, then stalled to think as she pulled it all back and put it back in the elastic. "How are we getting over to the other side?" She didn't have a choice. She had to get the others to safety.

"Dad and I will take care of that. Jay and your father came up with the plan, we just have to follow it." He glanced at the barn. "Be ready to go first thing in the morning."

Kobie nodded, "yeah. Did you get me that stuff?"

Fischer pointed to the bag on the ground where he'd been standing then reached into his pocket, "you should have said something if one of you are injured."

She grinned, "we're not. Keep it, give it to whoever they send for us."

He looked at the tube in his hand and then back to her. "For what?"

She chuckled softly, "they'll send a male, he needs to put a dab under his nose."

"Won't that fuck with his sense of smell?"

She tucked her hands into the pocket of her jacket. "Yes, and that's the point." She motioned to the barn with her chin, "we have no idea when Annamarie and Nichelle will come into their first cycle or shift, so—"

"Ah. Got it." He took the cap off and smelled it. "Jesus." He capped it and then stuffed it in his pocket, "that will do the trick."

"It always does." She turned and looked back across the field. "We squeezed about six tubes of it all around the farm before we came over here." She sucked in a breath and cleared her throat. She wanted nothing more than to go over and check if any of them had come back, but after they'd found the three bodies of their men, she knew she had to get the remaining members of the clan out of there. "Were you able to get their bodies out of there, so no one could find them?"

"Yeah. We buried them in the old meadow."

She let out a shaky breath. "Thanks. I'll tell their mates they were buried with respect."

"Do you need anything tonight?"

She knew the food he'd given them was probably still sitting there uneaten. It was hard to force anything down when your universe had just caved in around you. Clearing her throat, she shook her head and turned toward the barn. "No. We'll be ready before dawn." She couldn't look at him and see that expression on his face again. "Thanks, Fish, for everything."

Going through the door, she turned and locked it again. Cortney met her. "Everyone resting?"

Cortney nodded and flipped her long hair out of the way. "Finally, yes." She glanced at the door, a hopeful look on her face.

Kobie shook her head. "Fish buried the ones we found." She cleared her throat, trying to prevent her voice from cracking with emotion. "His dad and he have been taking turns driving over," she shook her head slowly, "no sign of anyone else."

"I tried calling all the numbers we had. There's no answer." She held the cell phone out to her.

"Did you take the battery and card out of the phone after?" Kobie took the phone and stuffed it in her pocket. Fish had given it to her, along with the numbers he knew.

"Yes." Cortney handed her the card and battery. Then put her hand over her mouth. "I don't know what to tell Daisie about her father."

Kobie turned and looked over to where the girls slept.

Daisie was nine and probably the biggest ray of sunshine on the entire planet. The combination of her big blue eyes and shiny strawberry blonde hair just hit you in the heart when she looked at you. "Nothing for now." Kobie took her elbow and guided her further away from the others. "Jay and Dad had an emergency plan lined up for the clan."

Cortney looked surprised for a second. "I suppose it makes sense our Alpha would think of that." She glanced over at her daughter again, then used her fist to wipe a tear off her cheek. "At the rate members were vanishing."

Kobie nodded. "We're going across the border with the protection of the Alliance."

"The border?" Cortney's voice cracked.

"Fish will keep checking for any that return." She had to believe some of them would make it back. "They'll join us when they do." She inhaled a deep breath and exhaled slowly, trying to keep herself calm. "We can't stay here—if they come back..." She couldn't finish.

"I know." Cortney nodded. "When?"

"Dawn." She placed her hand on the other woman's arm. "Go get some rest." She glanced up to the top of the mow. "Torrey and I will take watch until dusk." She waited until she left and went over to where the others were sleeping. Taking a deep breath, Kobie turned and started climbing the ladder to the mow. She'd fill Torrey in on the plan after she checked out the loft door and made sure that there was no one in sight that shouldn't be.

Opening the door a few inches, she looked out it. Cortney and Torrey were technically her elders, but they both had daughters to watch over, so Kobie took it upon herself to take the lead. The others followed suit. Until her father or brother came back, she was the leader of the clan. Despite the other two women being seventeen and seven years older than her twenty-three years, they respected Kobie would do all within her power to keep everyone safe.

Leaning closer to the opening, she inhaled deep and took the scents into her system. She closed her eyes and took a moment to process the many smells. Opening her eyes, she glanced across the mow at Torrey and shook her head. Torrey gave her a quick nod, telling her all was clear on her side too.

Getting up, Kobie walked carefully over the tiered bales to the opening on the other end, she'd spend the next twelve hours walking in a circle checking every direction if she had to. She touched the pocket with the phone in it and wanted nothing more than to call her brother again. She knew she shouldn't. Couldn't.

As she looked out across the barren field, she clenched her jaw. *Jay, you better get your ass back here.* She wanted her father to return too, but she needed her twin in ways she could never explain to anyone. They had a connection, something that had bound them together before they were born. She smiled despite the ache in her heart. Hunting with her brother when they shifted was her most favorite thing on earth. They were in total synch with each other, like they were of one mind.

Sniffling past the emotion, she closed her eyes to inhale the air outside. She had to hold on to the hope that her brother would contact Fish as soon as he was able. She inhaled slowly. *If you need me, I'm there, Jay. Always.*

Chapter Three

They were late. Blair got out of the van and went to the front to look along the road. He scoffed and glanced around, this was a path, not a road. Pulling out his phone, he brought up the email from Devin, he knew he was at the right location—he read it quickly again, and he'd been early. Tucking his phone back in his pocket, he opened the van—which he still couldn't believe he had to drive. It was like he was a soccer mom or something, only he wasn't a mom or a female, and he hated soccer. Grabbing the map, he opened it where he had it creased and studied the route again. He'd already come up with about six alternate plans, just in case he needed them, he had no details on what had happened to this clan, but he would make sure he got them all out safely.

Right now, he was running on pure adrenaline, and thankful for it. He'd driven straight through after he'd picked up the van. It had been a long drive, but with so little detail, he didn't want to not be here on time and leave them stranded in uncertain circumstances. He had a twenty-minute nap when he got here, just enough to keep him going.

Devin said eventually they'd be going to his campground, but they had to be checked out prior, so Blair was to take them to a new location they'd set up. One in the middle of nowhere, about halfway between Gage and Devin's places. He was okay with that, he preferred the middle of nowhere to populated areas.

Grabbing his pack, he stuffed the map in and then looked at the stack of blankets he'd gotten, along with water and some basic snacks. They could pick up anything else required along the way. He had no idea what state they would be in, hell he didn't even know where they were from or what they were running from exactly.

Closing the door softly, he inhaled and focused to see if he could scent any change in the area. Nothing. Jamming his hands in his pockets, so he wouldn't check the time again. He looked to his left, then slowly to his right. The sound of a vehicle had him straighten, his cat rubbed along him, alert and ready as well.

The SUV stopped and a man jumped out of it, leaving it running, the door opened and hurried toward him. Blair looked at the vehicle. No one else was inside. *Shit, something is wrong.*

"Are you Blair?" The guy approached him fast.

Blair's cat didn't like this at all.

"You are definitely a cat, damn, sorry to rush at you, I'm Fischer." He looked over his shoulder. "Pretty sure we were being followed, so I detoured past the turnoff and dropped them off." He pointed to the treed area. "Kobie is leading them through there to meet you here."

He knew he was a cat? Did that mean this clan was cats? Blair inhaled subtly; Fischer was a one-form. His confusion must have shown on his face.

"Yeah, I'm a one-form. Grew up with the Alpha's son." He pulled something out of his pocket and held it out to him. "Kobie says you have to dab this under your nose—" he looked apologetic, "there are two women close to their first cycle…"

Fuck. Just what he didn't need to be contending with. Blair took the tube and opened it. Then held it away from him as long as his arm could manage. "How the fuck am I supposed to keep them safe if I can't smell?"

Fischer started backing toward his vehicle. "Kobie will do that," he smirked, "best hunter in the clan."

That made Blair feel better, not much, but if his senses had to be crippled, having their best hunter alongside him was better than nothing.

"I gotta go. Get back out on the main road in case they're still looking. I'll lead them in the other direction, buy you some time."

Blair nodded.

"If I know Kobie, they'll make it here in about fifteen minutes." He paused halfway in the driver's seat, looked like he wanted to say more, but didn't.

"They'll be safe," Blair told him and he meant it.

"Tell Kobie if any of the others come back, I'll hide them until we can get them out of here." He got in and made fast work of turning around and leaving.

Others? What the hell was going on? He looked at the offensive tube in his hand. Did he have a choice? No, not really. If his cat was distracted with some female in her cycle, it would make this trip ten times harder, not to mention it would piss off any of the males with them if his cat was flirting with their females. He looked at the van. Yeah, cramming ten bodies into that for a long drive was going to be hard enough, never mind distracted cats. This Kobie guy must have balls of steel to request he use this crap and impede his most important sense. Blair shook it off, he'd probably do the same to protect his clan. He had to respect that he was just looking out for what remained of his clan. "Shit." He opened the tube and put the smallest possible amount he could on the tip of his finger. "This is going to suck." He hissed, then chased his head as he leaned back away from his hand, reaching to touch under his nose.

Almost fifteen minutes on the dot, Blair heard movement in the trees. He inhaled and immediately regretted it. Sucking more of the offensive scent into his body. He went around and opened the side door of the van. If someone was looking for them, introductions would have to wait until he got them the hell out of here.

His cat was freaking out inside him. He didn't like not being able to smell. When the sound got closer, Blair hunched down, ready to spring in case the clan members weren't causing the barely audible sounds.

A woman with long brown hair stepped out of the thick growth. She had a small girl with strawberry blonde hair and huge frightened blue eyes in front of her. Blair stepped down into the ditch and held out his hand to help them up it, "It's okay, honey," he took the little girl's hand, "I'm Blair and I'm taking you somewhere safe," he kept his voice soft and light.

"I'm Daisie." She said in a shaking voice.

He was sure his heart just cracked a little inside him. "Hop up in and get comfortable." He helped her and then turned to the woman and nodded as she climbed in and pulled the child onto her lap. "Are the rest close?"

She nodded, "Kobie spread us out to keep the sound to a minimum."

Blair didn't pause to chat. He went back to the ditch and squatted down watching and listening. This Kobie guy was smart. Keep the sound from traveling, send the women and children first so he can watch over everyone. He felt a small measure better about not being able to smell. The brush moved and another woman with an older girl came out. No mistaking these two for mother and daughter with their matching curly hair.

He held his hand out to the teenager. She looked exhausted. "I'm Blair, take my hand." She hesitantly took it. He pulled her up out of the ditch. "Water and snacks are under the seats." He released her hand when he was sure she had her footing, then turned back to the mother.

"Franki slipped and has a gash," she pointed to her arm as she climbed into the van.

Blair nodded and reached in under the front seat and pulled out a first aid kit and held it out. "Fix it up when they get here."

The woman took the kit. *Fuck, the scent of blood would be like a damned beacon.*

"Kobie took off her shirt and wrapped it," Daisie told him as he turned back to the ditch.

He winked at her. "Smart move." He stepped back over to the ditch. *Her shirt?* He had to have heard that wrong.

Two more women stepped out of the foliage. One of them had dyed red-streaked hair and was holding the arm of a short blonde woman as she held her wrapped arm. Franki was a woman. He hadn't caught that part. Snapping out of it, he slid down the ditch and held out his hand to her. "I'm Blair, we have a med kit in the van."

The one helping her let go and climbed up the incline. "Kobie dosed any blood on the ground with rubbing alcohol."

He took Franki's elbow and helped her out of the ditch. He'd never thought of using rubbing alcohol to cover scents, but it was a good idea, and he hoped it worked.

"Annamarie was freaking out, so Mika is dragging her along," Franki told him.

He glanced at the van again, deciding the one with the dyed hair was one of the cats close to their first change. She had to be around eighteen, nineteen. Hopefully, her cat would figure out now was not the time to introduce her to their world. Stopping for an inevitable first change was not something they had time for. Of course, if he could fucking smell, he'd know how close she was.

Blair hoped as he'd never hoped before that Mika was a man, otherwise, his tense guts told him he was going to be transporting nine females many stressful miles. He released her elbow as she got in the van.

Hurrying back when the vegetation moved, he waited at the bottom for the next ones to arrive. A woman with short brown hair, around twenty, huffed out a breath as she cleared it. She turned and gave the older woman with long red hair a glare of attitude. Mika was not a man.

"Come on." He did not have time for haughty girls. The upset one took his hand, then assessed him and gave him one of *those* smiles—the kind the old Blair would have lapped up like a starving kitten. He pulled her up the incline and then released her hand as soon as her feet were on level ground. He was almost thankful for the stink under his nose right now. His cat did not need to know about the pheromones he knew she'd be tossing at him right now.

He turned back to Mika. She was in her late twenties if he guessed right—and when it came to females, Blair was usually right on the money guessing their age. Taking his hand, she gave him a brief nod and then looked at the van.

"We should dump the seats, there'd be more room." She stepped to get in the van.

"Leaving seats laying here would be a flashing sign." He said quickly, then turned back to the growth, watching.

"Good point," Mika said from behind him.

Before Blair could think of anything else to say, a tall woman cleared the growth. She was wearing jeans, a jacket, and just a bra underneath. Turning her back to him, she reached out in front of her and backed up the incline while spraying over her tracks as she went. He would have tried to scent what she was misting the ground with but knew the only smell he'd pick up was that god-awful ointment again.

Backing toward the van, he looked all around them. Opening the passenger door, he reached over and opened his bag, pulling out the first shirt he found.

Kobie reached the van and then finally turned to look at him.

Blair's heart did this hard stop in his chest. She had dark blue, almost black eyes, combined with her high cheekbones and pouty lips. She was probably the most exotic-looking she-cat he'd ever seen. His brain snapped back to functioning, and he held out his t-shirt.

Stuffing the spray bottle into her backpack, she took it. "Thanks." She yanked off her jacket and tossed it in the van and pulled the shirt over her head. "How's the arm?" She looked in the van.

Mika nodded as she wrapped it. "It's not bad."

"Good. There's no time to shift and heal it, so hang on, Franki, just keep an eye on it." Kobie leaned over and grabbed a bottle of water, then took a long drink of it.

"Sorry," Franki mumbled, "I know better."

Capping the bottle, Kobie shrugged, then reached up and pulled out the elastic holding her long, almost white, blonde hair. Shaking her head, she pulled a small twig from it and then tossed it in the van instead of the ground.

That told Blair she knew a lot about hunting and tracking.

"Grab a nap when you can." She told the women, "Nichelle, you have the first watch," she pointed behind the van, "I don't care how insignificant you think it is, you tell us what you see."

The one with the dyed hair nodded her head and then shifted in the cramped space so she was looking out the back window.

With an abrupt nod, Kobie closed the door and then finally looked up at Blair for more than a second. "Thanks for being here."

Blair nodded, then wiped his wrist under his nose, wishing he could smell.

She shrugged and brushed by him and climbed in the passenger seat, then pulled out the spray bottle again. "The ointment was necessary."

Blair watched her spray where she'd been standing, then held the bottle out to him. "I get it. I don't like it but understand why." As soon as she closed the door, he sprayed the ground and backed around to the front. He didn't know where he'd stood or not stood since arriving, so he pulled the tube of gunk from his pocket and squirted some on the ground. He doubted even a torrential rain would wash *that* scent away. Climbing in, he handed her the bottle and tossed the tube on top of his bag.

Holding his hand out, he watched as she looked at it for a moment. "Blair Elden."

She looked at him for a timeless moment, making him feel like he'd just been thoroughly judged. Placing her hand in his, she gave it a half shake, then pulled it away. "Kobie Sorum."

Starting the van, he pulled away without leaving a tire mark behind.

"You're part of the Alliance?"

He glanced in the mirror to see all the women watching him, waiting for him to answer Kobie's question. "Not directly, no. The king's son asked me to come to get you."

"That's a compliment." She stated in a serious tone.

Blair shrugged, "He knew I'd get you out safe." He glanced to see her nod as she watched out the window. "Look," he looked at the tired, scared women behind him, "I know you're beat, but I need some details." He cleared his throat and checked the side mirror. "I feel like I've been sent in blind here." He gave her a quick look, "your one-form friend said you were being followed." She gave him a slight nod. "By who?"

He heard her blow out a breath. "I'm not sure. My father, the Alpha, and the men didn't share the details with me. It's been an ongoing thing though, as far back as I can remember—" she gave him a hard look, searching his face for a second before he looked back at the road. "Women and children were being taken…"

Blair swung his head and looked at her. "Fuck." He said in as quiet a voice he could manage. "Tomas." *Fuck!* He looked back at the road quickly. "Does anyone have a cell phone or any sort of electronic gear with them?"

"I just have a phone; the battery and stick are out of it," Kobie said quietly.

"Toss it all out the window." He knew his tone wasn't pleasant, but he'd just found out they had handed him an impossible task. He liked how she immediately followed his instruction. "So did your Alpha send you…"

"No. This was a contingency plan set up with Fischer—I didn't know about it." She cleared her throat. "When we— found our men that were on patrol, I gathered up the others and got out of there."

He didn't need to ask if the men were alive. "The rest of

your clan go after them?"

"They left and said they were going to get the others—four days before we found the patrol. We haven't heard a word from them since."

Blair nodded and glanced in the rearview mirror to see the little girl looking at Kobie. "I get it." He said quickly so she wouldn't have to say anymore in front of the child. Glancing at the speed he was driving, he put his foot on the accelerator. This changed his original route back. He motioned to his pack, "grab the map out of there, we need to take the most remote route back."

Kobie listened and opened his bag and pulled out the map.

"You navigate." He told her. Grinding his teeth, he went over the routes in his head, trying to find the nearest location he could stop and call Gage. He was going to need some kind of backup on this. "I need to make a quick call." He glanced in all the mirrors as he slowed again. "See how soon I can meet up with someone along the way." He chanced a glance at the woman beside him, expecting panic to be on her face. She only nodded and then looked at the map again.

Stepping out of the van, he closed the door and hit send. Being on the outside or not he knew all the shifters in that van that had reached their first turn could still hear him, but it was for the sake of the four he knew hadn't that he tried to keep his voice down. He wiped at his nose, waiting for Gage to answer.

"Blair?"

"Fuck, Gage, this is a shitshow," Blair said quietly.

"What's wrong? Did you pick them up?" Gage sounded like he was running.

"Yeah, I got them." He glanced over his shoulder at the passengers, "all nine *females*."

"They're all women?"

"Women, girls, and a child." Blair clarified.

"Are they okay?" Gage said something he couldn't hear. "We were just about to head home, hang on, Devin's right here." He heard more sounds. "You're on speaker."

He didn't waste any time on greetings. "They're searching for them. The contact had to drop them off to run through a bush because they were being followed." He heard a few curses but didn't know who said what. "It's Tomas, Gage, I feel it to the core of my soul."

"I spoke to Jesse, and he confirmed the Alpha had been communicating with some of the council members in the Alliance," Devin's tone was hard, "and yes, we believe it was part of Tomas' association they were dealing with."

"They're all females." Gage blurted out.

"Fuck." Devin hissed. "I was told their best hunter was with them. What do you need, Blair?"

A fucking miracle. Blair glanced in the van to the anxious faces watching him. "Oh, their best hunter is, and she knows her shit. I'm going to back road it as much as I can, so I don't have an exact route. How close is *anyone* that can lend a hand?" He heard a commotion. Presumably, they were pulling out a map.

"Closest, right now with everything going on is roughly six hours out…"

Blair closed his eyes and blew out a breath. He opened his eyes and then turned and slowly surveyed all around them. "Okay, text me any locations and numbers from here to that house you set up." He rubbed his hand across his nose again, wishing to fuck he could smell. "I'm going to be moving fast and crazy as long as I can."

"Check-in when you can," Devin said. "I'm calling Dad and filling him in."

"Their contact said more might return." He looked at the little girl. For her sake, he hoped it was true.

"Okay, I'll tell him. See if we can get someone from down there checking into that." Devin said quickly.

"Blair," Kelsey sounded like she was holding the phone, "be safe."

"Always, sweetie." He said automatically then clamped his tongue between his teeth because he had replied like that. "Gotta get moving." He hung up and opened the door. Tossing his phone on top of his bag, he had the van moving before his door was closed. "The Alliance is going to alert all clans along our trip, so we have a backup if we need it." He glanced at Kobie. She only nodded and kept looking out the window.

"Thank you." One of the women behind him whispered.

"I'll get you there safe." He said and hoped to hell he could manage it.

"You must be a fierce warrior to be sent alone."

He didn't need to look to see who said it, he knew the voice went with the flirtation he'd gotten from Annamarie. Opening his mouth to answer her, he snapped it shut again. He would not feed her little infatuation.

Devin and Gage had been just as shocked as he was picking up all females. That made him feel a little better, not by much though. He also knew the only reason he was alone was because of all the other shit happening, and they hadn't been given all the details.

Chapter Four

Kobie looked over at Blair again. She did that a lot more than she should be. She'd known they would send a male, what surprised her was they'd sent a young one and so far, she was impressed with him. He was around her age, but there was something harder about him. She looked out the window and rolled her eyes at her brain's stupid side trip, aside from the muscles she was sure were under his clothes. But there was something darker in there that you didn't see with most men their age. She inhaled and could only smell his scent on the shirt he'd given her. Did they have to send someone so damned sexy? She blew out a breath, trying to keep her body from betraying her to the shifters sitting behind her. She smirked. At least *he* wouldn't smell it.

She glanced once more, then looked away. His hair was even whiter than her own and spiked up messy like he spent hours running his hands through it. It was so different from the slicked-back, neat hair on the men Kobie was used to being around. His eyes were the palest blue. She thought he was looking right through her each time they connected with her own.

His phone rang and startled her.

He answered it quickly. "Yeah?" His brows furrowed, and he gripped the wheel tighter and kept driving fast. "When? Is everyone okay?" He glanced in the side mirror, then at the one on her side. "Don't go back, find somewhere to hole up and call that number again and tell them…" He held the phone out and glanced at it before putting it back to his ear, "yeah I'll tell her." He hung up but continued to hold his phone. He held it out to her. "Check these on the map and see where the closest is."

Kobie took the phone but continued to look at him. "What's happened."

His pale eyes connected with hers briefly. "That was your friend, Fish. Someone tore apart their place before he got back," she sucked in a breath, "his father was at your place checking for others."

"Was there anyone?" She held her breath.

Blair just shook his head and didn't say anymore. "Check those locations." He glanced in the mirror to see all but that teen Nichelle was napping. "We may need to dump the van and go cross-country to stay off their radar."

She watched him for a moment, then glanced at the others behind him. "We'll need some packs and supplies if we're doing that."

"Will they be able to?" He asked in a hushed voice.

Kobie opened the message on his phone and set the phone on the map on her lap. "Yeah, Daisie could run for days if she had to."

"If they found your friend's place, they're going to figure out you crossed the border." He reached over and placed a hand over hers until she looked at him. "Tomas' organization is huge. He has the resources to track you from one end of the globe to the other."

Her heart picked up the tempo. What he was saying sunk in. This Tomas person would find them anywhere they went. She appreciated his complete honesty with her, even though it scared her. "You and I will get them to our destination."

Blair watched her for a second more, then squeezed her

hand and released it.

She looked back at the map.

"How do I get this shit off my nose?"

She smirked at his distraught tone.

"Look, you're just going to have to trust that I can control myself and my cat—" he made a sound of exasperation, "I've had years of fucking practice with *that*, but I need all my senses to get us through this."

Kobie blew out a breath. He was right. She didn't know him, but she trusted him, and from the signs her cat had been conveying, so did she. That was surprising. They just met. She'd never been conflicted with her cat, ever. Leaning down, she opened her pack and pulled out a wipe. Grabbing the bottle of alcohol, she sprayed the wipe and held it out to him. "It will burn for a few seconds, but in a few minutes, you'll be able to smell again."

Blair raised an eyebrow as he took it from her. "Thank you."

Kobie nodded, "just don't cross me, you won't like the outcome at all."

He glanced to the road, then back to her. "Warning received." He smirked at her. "Find the nearest town on there. We will make a quick stop and get everything we'll need." He didn't even look to see if she was paying attention, just rubbed at his face with the wipe.

She smirked when he winced as the burning in his nostrils hit him. Kobie had tried it on herself before to see how effective it was, the ointment, alcohol, all of it, so she knew his reaction wasn't exaggerated in the slightest.

"Nasty." He said quietly but did it again to make sure he got all the ointment off. Kobie looked behind her to see Nichelle give her a shocked look. Kobie didn't need to voice why. She knew the younger woman had been listening to them the whole time. Whatever it took to get all of them to their destination safely, Kobie would do and then some.

Chapter Five

Blair stood on the curb where he could watch the six still in the van, keep an eye on the three in the store, and survey any movement around them in this tiny town. His cat wasn't happy with this situation.

They'd been driving for two and a half hours. Priority had been a quick stop for gas and the game of bathroom tag. He rubbed his hand over the top of his hair. Only fate would put him in this situation. His cat had conveyed the emotion of *what the fuck* when he could smell again as they were driving. The blended scent of nine females had been more than even his cat knew what to do with.

Turning, he checked the other direction, then glanced in the store's window. Kobie, Torrey, and he thought her name was Cortney were at the cash now. Daisie had woken from her nap about forty-five minutes ago and talked non-stop. He knew their names, approximate ages of everyone, their personal preference for food, flowers, and how bad cussing was—even if he was a boy, it was bad.

He glanced in the van at her. She was still chatting up a storm. How had they taken her through the bush and kept her quiet? He had no idea but hoped they were able to do it again.

If his calculations were right, they had another hour of driving, and then they were going to be going cross-country on foot.

Cortney came out and gave him a quick look. "Prepare for the drama." She whispered.

He frowned and watched her open the van door. "Annamarie, Nichelle, you get the bigger packs." She tossed the backpacks in.

"What? Why? Oh my god. I'm a pack mule." Annamarie whined.

Blair put his head down and rubbed his jaw so the smirk on his face wasn't visible as Annamarie was still mumbling about having to carry a backpack instead of a smaller portable pack that you'd wear around your neck in cat form—to which Nichelle reveled in telling her she could carry *when* she could shift.

He looked up to check around them and noticed an older couple coming along the sidewalk. Out of the corner of his eye, he saw Kobie and Torrey come out of the store with the rest of their purchases. He gave Kobie a quick, exaggerated wide-eyed look, then glanced at the couple. A van and nine women were something *anyone* would notice seeing.

"Got everything, honey, we'll be able to hit the trail now," Kobie said, pausing beside him and smiling up at him like they were a couple.

Blair smiled, and it was real. She was sharp. That was a huge blessing in his mind.

"Brave man."

He turned to look at the older gentlemen. "Wilderness survival." He blurted out.

The man chuckled, "Hope *you* survive it." His wife swatted him, then gave him a gentle nudge to keep walking.

As soon as they were gone, Blair stepped over to the van. "You get the protein bars and jerky?" He couldn't think of anything else to help with the shifts they may have to do.

Kobie nodded, "yeah, juice pouches too. They take up less space."

"I'm going to have a backache," Annamarie complained.

Nichelle took the bag Torrey held out and looked at the other girl, "well at least you'll be *alive* to *feel* your backache."

Blair was really liking Nichelle's attitude.

Annamarie's expression changed to guilt, then sorrow. She nodded, without further comment.

Blair knew he shouldn't give them false hope, but he couldn't handle the emotions suddenly coming off them. They were suffocating him. He climbed into the driver's side and turned around when everyone else was back in. "My friend has sent people from the Alliance to look for the rest of your clan." It wasn't a lie.

"Do you think they'll find them?" Nichelle gave him a pleading look, her dark blue eyes asking him to lie if he had to.

"They'll have answers for you by the time we get where we're going." He said and left it there. He knew they'd find them or find out what happened to them.

"Will they bring my daddy back?" Daisie asked in an excited voice.

He almost lost himself in her big eyes, before he could think of anything to say her mother interrupted.

"Let Blair focus on driving, okay, we'll chat later."

Daisie nodded. "Okay. I can't wait to be in the trees again."

Turning, Blair caught the look Kobie gave him. Yeah, he knew it was dumb to say anything to them that would give them too much hope. He inclined his head to her and turned away as he started the van. It would be late afternoon by the time they reached the point they were going on foot. He watched every car they went by as he left the small town. If they were lucky, they'd meet up with the other clan before dark—if they weren't lucky, it was going to be a long, sleepless night of standing guard.

"Here's your change." Kobie held out the money. "I can't believe I didn't think to bring a bank card or anything."

Blair motioned to the glove box. "It's not mine, it was in the van when I picked it up, so it's Alliance money. Put the envelope in my pack." He watched as she took it out and put the change in it. "And I'm pretty sure shopping was the last thing on your mind when you got everyone out of there."

She looked over at him, a sadness in her eyes.

He gave her an earnest look. "You did good." He whispered.

She inhaled a deep breath and then nodded her head.

Blair turned back to the road. There had to be an emotional tidal wave inside her—but he couldn't pick up on it at all. Her father, the Alpha, was out there somewhere, and she had no idea if he was alive or what. He glanced in the mirror and watched the fifteen-year-old, Kasia. She hadn't uttered more than two words the whole time. Her mother, Torrey, had a haunted look in her eyes. He wondered if one of the men found dead had been her mate. He glanced to Kobie. He needed a moment alone to get more details. How he was managing that, he had no idea.

"Rest now," Kobie said in a commanding tone. "We're going to hit the ground running as soon as we're in the bush." That part was a bit softer.

"How long do you think it will take us to meet up with that clan on foot?" Franki asked.

Kobie looked over at Blair. He paused on her expression for a moment, surprised she was deferring to him to answer. Glancing at the road for a second, he looked back at her. "I can't say for sure, I don't know the terrain, but I'm hoping we'll find them before nightfall." No one made any further comment. Blair checked his phone. He'd hoped Devin or Gage would send him some sort of update by now.

He slowed down and watched for a place to pull the van off the road. This area was thick and a good place to slip into the brush leaving no evidence in the direction they'd gone.

"Up there," Kobie said softly.

He looked where she pointed. It was a small path into the bush. "We'll leave the van there." Leaning forward, he turned on the GPS and hoped there was enough signal here. He didn't like just dumping the Alliance's van in the middle of nowhere and walking away.

Kobie leaned over and brought up the map on it so it would give rough coordinates. "Are you sending them coordinates from this?"

"Seems like the thing to do." He said as he pulled the van in as far as he could and put it in park.

"There's a small compass in my pack. Find Northeast on it. We have to stay on point all the way there from here." He took the map from her and glanced at the GPS before he shut the van off. Picking up his phone, he typed the coordinates in a message to Devin. The signal was faint, but it would still send as soon as there was one.

Climbing out, he stretched and rolled his shoulders before looking at the map. It took him a moment to find their location on it. Living where he did, it was easier for him to find unmarked roads and trails from the color keys on a map than it would be for others. He glanced over to see Kobie turning slowly with the compass. Most shifters didn't carry a compass with them. Then again, most hadn't tried to compete with Calum Dante in the middle of a three-hundred-acre bush before. That man and his cat were insanely good at traveling in a forest so thick there was nothing to give away a direction, but he always found the predetermined location every damn time.

"Got it." Kobie pointed.

"Give the compass and map to someone that isn't shifting, so they can keep us on course." He typed a quick message to Gage, telling him they were heading into the bush now and would try to update when he could. He hit send and watched to see if it sent.

"I'll take the compass and map." Cortney went over to Kobie.

"I want to help too." Daisie got out of the van and bounced.

Blair smiled down at her and then held out his phone. "I have to turn the ringer off because we can't let anyone hear us, but I need to know if I get any calls or messages."

She gave him a serious nod. "I'll keep it in my pouch and check *all* the time."

He winked at her and watched her put it in the front pocket of the small pack she had around her waist. "Thanks, honey." He watched the others as they prepared packs or backpacks. He wasn't sure how many were going to travel on four paws but hoped at least a few would. The more scenting around them, the easier this would go.

Kobie rolled up her jacket and held it out to Nichelle, who put it into her backpack. When the teen moved over to take Mika's jacket, Blair took that opportunity to go over and talk to the leader among the women.

Kobie looked up at him as she took off her hiking boots and tied them together.

Blair sat on the ground and took his boots off. "The men you found," he said in barely an audible voice, but knew she'd hear, "any of their mates?"

Kobie tied her boots to the pack and then took off her socks. "Two were." She motioned with her head to where Torrey and Mika stood. "Fish went back and buried them." She said with barely any voice at all.

Blair nodded. There was nothing more he could say about it. "The others?"

Kobie paused and looked at him. "My father, my brother, Cortney's mate, and fifteen of our men never came back." She reached into the bag and pulled out a hunting knife. "Ten women and young males went missing before that in the last year." Standing up, she looked over at Cortney and held up the blade.

Cortney came over and took it. She glanced down at him, "Daisie won't make a sound once we're moving."

Blair nodded.

Mika came over and leaned down and pulled a knife out of her boot and gave it to Cortney as well. "Torrey and you shifting?"

Cortney shook her head, "No, we'll stay like this and keep watch over the four girls."

Mika nodded, and then just stood there.

All of them looked down at him. It took a few seconds to

sink in that they wanted him to make himself scarce so they could strip down and shift. Clearing his throat, he motioned to the van. "I'll go shift over there." Getting up, he made fast work of getting there. Grabbing his pack out of the still opened door, he tucked the keys under the mat and closed the door.

"Should we take the blankets?" Torrey asked, looking at him through the window on the other side.

"As many as you can, in case we don't meet up before night."

She nodded and reached back into the van.

He watched the young teen, Kasia come over to the van. She opened the door and pulled out his backpack. Coming around, she took his boots from his hand and tied them to the backpack, then slung it over her shoulder.

"Thanks." He'd actually planned to leave it behind, but the change of clothes and other gear inside could come in handy.

"I just want to do something to help." She said quietly, with no emotion in her voice at all.

"I appreciate that honey, I really do." He gave her a soft look and for a second, the pain eased in her eyes. With a nod, she turned around and went back to the others.

Pulling his shirt over his head, he rolled it and jammed it into his small pack. He wanted to believe it was going to be as easy as a run through the bush to meet up with this other clan and then all the weight would be off his shoulders, but his gut was telling him that wasn't how this was going to go down. His cat was so silent he had to wonder if they slept when they weren't on the outside.

Shucking his jeans off, he rolled them tightly and stuffed them into the pack, and then zipped it up. Adjusting the long strap to its full length, he put it over his head and one arm through it. On his human body, it hung to his waist and made him look like he was wearing a purse. Shaking his head at his own ridiculous thought, he shifted in the next moment.

Chapter Six

Forcing his cat body to stand there for a moment, to make sure all the others had changed, he took time to memorize scents. He went around the van toward the women standing there. Nichelle came out from behind one of the bigger trees, stuffing clothes into her backpack. Zipping it she put it on her back and then paused and smiled at him.

"You're pretty." She said with a grin.

Blair snuffed, trying to show his dislike of being called that. Pretty—why did women say that about his cat? He was one of the largest males in his clan in cat form. How did that even come close to pretty?

He chuffed at her again, and she smirked.

"Daisie…"

Daisie didn't care that he was a large animal. She came right up to him and looked into his eyes. "It *is* you." She said, then smiled. Leaning forward, she rested her forehead on his for a second. "You're Kobie's opposite." She grinned at him again and then took her mothers, hand and walked away.

Blair had no idea what that could mean. While she'd been all up in his face, two other cats had come around the tree. It took no guessing to figure out the dark orange female was

Mika. It matched her hair perfectly. The other one was darker, almost brown in areas that had to be Franki. Blair assessed how she was walking. No limp. The shift had solved that gash problem on her arm.

When the last cat came out from behind the trees, Blair had to work hard to not gape at her. Did cats even do that? He had no idea. Where Blair was mostly white with black stripes, Kobie was black as night with white striping. He glanced at Daisie, who nodded at him and smiled. The child was right; they were exactly the opposite coloring. She was long for a female, but then she was pretty tall in human form as well.

Kobie looked at the two female cats and chuffed twice then looked in the direction they were going. Both turned and bound into the trees. That made it easier for Blair, he had been trying to figure out if he should scout or hang back with the others.

Kobie walked over with the serene grace of a cat and paused a few feet from him. She was giving him the same appraisal he'd given her. With a whisper-quiet yowl, she took off to his left to check that area.

Blair has to override his cat, who wanted to follow the intriguing black tiger she-cat and romp around in the forest with her. He watched the others move. That's what he didn't need, his cat interested in Kobie's.

It impressed him how he couldn't hear any of the girls walking. They had been trained well. He lifted his head and scented the air, checking for anything that was wrong.

He started following the others, keeping his ears tuned in to the surrounding sounds. Sure, Kobie was an interesting woman, was unlike any he'd met before, but a female was off the list of things he needed to be thinking about right now. He stopped and checked the air around them again. Then he just stood there when he realized he hadn't been mooning over Kelsey in hours. Chuffing quietly, he started walking again, *been a little busy to stop and mope, idiot*. Mika came bounding back from the left and he realized she'd gone in a full circle. She followed alongside him. Giving her a quick look, he moved faster. He needed to see for himself what was up ahead, no more surprises, this day had had enough of those.

He wasn't sure how much time had gone by. When they came to a creek, he stopped to get a drink. The women on two legs opened packs and offered drinks and a snack to the others. Nichelle followed Kobie over to a darkened area. A few moments later she came back out. Blair checked all around them and then turned to see Kobie, in jeans and a t-shirt. *His* t-shirt. She took the bar and water Torrey held out. Then went over and got the map and compass from Cortney and sat down on the rock near him. "I'll check how we're doing."

Daisie came over to him and held up his phone. "No messages or calls." She informed him.

He had enough time to see how long they'd been walking before she stuffed it back into her pack and went back over to her mother.

"We're still on track." Kobie said and took a bite, "still a way to go yet." She looked over at him. "Think they'll message us? The clan we are meeting."

Blair trusted she could read a map. He chuffed softly at her. That was the plan and reason he'd messaged Devin the location of the van, so he knew when they left.

Kobie looked around them. "I don't know, Blair, my gut says something is off." She stood up and motioned to Franki to go look around. The she-cat bound away from the creek.

Blair didn't want to admit it, but even in cat form, he was antsy. Getting up, he went over and nudged her leg with his head, then looked in the direction they'd come.

"You going to double-check we're not being followed?" She nodded. "I'll keep us moving in the right direction. Be safe."

That she understood him made this simpler. Blair inhaled deeply, then regretted it. *Shit, she smelled appealing to his cat, even in human form. Fuck.* No time for *that*, he thought quickly and then took off to backtrack where they'd been.

The next quick break they took was because they stood in front of a ravine. Blair went over to the edge and looked down at it. The girls wouldn't be able to make it down. He looked over to the other side. He doubted even in cat form he could make it up the other side. Kobie came over beside him and looked. He turned to see Cortney was coming over carrying the map.

She pointed to her right, "we're going to have to go up and circle back," she pointed to where it looked like the ravine leveled out again, "then get back on course." She glanced over at her daughter. "That climb will slow Daisie down."

Blair chuffed at her twice, then ran over to the trees.

Coming out with his jeans on, he went over to Torrey, who was holding out a drink and a few bars for him. "Stop and refuel, ladies." He said quietly. Dropping his pack on the ground, he sat down. Taking a bite of the bar, he looked at the hill they'd have to go up. "Can I see the map, please?" He waited until Cortney brought it over.

"I've been watching, there's no other way around it."

He nodded, "I knew it wasn't going to be easy." He motioned around them, "but in a car on the road, we'd already be found."

She nodded and then motioned for Daisie to come over.

Daisie did, holding out his phone as she did. "Thanks, honey." He smiled at her.

Kobie came over as she zipped up her jeans and sat down. "How are we doing for time?" She looked up at the sky, assessing the time of day for herself.

He finished chewing the chalky bite before glancing at his phone. "All things considered, not bad." It had taken them over two hours to get this far. The terrain had been a lot rougher than he'd expected. He looked at his phone again. There was a signal. "We should have heard from someone by now."

Franki came out and stumbled a few steps.

Blair watched her for a moment. "Get some of the jerkies into you, Franki. If you're not steady, you'll have to stay on two legs for a bit."

She nodded and took the food Torrey offered.

"I can change if Franki's unable." Torrey offered.

Blair looked over to Franki, "let me see if I can reach someone. No sense in all of us exhausting ourselves if no one is there to meet us." He met Kobie's look before he opened the screen and typed out a message to Devin. *Rough trek through this bush. Going to be another few hours, at least.* He hit send and then took another bite. He hated protein bars, but he wasn't sure how the women would react if he booked it through the bush looking for a rabbit to eat.

Torrey offered him some jerky as if she had read his mind. "My mate hated those bars too." She mumbled, then walked away.

His phone vibrated in his hand. He lifted it and read the message from the prince.

Abort! We can't reach them. Last communication said choppers were circling their area.

He read it again. "Fuck." He said under his breath. *New plan?* He hit send a little harder than necessary, but it was that or toss the phone down into the ravine.

"What is it?" Kobie leaned closer and spoke in a hushed tone.

Blair turned the phone and let her read it.

Her face blanched, and then she looked up in the air. Standing up, she motioned to the bush. "Everyone, move back into the cover of the trees."

Everyone listened without hesitation. Blair stood up and grabbed his pack. He watched the signal bar on his phone as he went, making sure he didn't lose it. He stepped back into the shelter of the trees and avoided looking anywhere but at his phone. He didn't need to see the anxious and worried look on the women's faces, he could feel them.

Not sure yet. Just stay put for a few. That was the response he got back.

Blowing out a breath, he rolled his shoulders to release some tension. There was one person he knew that would have a plan immediately in a situation like this. He really hated to disturb him, but he had nine people and nowhere to go. They didn't have enough supplies to stay in the bush indefinitely. Opening the contacts, he brought up his name and hit dial before he could change his mind.

The phone rang three times. "Hello?"

"Cal, it's Blair."

"I know or I wouldn't have answered. That idiot prince and his sidekick, your boss, keep calling—at all hours."

Blair smirked, despite the mess he was in.

"What's going on? You go pick up those people?"

Blair looked around at the women watching him. "Yeah, and we're in a bit a fix now."

"What happened?"

"Okay, summary, Tomas' people *are* involved, they were being followed. We ditched the van and have been trekking through the bush. We were supposed to meet the closest clan to here, but Devin just sent a message to abort."

"Fuck me." His tone was a lot deeper now. "Is everyone in good health?"

Blair nodded and looked at the ground, "Yes, all nine women, girls, and one ray of sunshine are healthy."

"They're all females?" He heard Calum blow out a breath. "Tomas isn't going to quit."

"I know. I'm open to suggestions, here." He glanced to Kobie, who looked hopeful.

"Okay, text me your location as best you can guess and give me ten minutes. I'll come up with a plan of action and I'll…" he heard a feminine voice near to Cal, "*we'll* head to you."

Blair closed his eyes, relief filling him. "Fill Gage and Devin in, please. I think they were trying to figure out a plan."

Calum laughed, "amateurs. I'll talk to you in a few minutes."

Blair handed the phone to Kobie. "Can you text our location to that number? I need to go," he motioned to the tree.

"Yeah." She took the phone. "This Cal is going to call in the troops to help?"

Blair walked backward toward the tree. He grinned at her. "No troops, he *is* the calvary." He barely got out of sight when she called out to him.

"Blair?"

"Yeah?" he held his breath and hoped it wasn't Cal messaging saying he was out of ideas. "Your battery is getting low."

Blair grinned. "There are two more in my pack. Switch it out after you send him the coordinates." He had to go to the bathroom, but he needed a moment to rest his forehead against the bark of the tree and hope like he never had that he could get them all out of this.

Chapter Seven

Calum had called back with a plan and a lot of advice that Blair was more than happy to accept. They still had to climb that hill, but they were now heading Northwest once they reached the top of it. He didn't know what maps Cal had, but he could tell him what kind of terrain they were going to be traveling over. He'd also suggested most staying on two legs because they didn't have the food to sustain shifting back and forth for another day—or send them off to eat whatever kill they could find in cat form because lighting a fire was out of the question. Mostly, Blair had thought of all that too. He just felt better telling the women and saying 'Cal said' instead of forcing his ideas off on them.

They found a secluded, semi-sheltered area to bunk down for the night, and *now* his nerves were strung right out. He needed rest, but they needed rest more than he did, so he took the first watch and was trying to let the ladies sleep as much as they could.

He heard movement from behind him but didn't take his eyes off the area below the incline. If anyone were coming at them, it would have to be from that direction—unless they could fly, and he silently prayed Tomas didn't have any flyers.

"Bet you're wishing you were at home right now doing whatever it is you do," Kobie spoke softly and sat down beside him.

He shrugged, "I wasn't at home when I got the call. I was helping at the farm that's my clan's."

"Your clan's not all together?"

"For the most part, the largest financial support for them is through the Alpha's family business, so I live and work there." He inhaled slowly and then regretted it when all he could smell was her. She smelled just as appealing in human form. His animal brushing along him confirmed that opinion.

"What's the family business?" She kept her voice so quiet, even the shifters sleeping behind them wouldn't hear.

He glanced at her to see her hair was down and half-covering her face as she looked around them. She was lovely to look at; he decided. "We repair and rent out big equipment," he shrugged, "like stuff for construction, drilling…"

"It's a remote area?"

He grinned and motioned around them, "like this only with more bogs and small lakes."

"That's nice." She said nothing after that.

"How are you doing?" She had to be hurting, not knowing what was going on with her clan. He knew their fate would not be a good one but wasn't going to refuse that.

"Holding it together." She spoke quietly, then cleared her throat softly. "I think," she blew out a breath, "my brother is still alive." Her voice cracked at the end.

Blair watched her, not sure what he should say. His cat was so still it made him nervous.

"We're twins." She whispered, "I think I'd feel this void inside me if he weren't."

Blair reached over and picked up her hand, then leaned closer and lifted her chin so he could see her face. "Then believe he is if that's what you need to keep going." He, more than most, would understand that you needed a purpose to move forward sometimes.

Her dark eyes searched his for a moment, then her lips

quirked like she wanted to smile but couldn't quite do it. "You are not what I expected when Fish told me they were sending someone from the Alliance."

Blair gave her hand a squeeze before releasing it. "Better or worse?" He sent her a playful, cautious look.

"Better." She grinned. "I expected some hard-ass, aging man, who would bark orders at us."

"And you were prepared to put him in his place?" He raised an eyebrow at her, then remembered he needed to keep watch and looked back out in the night.

"You know it." She laughed softly. "Go take your run and check the boundaries and then grab a nap, I'll keep watch."

"Did you rest at all?" He wasn't sure how long he'd been wandering around quietly.

"A little." She cleared her throat. "Sleep isn't going to find me anytime soon."

He didn't want to put the pressure of watching over everyone on her, but he also understood when you had emotions riding you. He doubted he'd sleep, but he would go stretch out for a bit after he shifted and did a thorough check of the area. Getting up, he gave her a quick look. "If you get tired, come and get me." He didn't wait for an answer, just headed out of sight so he could strip down and shift.

Running the full perimeter, he was satisfied that there was nothing but nature out there. He went back toward the others. His cat decided he needed to see the pretty white-haired woman one more time and then Blair found himself making a hard-right turn when the site was in view. He hoped there was no blood all over his face from his midnight snack a few minutes ago. The women might get by on protein bars and jerky, but he needed real meat to sustain the length of shifts he'd been doing.

He slowed his cat when Kobie was in view. Her expression made him glad his insubordinate side had decided on this visit. She looked so forlorn and lost right now it made his heartache. Creeping closer, like he was stalking her, he crouched lower.

He didn't make a sound but saw her inhale subtly and then turn in his direction. When she cocked her head to the side, he knew she was onto him. Straightening, he walked over to her and sat in front of her.

"Feel better?" She smirked at him.

He snuffed loudly as a reply.

She looked over at him. "Your coloring surprised me." Her dark eyes connected with his again. "My brother is fair like us, but he's still orange when he shifts."

That surprised him. Usually, a person's hair hinted toward their coloring when they shifted.

"I like that I'm different." She smiled briefly. "Is the rest of your clan your coloring?"

He gave his head a shake. Gage was whitish with brown tinges, but Blair was the only pure white Bengal in that he knew of, well, was until he'd seen Kobie's coloring.

Reaching out, she ran her hand along his jaw. "Go grab some rest, Blair, if you're exhausted and falter, I'm going to crumble."

As he walked back to where he'd left his clothes, he tried to figure out what that meant exactly. He had been anything but calm and cool since that Fish guy had shown up. Maybe a quick nap would be a good idea. His mind was bogging down.

Kobie watched him come out of the trees and walk over to where the others were sleeping. She was glad it was dark and no one else was around. It allowed her to admire his shirtless form. With the sculpted muscles in his back, there was no question that his job was very physical. When he walked, it looked like he was stalking prey, each foot was placed silently on the ground. He'd sleep on the very outskirts of the area everyone was in. She knew it. She blew out a breath like she'd been holding it all day and opened her pack. Pulling out the small bottle, she looked at it. The oils were almost gone, and then what? It's not like she had time to run back to the house and grab some when she realized she had to round everyone else up and run. She glanced back his way again and opened the bottle. Dabbing the smallest amount on her fingertip, she rubbed it on the main pulse points on her neck. Stuffing it back into the pack, she pulled out the small bottle of rubbing alcohol and rubbed it on her hand. She'd have to wait a few minutes to be able to smell around the area clearly.

She looked up at the sky like she knew there was a god up there, even though she didn't believe in that stuff. *Why now?* The sexy, noble Blair Elden was her mate, she was sure of it. She used oils so no male could 'scent' her, but she could smell him from twenty feet away. She knew for sure because no male had ever really appealed to her, human or otherwise, in the way he was.

Kobie had known the second she'd stood beside him at the van. At first, she'd tried to tell herself it was the adrenaline of the situation and then that it was her emotional vulnerability with everything that had happened. Lies. All of it. She'd never been the type of girl that hoped for a mate to 'complete' them. She liked how she was now. Running earlier, she tried to figure out if walking away was a possibility after finding your mate— she didn't know enough about it.

Standing up, she looked down the slope. When she'd been in cat form, all *she* wanted to do was rub herself all over his gorgeous white coat. Biting her lip, she glanced back to make sure everyone was still asleep. *Jay, you better be in one piece and get back to me. I'm in trouble here.* Not that her brother was going to be any help at all. He was the very definition of dorky, awkwardness unless he was his cat. Sometimes she thought she liked his cat more than when he was in 'normal' form. She grinned and shook her head. Yeah, she might need a quick nap soon. Her brain was out of control. Her freaking life was so far out of control she had no idea if she was ever going to get it back together again.

She heard whimpering and immediately turned around. Daisie was standing there, rubbing her face. She'd probably had a nightmare. Before she could move, Blair was on his feet and scooped her up into his arms. He went back over to where he'd been laying and lay back down, cradling Daisie in his arms. Kobie's heart thudded in her chest. "Where the hell are men like you made?" She more mouthed than spoke.

Chapter Eight

They'd started out just after dawn. No one could sleep any longer than that. Blair had made all the women that could shift go out and eat some local wildlife—Kasia, Nichelle and Annmarie thought that was 'gross', Daisie thought it was cool. Blair was certain once Daisie was old enough to shift, there would be no one that would ever catch her again.

He watched Daisie stumble twice, going up over some thick roots on the incline and bound over to her. Making a soft prusten sound at her, he crouched down, hoping she would understand. She looked at him, then turned to her mother.

"He's offering you a ride, baby." She said, giving Blair a look of appreciation.

"Really? Even Daddy won't let me ride anymore." Daisie got up on his back carefully and leaned forward, so she was draped over him and not holding on with handfuls of hair. He was glad about that.

"You're getting too big, but this is a special circumstance."

Blair was a little unsettled by the weight of her on his back for the first few steps but decided it would speed things up and prevent her from getting hurt, so it was acceptable.

He went ahead of Cortney until he was alongside Torrey.

He chuffed quietly, and she lifted the map and looked at it.

"We're on course." She said quietly.

Glancing back at the others, he saw they were keeping up fine. Kobie was at the back in her cat form, and she paced back and forth like she wished everyone would run full speed, so she didn't have to walk along so slowly.

"Thank you," Daisie whispered, leaning closer to his ear. "I'm tired and thirsty, but don't want to bug Mom right now." There was a pause. "She's sad."

Blair picked up speed, so she would have to hug him to stay on. He couldn't hear about sad moms from brave children right now. He'd never make it if he did. As it was, he felt like he was barely holding on during all of this. Now he just wanted to run full speed, but the child on his back squeezing him kept him cautious. Another hour and they should almost be at the point Calum said he'd meet them at. He really hoped he was there and that he brought his mate—one female on his side would be very welcome right now.

Blair paced around the area the others were resting in. The younger ones had started lagging further and further behind, so Cortney suggested a brief rest. They'd reached the top at least. He moved through the trees and stopped when he could see the terrain going down. According to Torrey, they were close to where they needed to be. He inhaled slowly, searching for any trace of scent that told him Calum was waiting below as planned. He didn't pick up anything. Knowing Calum though, he'd be two feet in front of them before they could sense him.

Going back to the group, he surveyed their state. The only one that hadn't shifted back was Kobie and the way she was pacing along the ridge to the right, she was just as anxious as he was. Daisie was rested after her ride up here. He didn't mind doing it but wouldn't be offering that again unless there was no other way. He didn't enjoy feeling weighed down.

A high-pitched screech had him bolt toward Daisie. "Snake." She screeched again and stumbled backward—right toward the edge.

In a blur, he watched Kobie come out of nowhere and knock her back away from it. Then, as if in slow motion, he watched Kobie disappear over the edge. He leaped over and looked down. She was laying at the bottom of a thirty-foot drop. She wasn't moving. He searched for a way down to her.

"Kobie!" Franki called down.

She moved but didn't get on her feet.

Blair growled out an order he hoped she heard and understood, telling her not to shift. Without hesitation, he jumped down to an outcropping. His paws slid along it, almost sending him tumbling off it. There was another one and then a tree he could use. Springing down to the next one, he twisted and headed for the tree. He hit it and swayed over as the tree shifted from his weight. Not pausing, he used his claws and tried to control his slide downward along any branch he could hit. At the end of the branches, he hung by one paw, dangling out of the tree. He was going to have to do some acrobatic shit to get down from here. His cat wasn't happy with this situation at all. It took hard focus to get him on the same page with him. He retracted his claws and was free-falling fast.

Hit paws smacked the earth with enough force they stung. Not caring if they were bleeding, he ran the last ten feet to her and shifted fast. "Don't shift." He ran up behind her and leaned over her. She was breathing too fast. "Stay calm, Kobie, don't shift. Let me check if anything is broken. You can't shift if anything's broken." He tried to keep his voice calm, even though he was freaking the fuck out on the inside.

"That's it, okay, check your breathing—any ribs hurt?" He ran his hands along her front legs, then up her shoulders. He felt nothing out of place. Unclasping her pack, he pulled it out of the way. "You're doing great. Can you lift your head?" She moved slowly and lifted her head off the ground. "Everything feeling okay?" She didn't make a move or sound to tell him otherwise.

"Let me check your back, just keep breathing steady." He glanced up to see everyone watching down over the ledge.

"Keep going toward Calum." He called up to them. Running his hands down her spine, other than unbelievably soft fur, he felt nothing else. "His mate is a healer." They didn't move. "We'll catch up. I'll get Kobie back up there and we'll catch up."

He must have sounded convincing, because one by one, the heads disappeared. "Okay, move your back legs. Any pain?" He watched her for signs of discomfort. "Okay, shift back and we'll rest for a few."

Leaning back, he pulled his jeans out of his pack and pulled them on as he heard the popping of her bones reforming. He held out his t-shirt, keeping his eyes closed as he waited for her to say something. She pulled it from his grasp.

"I'm okay." She said breathlessly.

His eyes opened, and he assessed her slowly.

"I think I just scared myself into shock." She sat down, pulling her legs beneath her.

"Scared you?" He looked up at the top ledge. "I just tried to make my cat learn how to fly to get down here." He pulled out a bottle of water and sat down. Grabbing a protein bar, he tossed it to her.

She looked all around them. "How are we getting back up?"

Blair took a long drink while looking along the ridge. "I have no idea." He grinned at her wide-eyed look, "what was I supposed to lie?"

She took the bottle he held out to her, "maybe pretend to have an idea next time."

He shrugged, "I've recently learned that it's the straight-up truth that keeps me in one piece."

She raised an eyebrow at him, "Sometimes the truth just creates more problems." She looked up again, then got to her knees and pointed. "Think we can get up there in cat form?"

He turned to look at the area she pointed to. "It will be a workout." He didn't like how loose the soil looked along the slope, "but we'd never make it using hands." *The truth just creates more problems?* With his chin, he motioned to the unopened bar she held. "Get that into you, I'm going to go take a closer look." He took a bite of the dust bar in his hand as he went toward the area she pointed to. It was possible, there was enough growth going up it they would have small areas to rest and get a foothold, but damn, it was going to take some balance. *What truths was she hiding?* He blew out a breath before taking another bite. His cat was not built for acrobatics—but there was no other way up that wouldn't take them an hour to backtrack.

The first ten feet were the easiest part. After that, claws and strength were the only things that prevented them from crashing onto the ground floor below them. He watched as she pulled her cat up onto a small chunk jutting out. His paw hurt holding most of his weight dangling here. Personal space or not, he had to pull himself up and crowd her.

Finding footing, he gave himself thirty seconds to prepare for the next leap. Kobie leaned into him, making sure not to push him off balance and off their tiny mid-air island. He made a soft noise, trying to encourage her to push onward. They were almost to the halfway point of the climb. After the next spot protruding out enough to use to climb further, the angle of the incline was more sloped inward and not straight up and down to the floor beneath.

He felt her side huff out a few times as she built up the courage to make the jump. The muscles in her powerful back legs tensed three times, then she sprung upward. She almost missed the lip of the next landing. Instinct had him leaning out precariously near the edge of his foothold in case she slipped back down. As she slid, she dug her back paws into the parched earth and slowed her body enough to get a better grip above.

Blair hadn't realized he was holding his breath until his sides heaved to suck more air in. He called out a quiet prusten, so she'd keep going. There was no way two of them could stop in that small space.

Blair clawed his way over the top and then dragged his large body away from the edge. Kobie lay there a few feet away, her sides heaving as she caught her breath. She sat up and looked at him, her incredible cat eyes telling him that was the first and last time she'd ever do that shit. He chuffed twice, letting her know he agreed. Getting up, he moved over and bumped her with his head. They had to catch up to the rest. It had occurred to him while cursing the stupid idea of climbing that, that he hadn't told the others if they encountered a jaguar or two, that they were friends. That's the last thing he needed in his world right now was a bunch of female tigers to attack Calum, or worse, Calum's mate.

Kobie got up and sniffed the air, then started moving with sure steps in the direction the others had come. Blair paused and checked for scents down the slope the group had climbed. There was nothing out of place. This bit of good luck would not last. He felt that truth to the very bottom of his soul.

Chapter Nine

By the time they caught up to the others, Blair had gone through a whole gauntlet of emotions and that alone put him in the mood where he just wanted to kill something. He had had the realization that Kobie could have died in that fall—then what? He didn't know, but he'd had to reign in his cat as they processed that thought. Next, it was that Daisie could have fallen—he wasn't sure, but his own feelings on that weren't much better than the idea of something happening to Kobie. He didn't know what in hell was going on with his head, but it needed to smarten up. He didn't have time for all this emotional shit. He had nine other lives to get to safety. This was no time for feeling all this other crap.

Once assessing that everyone was fine, Kobie chuffed her intentions of leading and took off down the incline. Despite his internal chastising, Blair hung back for a minute and checked that Daisie, was in fact, fine. He even gave Annamarie a quick once over to make sure she was well—unhappy with the state of her boots, but otherwise, she was in good health.

Turning, he scented the direction Kobie had gone and then took off as soon as he processed another familiar smell. Calum was close by and another jaguar. Even though Calum was his friend, and his cat knew the other man's the scent still registered as a danger. Someday he'd build up the courage to ask Calum why that was, but for now, he just had to catch up to the crazy fast she-cat. Her speed, along with other aspects he was finding, filled him with pride that she was as incredible as she was.

He cleared a heavy vegetation area and came to a quick halt, paws sliding on the dried needles covering the ground. Kobie was hunched down, ready to spring, her ears flat on her head. As Calum cleared the bush on the other side, Blair leaped toward Kobie and placed his body in her path. Bumping her, he gave her a not so gentle verbal command to stand down.

Calum stopped and sat right where he stood, Blair could see his amusement even in his cat's eyes. The look told him he was amused that the spitfire of a female was ready to take him on to protect her clan—or he was laughing at Blair because of the predicament he'd been through the past few days. He wasn't sure which.

Nudging Kobie with his head, he got her to turn around and head back to the others. Once she started moving, Blair watched Calum look behind him as a huge black jag came running out of the trees carrying a backpack in her mouth. Calum swung his head and looked back at Blair as if to say, 'she insisted on bringing it'. A lot had happened in his friend's life too, it seemed. He looked forward to the distraction of hearing about it.

Turning, Blair took off in the direction Kobie had gone. He knew he didn't need to lead the jags to the others. It was Calum, he would know their exact location.

As he reached them, he could hear their chatter. For a group of shifters, they too often forgot about making too much noise when they otherwise should be quiet. Stopping out of the way, he shifted back and got dressed. His legs reminded him with each movement how much he'd been doing in cat form since he met that Fish guy on the side of the road. His cat might take it all in stride, but it left his human form with stiff and sore muscles.

He went around the tree to see Kobie still in her cat form. She spun toward him and even from this distance, he could see she was unhappy about something. He barely got to sit when she bound over and knocked him onto his back and held him there with one large, firm paw. He frowned. She couldn't be this pissed that he'd stopped her from attacking his friend. "Hey…"

"Blair, you had two phone calls." Daisie came bounding over. "Mom read who called for me. I think Kelsey is a pretty name and," she held out the phone, "Layna too."

Shit. He turned and looked up at the she-cat giving him a hard look. She gave a low yowl at him and then released him and walked into the trees. He blew out a breath and glanced to see Calum leaning against a tree with his arm around a woman with long black hair. "Thanks, Daisie." He held out his hand for the phone and sat up. Out of the corner of his eye, he saw Kobie come back and almost wished it was the cat returning, the look she gave him was not friendly. He did not know why she was mad—okay, getting calls from two women in the past hour made him look like some kind of playboy, but there were explanations. Getting up, he looked over to see Calum's amused look. *Shit.* He'd missed a step or something somewhere.

"This is my friend Calum and his mate…" He had no idea what her name was.

The woman smiled, "Shaelan." She held up the backpack. "I brought stew and," she smiled, "coffee."

Just like that, she was everyone's favorite person. Blair stood back as *all* the women chatted quietly. He felt Calum come up beside him.

"Feel like I missed something," Calum said softly.

Blair snorted, "same."

Calum chuckled. "Go grab some stew and we'll find a spot to keep watch," He shrugged one of his big shoulders, "let them rest up before we hike down." He glanced in the direction they'd come from, "there's a few rough spots."

Blair gave him a blank look. "I've already done my acrobatic moves for the day."

Calum grinned and rubbed his hand along his jaw. "I might need details for that."

Pushing away from the tree, Blair motioned to Shaelan with his chin, "yeah I think I need some too."

They sat in a location where they could see in all directions and keep an eye on the women.

"Did Dev and Gage know they were sending you to fetch nine females?" There was no hint of humor in his tone.

Blair swished the cold coffee around in the cup before drinking the rest. He shook his head, "no. They were as surprised as I was."

Calum said nothing for a few seconds. "You know the chances of any of their clan returning is pretty fucking low, right?"

Looking over to where Kobie was, he nodded, "Yeah." He motioned to her with a jerk of his head. "Kobie thinks she'd know if her twin was dead though."

Calum blew out a long breath. "It's possible, stranger things have happened." He looked all around them for a moment. "I made a quick call while Shae was getting everything ready." He looked over at his mate, "Dev's dad says it is part of the Tomas group that has been taking their clan members."

"I figured as much. As soon as Fish told me they were being followed and saw it was nine females, my guts hardened."

Calum nodded, "Yeah and we're not in the clear yet." He pointed in the direction they'd met up. "We'll get down to the bottom and then stay there the night. We left some supplies down there hidden, but Jesse won't be here with transportation until morning." He looked at him and grinned, "but I thought you could use some backup before that."

Blair shook his head and leaned on his knees, "yeah." He rubbed a hand through his hair, "I'm so far out of my league here." He shrugged, "I thought, yeah, go pick them up and drive them to another location."

"Well, if they'd had all the facts, they would have sent

someone else with you." He paused and visibly inhaled, "Tomas has us running in so many directions right now, my gut says it's on purpose, my head says it's because he's desperate."

"So which is right?" Blair checked on the women again, his eyes lingering on Kobie longer than the rest.

"Both. He's desperate, so he's trying to keep us running in circles." He gave him a steady look, "But you got them this far on your own, so no, you are not out of your league doing this." Calum nodded slowly, "most would have tried to outrun them on the road, but you had the sense to throw several thousand trees in their path instead."

Blair smirked, "and a few ravines." He sobered quickly. "I was just trying to clear my head…"

"How's that going?" His tone was serious.

Blair snorted softly, "I don't even know anymore." He looked back over at Kobie and Daisie standing there with her, "but I've been too busy to get hung up by it for the past few days."

"Good." Calum nodded his head once, "she's someone else's mate, you knew that going in and knew the eventual outcome."

Blair nodded. None of it was wrong.

"Besides, I think you might have something new to contend with," he made a point of turning his head and looking at Kobie slowly.

Blair gave him a blank look for thirty seconds. "Why?" He looked from Kobie back to Calum.

"I'm no expert, but her reaction to two women phoning you was a pretty good indicator."

Blair snapped his head back to look at Kobie. She was smiling at something Shaelan said. "No, what? Do you think she was jealous? There's nothing between us." He knew that was a small lie. She was spectacular, and his cat was besotted with Kobie's. He turned back to Calum, who just raised one eyebrow and looked at him. Blair shook his head, "you think it's more?" Blair smirked at him, "I'd know, I would scent it—

my cat would *know*."

Cal crossed his arms over his chest and stared out into the trees. "Would you? Those perfumes or oils she's wearing are pretty fucking strong. Lemon and something sweet…"

"She's wearing perfume? Anyone that can shift knows that will mess with their animal form—" He blew out a breath, "she had me put this rank shit under my nose before they got to me so I couldn't smell anything but that—a few of the girls are close to their…" Blair stood up and put his hands on his hips and stared down at the ground, "holy shit, Cal," He looked at the big man, "she does this thing with rubbing alcohol to cover their tracks and it works—"

Calum stood up, "you think Tomas' people know about it?"

"It's the only thing that would explain why we always lose their scent."

"Shit." Calum pulled out his phone, then motioned to the others, "get everyone ready while I message Dev, we need to get moving. If they are following you, they could be here already."

Nodding, Blair turned to go over to the others. *Why would a shifter wear perfume? Was it another thing she used to keep people from scenting her cycles? No, then the others would be too, and he knew they weren't.*

Shaelan came over to him. She looked to Calum, "I know that look. What's he plotting now?"

Blair grinned, "no plotting, more like answers to a problem we've been trying to solve for a while now."

"What problem?" Kobie came over.

Blair motioned around them. "Not this one, another one we've been trying to figure out for a while."

"With the missing women?" Shaelan asked.

Blair gave her a surprised look; the fact Calum had shared information told him that having a mate had changed the man he thought was unchangeable. "Yeah. We've tried tracking them and lost them in the middle of nowhere." He gave Kobie a look, "I told him about you and the rubbing alcohol."

She nodded. "It works better than anything else I've tried."

"Did you discover it by trial and error?" Shaelan asked her.

Kobie shook her head, "no, one of the elders told me about it, so I tried it to see."

Calum came over and looked around, no one was ready to go.

"Got distracted." Blair said, then motioned to the others and spoke to Kobie, "we're heading out."

Calum looked at his mate, "I'll shift along with Blair to track anyone else out there."

Shaelan nodded, "at least I can wear the backpack on my back this time." She gave him a soft look and went over to help the others get ready.

"I'm shifting too." Kobie gave Calum a look, daring him to say otherwise.

Calum inclined his head.

When she walked away, Calum looked at Blair, a half-smirk on his face.

"Alpha's daughter," Blair said softly and then turned to go get his pack.

Kobie followed a good enough distance behind Blair that she could still scent everything around them as they went down to the bottom of the mountain. Reacting like she had when Daisie had told him who called wasn't her best moment. If she hadn't been in cat form, she would have handled it differently. She paused and looked behind them, then continued when she noticed nothing out of place. Who was she kidding, she would have reacted worse in a two-legged state, because at least as a cat she couldn't *say* what she had been thinking?

Blair stopped and looked back at her. When he continued to stand there, she picked up the pace, so he'd start moving again. He waited until she was beside him to walk again.

What was she doing? Kobie didn't know the man. She'd only just met him, and really, maybe this Kelsey and Layna were sisters or something. She'd overreacted, and it had happened before she could stop it. If she wasn't exhausted, anxious, and worried, she was sure she'd have a better handle on her emotions. Or hoped she would.

She should just tell him what was going on. That would be the simplest solution. Tell him he was her mate and her cat had her doing things that were—unpredictable. If she could roll her eyes in cat form, she would have. Telling him was the worst possible thing she could do.

Calum came running past her so fast she startled. Stopping, she turned to see him running fast through the area to her right. She took in the scents and couldn't smell anything off. Blair came over and bumped her with his shoulder, telling her to keep going and let Calum be Calum. Hesitantly, she turned and ran up to the front so she could watch in that direction.

She noticed Shae give her backpack to Torrey at the same time Franki was passing hers off to Nichelle. Both women were ready to shift now if necessary. Shaelan watched to her left, barely looking in front of her again. She wasn't sure why her mate had taken off like that, but she would back him up if needed.

Pausing, she watched until Blair was in sight again. He didn't seem stressed out that his friend had taken off. She just needed this to end. She'd never been so off her game as she had been in the last few days.

Shaelan motioned to go through a small pathway, so Kobie turned and lead the group that way. She could smell that Calum and his mate had been this way before and wondered if they'd found a good place to stop before coming to meet them. These people were very well organized. It was the only thing that made her feel better that her brother and father had set up this emergency plan without telling her.

She walked through a group of trees to see a hollowed-out area that wasn't quite a cave about twenty feet ahead. It had a good place to sit on top to keep watch, and there was no way to get around it in any direction but head-on. Turning she glanced at Shaelan, who nodded. This is where they were staying until morning.

Chapter Ten

Blair paced ten feet in the other direction again. He turned and looked back at the entrance, where everyone was settled for the night. He'd seen Calum come out about an hour ago and disappear into the trees. If he was running the perimeter, then Blair would stay close by and keep watch. He wanted to shift and go for a fast run, burn off some energy and maybe put an end to this never-ending thinking. He didn't usually mind thinking things over, but this was getting ridiculous.

Giving his head a quick shake, he walked further away from the small cave to put some distance from the new reason his brain wouldn't shut off. He'd spent the entire evening stalking Kobie with his eyes, and he wasn't exactly sure why. He liked women, that was nothing new, appreciated all varieties—but this, this he hadn't done in a few years' time, and it was making him so uneasy in his own skin.

The last time he was this lost in his own head over a woman was with Kelsey—right after he found out she was off-limits. He caught himself wanting to look back to where everyone was and blew out an uneasy breath. *Knock it off. You should only be focused on getting them all out of here tomorrow.* Then what? He had no idea. Would he be asked to stay with them until they got everything sorted out? He didn't know.

Rubbing a hand over his jaw, he straightened and moved over to the left, so he'd have a better view of the area coming up to here. Why, he was now wondering, did it bother him that if he wasn't asked to stay with them? That was the plan—meet them and get them to where they were going, right?

A branch snapped behind him. He sprung around ready to fight if needed. Kobie stood there watching him.

"I didn't want to sneak up on you." She said in a hushed voice.

He relaxed—mostly and then nodded, "appreciate it." He stood there, wondering why she wasn't back with the others sleeping. "Can't sleep?"

She shook her head, "I did for a few minutes, I think." Turning, she surveyed all around them. "Calum out?"

Blair nodded, "he'll make a sweep of the entire area."

She came toward him, "he does this sort of thing often?" She stopped, leaving a foot between them. "Save people."

"Yeah." Blair tucked his hands in his pockets, trying to puzzle out why he wanted to reach out and brush the hair back from her face.

"Look," she clasped her hands in front of her body, a very submissive motion in their world, "I'm sorry about earlier," she looked down at the ground for a second, "when I stepped on your chest."

He honestly didn't know what to say. 'That's okay.' Seemed like it was inviting her to do it again and he still wasn't sure what had happened.

"I'm not—" she met his cautious look, "I don't know what happened," she lifted her hands out from her body and shrugged, "my cat," she frowned, "likes you," he raised one eyebrow to that, "I mean our cats seem to have a symmetry with each other." She nodded.

Blair just stood there, now curious to see where she was going with this.

"When Daisie started rhyming off women..."

"Kelsey is my boss' mate. I've known her since she was

fifteen." He said in a hushed way. It wasn't a lie, but he felt strange saying it. "Layna is the daughter of the man that runs the farm for the clan. I've known her since she was twelve." Again. Truth. His gut wouldn't let him add any more to any of that explanation. He needed to think through the truths he'd just spoken.

Kobie inhaled a deep breath and then nodded. "I shouldn't have reacted like that."

Blair tilted his head, trying to remember where that effortless charm was he normally had. "It's been a rough week for you."

She huffed out a breath but made no comment.

Now she stood there looking as awkward as he felt. Not sure what else to do, he turned and motioned in the direction he should have already checked. "I was going to check that area. Want to come?"

She nodded and started going that way.

Blair inhaled and tried to process all the scents the slight breeze was bringing to him, but all he could smell was lemon and rose? First, those were odd fragrances to mix, and second, Calum was right, she wore some kind of scent. He lengthened his stride so he was walking beside her again. "What's with the perfume you're wearing?" He waved a hand in front of his face. "It's messing with me picking up other scents."

She paused in step for a second, then sighed, "it's to keep me off male radars."

He couldn't help the surprised look on his face. "And that's an issue normally?"

Kobie nodded, then gave him a half shrug. "You never know, right?" She stopped and shook her head, "I shouldn't have it on right now," she motioned to the area in front of them, "not when you and Calum are trying to keep us all safe."

Blair's chest tightened at the despondent note in her voice. "We'll get it done, just maybe lay off it until we get back to civilization?"

She looked up at him and his heart jerked in his chest to see the anxious look on her face.

"Hey," stepping closer, he cupped the side of her face. "You're going to get through this. All of you are." He offered a brief encouraging half-smile.

Placing her hand over his that was still on her face, she nodded. "Thank you." Resting her other hand on his chest, she stretched until he could feel her breath on his mouth. She brushed her mouth over his and then leaned back, a shy look on her face. "I'm going to rest again."

As she walked back, without making a sound, he noted, all he could do was lick his lips and wish for a more thorough taste of her. Turning, he almost jumped into the tree to see a jet-black jaguar standing behind him. He didn't need to ask 'what', the expression was easy enough to translate, and he was right. He needed to get his head in the game. "I need to go for a run." Calum stepped aside as if to say, 'have at it'.

Kobie touched her mouth and then shook her head. What has possessed her to do something like that? Hadn't she just spent the last day telling herself to stay away from Blair? So what's the first thing she does once clearing the cave? Inhale and find out where he is. *Stupid.* Ignoring this mate thing wasn't as easy as she'd always imagined it would be.

When she stepped outside, she listened. There was no movement inside. Deciding she didn't want to lie down just yet, she went over to the side of the entrance and sat down. She'd barely had time to settle her breathing when Calum came walking out of the trees. He was wearing his jeans and carrying his shirt in one hand. As if she knew, Shaelan came out of the small cave. He smiled and held out his hand. Kobie had to curb the urge to sigh out loud with how in synch they seemed to be. Did she want something like that?

"Trouble sleeping?"

She realized Shaelan was speaking to her and nodded.

"You should try," Calum said quietly. "This isn't over yet."

"I know, I'm just too unsettled." Kobie offered what she hoped was a positive expression, even though she felt anything but.

Calum looked back in the direction he'd come. "Blair seems to have that issue too."

Kobie did not want to talk about Blair. She did actually, which is why she wasn't going to. "So, are you both from the same clan?"

Calum hugged Shaelan into his side while she chuckled softly.

"No." Shaelan whispered, "not even close."

"Oh, how did you meet?"

Calum closed his eyes and made a face.

"I actually found him chained to a wall," Shaelan said with a smirk.

"Woman," Calum growled playfully. "We've talked about this." He did grin, so Kobie doubted he was upset by it.

"No, mate, you talked about it. I never agreed once." Shaelan smiled at Kobie and then took Calum's hand and walked around the opening to go to the shelf above the cave.

Getting up, Kobie decided she didn't want to sit here within seeing and hearing distance of the two soft-on-each-other mates that wanted some time alone. Stopping in the entrance, she looked back into the trees and inhaled slowly. She could smell Blair's cat. Biting her lip, she told her own no when it brushed up against her softly. Kobie knew at some point it wasn't going to be that easy to contain her where the tall, sexy man-tiger was concerned, but until they were safe, there was no other option. Even then, she still had some thinking to do.

Chapter Eleven

Blair grabbed his pack and looked around. It was just dawn now, and the group was already up, and ready to go.

"I'm just going to check the area," Kobie said, standing up and walking away from the group.

He watched her walk away. Scowling at the ground, he turned and went the other way. He'd go watch down the trail. Maybe Jesse would get here early and come up to meet them. Calum said it was about an hour's walk to where they were meeting. At this point Blair could probably run it twice, he almost needed to. His mind had been swimming in so many thoughts since last night he didn't know where to start.

"You need to stop this."

Blair was startled and turned to see Calum leaning against a tree. He hadn't been there three seconds ago when he'd looked that way. "Stop what?"

"This constant brain ramble you have going on."

He looked at him, trying to figure out if it was that obvious that his head was a fucking mess.

Calum looked amused for a second. "My cat can feel it anytime we're in scenting distance—you are doubting everything you do, think and say."

Blair thought of denying it but knew better. "I'm just—" he looked in the direction Kobie had gone and then at the ground for a moment before he chanced a quick glance to the man in front of him. He wouldn't understand, Calum always had it so together Blair thought for sure he was part machine or something. "Kelsey, my head was a fucking mess with all of that going into this," he motioned to the group of women, the group he hoped was oblivious to the internal soup that was his very existence since their strong, beautiful, and independent leader had come across that ditch.

"And?"

He'd almost forgotten he'd been talking to Calum. "*And* it's worse now than it was." He paced away and put more distance between them and the group. He didn't need anyone hearing the bull he was spouting off. He felt Calum come up behind him. "Kelsey's been in my heart, in one way or another, since that scared, grieving girl was brought to the shop to live among us."

"I know."

He liked that about Calum. He didn't use ten words when two would do. Blair blew out a breath, "I know I was head over heels..."

"But now it's changed."

Blair nodded. "Something has." He glanced over his shoulder to see Kobie was back and smiling at Shaelan. He wondered what was being said for a second. It was like the sunlight had filtered all the way through every branch and leaf to shine just on her as it rose in the sky. He rubbed a hand over his chest and sighed again. "I feel," he looked at the other man, almost scared to say it out loud, "I feel like I'm cheating on Kelsey because I-I'm..."

"She's your mate." Calum motioned with his chin back toward the women.

Blair jolted and looked from Calum to Kobie again. He'd been thinking that, but still hadn't come to grips with that possibility. "My cat is some stranger to me whenever she's close. It's like-like…"

Calum laughed quietly. "You don't have to explain. As far as unusual shit happening, I've recently been through the gauntlet—of—I can't even explain. I've never been at odds with my cat like I was with the situation when I met Shae." Calum looked at him for a moment, "the pheromones skyrocket when you two are near each other."

Blair just nodded and kept bobbing his head like an idiot. He wasn't sure why he was, but it was better than standing there scowling at the man. "Yeah, I guess you have been through a bit," he was trying to ignore the pheromones comment, "but now," he rolled his eyes and sighed once more trying to blow out the stupid thoughts in his head, "*if* I can get over this emotional block or whatever the hell it is with Kels—" he motioned toward the women with a wide sweep of his arm, "she's an Alpha's daughter, part of an Alpha family," he didn't want to say it but did anyway, "even if they don't make it back to her, she's still..."

"Out of your league?"

Blair nodded, lifted his hand, then let it drop again. "I'm just—*fuck*," he chuckled at his own situation. Him bumbling around a woman was new. "I don't even know my original clan or anything other than my mother sent me away before she died." He looked at Calum, who stood there with his expression blank. He had no idea what he was thinking or if he was at all.

"All right." Calum motioned to the path that led up the incline.

Frowning, Blair started walking in that direction, having no idea why he was taking them to where they couldn't see the others.

"As you know, or maybe you don't, I do a lot of different things for the Alliance..."

Blair nodded, "yeah you're like superman or something."

Calum smirked, "or something." He shrugged, "I need to know about a lot of things that even most of the council aren't aware of."

That surprised Blair, but he didn't acknowledge it. "Makes

sense with some of the shit you have to do." He shrugged, "Gage has told us about some of it, after."

"I also like to know everything about anyone that has any sort of contact with Devin."

Blair nodded again. "Logical," like Calum always seemed to be.

"I know about your clan, Blair, your original one."

Blair swallowed but couldn't get a single syllable to come out of his mouth.

"Some of it you're going to wish I didn't tell you." The look on Calum's face was asking if he should continue or stop talking.

Shit. He paced away, then spun back around and looked at him. "Just tell me. I've spent the better part of the last fifteen years trying to think of reasons."

"Okay." Calum motioned to a log and then stood there until Blair sat down.

He didn't want to sit, but if the shit was so bad Calum thought he needed to sit, then he needed to sit.

"Your mother sent you to Ed's after your father was killed. She knew they would go after you and wanted you kept safe."

Blair sat there, just listening, trying not to react. He knew Calum would tell him slowly and let him digest or hoped he would. *Why would they go after me? I was two.*

"She died shortly after that. I'm not sure if it was natural causes or not." He didn't look away from him the whole time he was talking. "Your clan was still in the same area, there were around two dozen when last I checked on them."

Blair's expression was hard to guard at this point. His clan still existed.

"You don't want to go there. You do not want to meet them." Calum said in a low tone.

"I don't?" He rubbed a hand over his hair.

"No. Your clan was one of the first to work *with* Alberto Tomas—voluntarily..."

Blair jumped up. *Holy shit. My clan is part of the horrible shit that had been happening to shifters all over.*

"Your father and mother were against it. Tried to stop it and move the clan. That's why he was killed. Your father was the Alpha. *You're* from an Alpha family. Your brother is still part of *that* clan and is working with Aiden Tomas. If your mother hadn't sent you away, you would be working for Aiden Tomas right now."

Blair sat down; afraid his legs were going to give out. *Brother?*

Calum leaned against the tree and watched him. He was sure he must have had ten different emotions crossing his face all at once, but he just stood there and let him process without comment. When Blair took a deep breath, trying to find the words to speak. Calum straightened away from the tree. "An Alpha mate is fitting for you."

He couldn't think of a word to say. Before he could try, Torrey came running through the trees.

"Blair! Daisie is gone."

Calum spun around.

"She was right there behind me, at the side of the path talking about a flower and when I turned, she was gone."

Blair jumped up and started running back to the others. He stripped his shirt over his head and tossed it on the ground when he grabbed his pack.

"Hurry," Cortney grabbed Kobie's pack and tossed it to him. "Kobie just went after her. She told me to stay here…"

Calum was right behind him. "Everyone, get in the sheltered area." He turned to Blair as he pulled off his boots. "Go after her. I'll stay here and watch the rest."

Blair just nodded and ran over to the other side of the path. He looped Kobie's pack over his head as he undid his jeans. Stuffing them into his pack, he zipped it and shifted faster than his next breath.

Less than two seconds later, he was following Kobie, Daisie, and two other scents he didn't know. Two other shifters. They'd been on two feet when they'd taken her and then shifted. He couldn't be one hundred percent certain, but he was thinking wolf and some other canine breed. What he knew was when he caught up to them, he planned to take all his confusion and frustration out on them.

His paws slid along the incline as he went down it fast. How had they gotten this far so quickly? Bounding over a downed log and a few stumps, he caught something light-colored to his left. Landing, he turned to see it was Kobie squatting down behind a large vine-covered area. She was completely naked. Shaking his stunned brain into action, he leaped over to her, landed quietly, and then shifted back into his skin.

She held her finger over her mouth and then pointed at the vines.

Pulling her pack over his head, he set it beside her and ducked his head closer to look through the vines. Thirty feet on the other side of the thick foliage area stood Daisie. She had her arms crossed over her chest and stared at the wolf in front of her.

"I am not getting on your back again. I only did because he," she pointed to the jackal, "was going to bite me." Daisie finished. "So, bite me."

Atta girl, stand your ground. Blair leaned over closer to Kobie and put his lips against her ear, "I'm going to distract them, you shift and get in there and get her." He whispered in barely an audible tone. *She smells fucking amazing. The oils are gone after she shifts...*

She turned, her dark eyes holding his own. She looked like she was going to object.

"Kobie, just do it." He whispered but knew she would hear. "Get her back to the others, Calum will stop anyone that tries for her again."

The hard expression on her face softened. She nodded and placed her palm against his cheek. Leaning forward, her face almost touching his, "be careful," she whispered.

Blair's cat inside him froze when she brushed a kiss so lightly, he may have in fact imagined it against his mouth. He nodded. "Run fast." He told her.

He watched her shift back into her sexy white striped cat and then took his pack off and shifted. He'd always been warned if you fight, don't give them anything to get a hold of. Hopefully, he could find his pack after, the growth here was insanely thick. Before he could synch up with his cat completely, the traitorous creature rubbed his head along her shoulder. He needed to move before he did something really stupid. He bound out of the greenage into the open. The two other animals trying to corral Daisie spun to face him.

"Kick their butts, Blair," Daisie said loudly.

He looked at her long enough to assess she was all right and then vocally let the two animals advancing on him know they had picked the wrong child to mess with. He needed to get them to turn their backs to the shrubs so Kobie could get out without being seen. Daisie was smart. She would know to run to her as soon as she spotted her.

Blair had a lot more power than these two, he used it to spring and leap over them and land behind them. Both made fast work of spinning to face him. He hissed and issued one final warning sound, buying just enough time for him to see Kobie creeping out of the foliage and Daisie moving in her direction.

The wolf, ears flat, bared his teeth and utter a low growl. If Blair had been able to scoff in cat form, he would have. He had a shit ton of aggravation to burn out of his system and these two suckers were going to be his sacrifice.

Pouncing, he squashed the jackal into the ground and then used one of his large paws to bat him out of the way. Without pause, he turned and leaped at the wolf.

Chapter Twelve

Kobie ran as fast as she could. Her cat was torn between carrying Daisie back to safety and helping Blair. So far, she was listening and taking the child back to her mother. Daisie held onto the strap for her pack, but still had trouble sliding to the side as Kobie turned to go up an easier route to get back to the others. Cortney would be going crazy worrying about her. Those thoughts helped her stay on course and get back.

She put on a burst of speed as she went through the densely treed area before the incline to the cave. A large male jaguar met her halfway down the hill. She knew it was Calum and didn't pause to see if he was following or going to help Blair. She hoped for the latter.

Cortney came running out of the shelter and scooped Daisie off her back and went back to the safety of inside. Kobie looked back up the pathway.

"You should stay." Shaelan stepped out of the shadow of the entrance. "Blair is probably on his way back now."

Kobie looked at her, then back into the trees. Calum came bounding back at a full run and then right past her to check the other side of the trail. Shaking her head, Kobie went over to the side and shifted back. It would be easier to stay here if she was on two legs than her unpredictable cat was controllable. She didn't want to run back and end up distracting him. If anything happened to him, she'd be mad at herself for the rest of her life. Her cat was not happy they weren't going back for him. He had to come back. He had to be okay. She ignored the feelings of ire inside her chest. She shouldn't have left him. Why had she listened without question?

Torrey came out when she was walking back, carrying her shoes. "Daisie okay?"

Torrey nodded. "A little shaken, but" she shrugged, "you know Daisie—first thing out of her mouth was she was hungry." Torrey's voice shook as she spoke.

Crossing her arms over her stomach, she looked back, hoping she would see Blair's cat running toward them.

"He'll be okay." Shaelan came to stand beside her.

Kobie nodded, unable to find her voice to speak. He had to be all right.

Calum came out of the trees in his jeans. He glanced up at her but seemed to know not to tell her to come down and hide inside with the others. She wasn't moving until Blair was back—and if he took too long; she was going to find him.

Blair elected to jog and walk back to the cave. Something with his cat had almost scared him and he felt it was safer to stay on two legs, even though his bare feet weren't happy with that decision. He walked down the path and dropped the two packs from the other men on the ground. Calum came over and looked at them, a sober expression on his face. Blair jerked his head toward them. "ID's and phones." Calum raised an eyebrow and glanced at the borrowed shirt tied around Blair's arm. "It's not too serious."

Kobie came running down from the shelf and right for him. He wasn't sure if that was anger, annoyance, or concern on her face. She grabbed his hand and shoved it off his arm so she could look under the shirt.

"It's pretty deep. You need to hydrate, have something to eat and then shift again to heal it."

Shaelan looked at Calum going through the two packs and then came over and lifted the shirt away from his arm. "I can put a light stitch in it to stop the bleeding until you shift."

Blair nodded. He needed to stay on two legs for a bit. His cat liked blood, and he didn't need to be raging through the bush right now on a killing spree. He had no problems fighting for the right reasons, but the fury that had taken over his cat wasn't a good thing. He needed to think about that before shifting again.

"I'm going to call Devin and tell him about this." Holding up the wallets, he gave Blair a quick look, "we have addresses and new locations to check now." He glanced up the trail and sent Blair an inquisitive look.

Blair shook his head. "They won't be returning."

With a look of satisfaction, Calum nodded and walked down the trail.

"Find out where Jesse is too, Cal," Shaelan called after him. "I'll go get my bag." She went back inside.

Blair looked down at Kobie, "Daisie okay?"

She nodded and pressed the shirt against his arm again. "Is this the only injury?"

Blair gave her a brief nod. "I outweighed them by a lot, it almost wasn't a fair fight."

"Are they dead, Blair?"

The nerve in his jaw twitched while he decided if he should tell her the truth or breeze over it. "Yes. I threw the bodies over the ravine."

She inhaled through her nose slowly, then blew it out of her mouth. "Good." Without warning, she wrapped her arms around his waist and hugged him, pressing her cheek over his heart. "Thank you for coming to get her."

"Of course, I'd come." He held her. *This feels righter than anything I've felt in years.*

"I couldn't have taken both." She said quietly.

He didn't like the tone of shame in her voice. Blair leaned back and look at her. "No one expected you to."

"Hunting and tracking I know..."

He saw Shaelan coming back carrying a small bag. "You tracked them, I just followed you." It wasn't entirely true, but he didn't want her to be too harsh on herself. Most wouldn't have taken off after her at all.

"I'm going to keep watch." She released him and jogged away before he could say a word.

He could barely still long enough to have a few stitches put in his arm. Everything Calum had told him before Daisie was taken was now replaying in his mind, over and over.

Assessing there were two of the others watching in various directions, Blair walked away. The storm filling him was overwhelming. One problem being around so many other shifters were they would pick up on the emotions of others if they were strong enough.

He stopped when he was far enough away from the others and tried to breathe it away and settle down. He had a brother. A brother that worked for the Tomas family—voluntarily. He hadn't asked how old his brother was, obviously older than him, but by how much? He was from an Alpha family. His father had been the Alpha. He frowned, unless his clan, he shook his head. No, his clan was Ed's not that other one—if the clan he was born into functioned as most clans that meant his brother, did he want to know his name? He wasn't sure— his brother was Alpha of a clan that was responsible for a lot of the torment and heartache caused by the Tomas family.

His heart jerked in his chest. That clan was part of the reason Kelsey's parents were gone. He could never tell her. Would Kobie and her clan think less of him if they knew? He could tell no one.

Shaking his head, he looked down at his arm. He should go shift and heal this completely. He took two steps and saw the expression on Calum's face as he came back up the path. It wasn't good, that's all he knew. *What now?* Calum stopped and motioned for him to come down.

Glancing over his shoulder, Blair checked that Torrey and Kobie were keeping watch over the others. He walked toward him; a questioning look sent to the other man.

Calum shook his head and then stood there looking at his phone.

"What's going on?"

"Jesse will be here soon; he found a faster route." Calum motioned up the incline, "we'll go get everyone moving in a minute."

That was all good news, so what was the bad? "And?"

Calum nodded his head slowly, "*and* Kobie's brother was found." His tone was sober. "He's alive, but they're not sure if he's going to make it."

Blair looked over his shoulder to make sure they were alone. Running his fingers across his hair, he looked at Calum for a moment. "If I tell her, she's not going to leave."

"They're trying to stabilize him for transport." Calum looked up at the trees and then back at him. "Don't tell her yet."

Blair closed his eyes for a second, then opened them and sent him a blank look. "Secrets tend to come back and bite me *hard*."

Calum's mouth quirked like he wanted to grin but didn't. "If it comes to light, just tell her you were waiting for an update on how he was doing before telling her."

"We have to get them out of here." Blair paced a few feet away. "When they don't hear from those other two, they're going to send more after them, if they haven't already." He growled in the back of his throat. "They'll keep coming for nine females until we get them back to safety."

"May not stop even after we do." Calum motioned to go back up. "It's your call, but right now we need to get them down to meet Jesse." He looked at Blair's arm. "I'll stay on two feet until we reach the car."

Chapter Thirteen

Blair looked out the back window again. It was a good plan, having Calum and him follow them in Cal's car, but wished he had a bigger car. He looked at the big man driving. His seat back was so far back, he was half in the backseat. "I figured you'd have a truck."

Calum didn't even look over at him. "I need to get places fast more often than most." He shrugged one shoulder, "and this is fast."

Blair couldn't argue with that. He looked back at the van in front of them. There were no windows. That was a good thing. No one would know how many or who was in the vehicle. It still bothered him *he* couldn't see in it though. He looked over his shoulder again. "This was easier when I was the driver." He grinned and gave his head a shake. "I always thought you were a paranoid bastard, now I understand why."

"I'm not paranoid, I'm cautious," Calum said in a quiet tone as he glanced at the side mirror. "That white car has been behind us for the last half hour."

"I saw it." Blair motioned out the window. "There's not any main roads around here for them to turn off on though."

Calum tapped his phone that sat in the holder on the dash.

"Yeah?" Jesse answered.

"Slow down for a few and see if this car goes past." Calum glanced in the mirror again.

"And if it doesn't?" Jesse asked.

"Then pull over on the shoulder. I will not spend the next hour wondering." His tone was hard. "Don't hang up."

Blair liked how Calum hit everything head-on. Too many wasted time skirting around issues.

"If they do anything other than go by us, if they even slow down and look too curious, get a pic of their plate." He told him.

Nodding, Blair lifted his phone he'd already taken out of his pack. "They could be with Tomas and just tailing us in hopes they'll get another chance or find out where we're going."

"I thought that too." He turned his head and glanced at him, "I don't like not knowing things for sure."

"They going to pass?" Jesse asked quietly."

"They're riding our bumper right now," Blair told him.

"Pull over, Jesse," Calum said in a low tone.

Blair maneuvered to turn sideways in the seat as much as he could manage. He had the camera on his phone ready. The car pulled out and moved by them slowly. Two men were in it. Blair held his finger on the button and took continuous pictures. For a second, they looked like they were going to stop, then sped up and took off down the highway.

"You get their faces and plates?" Calum asked quietly.

Blair scrolled through the pictures quickly. "Clear shot of the passenger and the plates."

Calum undid his seat belt. "Give me five minutes and then go again, Jesse." He turned to Blair, "you drive, I'll meet up with you in a half-hour."

Blair opened his door, "I can go…"

Calum grinned, "my cat is faster." He got out of the car and grabbed his pack out of the back seat.

"You're going to run ahead of us?" Jesse asked through the phone as he leaned his head out the window and looked back at them.

Calum nodded and then jogged down into the ditch toward the trees that lined the highway. "I'll see you in a half hour."

Blair went around to the driver's side and then looked over at Jesse. Jesse grinned and shook his head. Getting in, he closed the door. "Leave the call going?" He asked.

"Yeah, until my fucking nerves settle down." That was the reply he got.

Blair grinned; he was glad he wasn't the only one strung out.

As they pulled out onto the highway, he was lost in his head. Knowing what he did now, going back to work at the shop seemed wrong. Blair was good at what he did, but his family— that clan he came from—he felt like he should be doing something to help put a stop to Tomas. He needed to talk to Gage and tell him what he was thinking. He should talk to Devin too, to see if he could work with the Alliance.

Checking in the mirror, he blew out a breath. He had to talk to Kelsey too. He understood she was mated, and he was— nothing but a good friend? Things had changed though, and he needed to tell her.

He glanced at his phone on the seat. Layna had called earlier again. Yeah, he needed to talk to her too.

Fuck. He had to talk to a lot of people all of sudden.

"Anyone tailing us?" Jesse's voice brought him back to what he was doing.

Blair checked the mirrors. "Road's clear."

"Good, let's hope it stays that way. I just want to get where we're going and have some backup."

Blair scowled as he looked at the back of the van. Who was the backup? Blair didn't care who it was, but he was staying with the women and making sure no one got near them again. "Yeah." He all but growled back at him.

"Calum's just checking to make sure that car kept going."

Blair stared at the phone, wondering why Jesse was telling him, then he heard Kobie speaking. He leaned closer to the dash so he could hear.

"He's very good at this, isn't he?" He heard her say. "Going to get people."

Jesse paused before answering her. "Yeah, he is."

It was true. Calum was good at it. Bair scowled at the road, bothered that she was talking about Calum. "I'll call if I see anything." He hung up the phone and then regretted it immediately. *That was a stupid move.* They needed to get where they were going and soon, Blair was slowly losing his mind in this compact car.

Kobie watched out the passenger's window when they pulled away. She'd been able to hear bits and pieces of the conversation that Jesse and was having. She was just about to ask who was running ahead when she spotted a black jaguar running into the trees. What happened that Calum was running ahead? Did that mean Blair was driving behind them?

She looked to the back of the van and wished for windows; she didn't like not knowing what was going on. Kobie still couldn't believe her family had this plan for her. She understood being the Alpha, her father didn't have to tell her everything, but her brother? They were the same age. How is it he knew, and she didn't? If there was one thing Kobie hated above anything else, it was secrets.

When her mother had disappeared five years ago, no one told her what had happened. Then another woman went missing a year later. It continued that way for a few more years until ten women and children disappeared in less than a year's time. She couldn't help wondering if her mother was with this Tomas person. Would it be a silly fantasy to hope she was still alive?

Glancing around, she noted everyone was napping or staring off into space—not that they had any choice. Blowing out a breath, she watched out the window again. She couldn't do it. Just sit here being in the dark.

Shifting forward, she cleared her throat so Jesse would know she was leaning right behind him now.

"Is everything all right?"

She watched him bob his head a few times, "Calum's just checking to make sure that car kept going."

"He's very good at this, isn't he?" He didn't reply. "Going to get people." She clarified, just in case he didn't know what she was talking about.

"Yeah, he is."

"I'll call if I see anything." Blair's voice came over the phone. She looked at the back of the van and wished again she could see—he didn't sound happy about something.

Turning back, she leaned closer to Jesse. "How long until we get there?"

"At least three hours."

"Oh, that long." She grimaced, "you've been driving a while today then?"

Jesse shifted around in his seat. "Feels like forever."

Nodding, Kobie sat back, "I'm just going to close my eyes for a few."

"I'll shout if there's anything you need to know." He told her.

She was tired, but she really just wanted to close her eyes and think. She had too much to think about and no idea where to start. Of course, if she could keep her mind from wandering back to Blair every two minutes, that would make it a lot easier.

What happened after they reached this place? Is that where they were staying? She didn't know. Was Blair staying when they got there or was his part finished? She didn't know how she felt about him leaving, although at this point with so much happening, she didn't know how she felt if he stayed either.

Opening her eyes, she checked on everyone again. This was going to be the longest drive ever.

Chapter Fourteen

Blair got out of the car and stretched. That was about all the car rides he could deal with for a few weeks. He was really missing his truck. Dropping his hands to his waist, he turned and looked around slowly. The house was enormous, which is probably why the Alliance had it, to house many shifters at once. A man was standing at the gate with an automatic rifle. Turning, he looked over to see a smaller building that may have been a small guest house at one time. Two men stood outside it, both had rifles. He wasn't a big fan of guns, but after the last few days, he was happy for the backup.

"First thing I'm doing is having a shower."

He turned to see Annamarie getting out of the van. He was happy to see the long drive hadn't dampened her dramatic flair.

"First thing you're doing is helping take the packs in and emptying them," Franki told her.

Catching a backpack that was tossed at her, Annamarie sighed dramatically.

"It's pretty here," Daisie said as she stood there hugging her mother.

Kobie climbed out next and Blair forgot everyone else around them. Even sitting in a van for that long, she looked great. He was suspecting he was biased or she always looked fantastic.

"Blair?"

Blair jumped to see Calum standing beside him, he pointed to the smaller building. "That's the guardhouse, where are the camera feeds are."

Nodding, Blair headed toward it. He'd go out and run the property shortly, but he wanted to see how safe this *safe* house was.

The house was huge, with many rooms. It was clearly just a brief stopping point for the shifters they brought here, though. The furniture was sparse. There was a big cupboard on the main floor with clothes of all sizes. The only part that seemed like it was a normal house was the kitchen. It was well stocked with all the utensils and wares a person could need.

After Blair wandered through the house and the immediate area outside, he met up with Calum, Jesse, and Shaelan standing talking quietly beside the fence at the back of the house.

He gave Calum a curious look.

"Kobie's brother is stable enough they want to bring him here, so we can move them together," Jesse said in a quiet tone.

"I wouldn't call him stable." Shaelan shook her head, "he's not in good shape at all." Nodding, she looked at Calum, "we're staying so I can look after him."

Blair watched the expression on Calum's face change and turned to see Kobie coming over.

"I wanted to ask—" she looked from one to the other, then frowned, "what's wrong?"

"They found your brother." Jesse received a look from Calum that said he should have waited to tell her.

Kobie sucked in a breath, "he's all right?"

The men looked at Shaelan, Blair felt like he was passing it off to her, but honestly didn't know how to tell her.

Clasping her hands in front of her, Shaelan gave her a gentle look. "He's in very bad shape. I spoke to Devin and honestly, it's a miracle he's alive."

Blair swallowed so he could force air into his lungs past the lump of apprehension forming in his throat.

"Did they just find him? Maybe it's not as bad…"

"They found him when we were leaving the mountain," Calum told her abruptly.

Blair closed his eyes and wondered why he would tell her that. Opening them again, he turned to see her facing away from them now.

"You knew?" Kobie spun toward Blair and glared at him.

How did she figure that out? Blair caught the cautious look Calum gave him as he guided Shaelan and Jesse in the other direction. He looked down at the angry dark eyes locked on him. "I knew they found him, and his condition was bad enough that they weren't sure he was going to make it."

Her eyes widened. "Why didn't you tell me? I would have…"

Blair leaned down and lowered his voice, trying to keep this under control. "That's why. You would have wanted to stay, then the others would have wanted to stay." She didn't look convinced, "we almost lost Daisie." He said it slow, reminding her of how it felt when it had happened. "Priority was to get *all* of you out of there to somewhere safe." The angry look changed little, but there was a quick flash in her eyes that told him she was reasoning with what he'd said.

"You still should have told me." Her tone was less hostile.

Blair took a deep breath and straightened. "I had to get you to safety, Kobie." He glanced at the door, then back to her, "I couldn't take a chance and wait around to see how soon he could be transported."

She bit her lip, her eyes still searching his face. "It's bad?"

Blair looked at the door, wishing Shaelan would magically appear again. Nodding his head slowly, he gave her a soft look, "it's bad," he motioned to the door, "Shaelan was just going to explain what the doctor told Jesse."

She took a ragged breath and hugged her waist. "I'm sorry." She nodded, "you're right, I would have stayed and put everyone at risk." Closing her eyes, she just stood there.

Blair rubbed his hand over his chest. He wanted to pull her into his arms and comfort her. His cat was silent inside him, not knowing what to do either. Just knowing she was upset. "It's your brother, I get it," he didn't really, "we also wanted more information before we told you." He watched her open her eyes slowly and look at him again. He could see the pain in them. "I didn't want you losing your mind not knowing a thing about his injuries."

She nodded, then looked at the door. "Were any others found?"

Blair tucked his hands in his pockets so he wouldn't hug her. "No."

Kobie blew out a loud breath, "Jay has to be okay." She motioned around them, "if my dad didn't make it, he has to be Alpha." She wiped a tear off her cheek, "I'm the only other relative left and I think my reaction a few moments ago proves I'm not Alpha material."

His cat brushed against him, prodding him to comfort her. "Hey," reaching over, he lifted her chin, so she'd look at him, "you got them out of there. Most wouldn't have managed that in this situation. Daisie is still here because you were right on their heels when they took her—"

"Blair."

Dropping his hand, he turned to look at Calum standing there.

"One of the cameras at the back of the property has picked up movement."

"Fuck. They can't have gotten here before us." He started walking.

Shaelan came outside. She gave Kobie an understanding look. "Come in and have some tea. I'll explain what's happening with your brother."

Blair paused and watched her go inside. He pulled his shirt over his head. "Tell the guards not to shoot me."

Calum chuckled. "Us. Not to shoot us." He looked over at Jesse, who saluted and walked toward the guards' house.

After running the property three times, he met up with Calum, still in cat form. From the way he was looking around and checking the air, he found nothing as well. They both turned and ran back toward the house.

Pulling his jeans up, he turned to see Calum scowling.

"I got nothing," Blair said and picked up his shirt and boots.

They rounded the corner of the house to see Kobie sitting on the step.

Blair blew out a breath and looked around. "Where are the guards if she's out here and there was a potential intruder?"

Calum made a soft growling noise. "I'll go ask them," he motioned to the small building across from the house. "You go explain why she shouldn't be outside."

Blair stopped and watched him keep walking. "And find out what the camera's picked up? Was it a bird, an animal, or what?"

Calum lifted his hand to acknowledge he'd heard and kept going.

Blair turned to see Kobie coming over to him.

"What was it?" The concerned look on her face made him a little less perturbed she was sitting there possibly putting herself in danger.

"We couldn't find anything." He stood there, refusing to give in to his cat's prompts to go comfort her worry. "You shouldn't have been outside," he looked around, "alone when there was a possibility of someone being on the property."

"I was worried about you." She stopped in front of him and hugged her arms around her waist.

It thrilled his cat to hear this, he was annoyed that he was happy to hear it and thus it softened the lecture he planned to give her. "While I appreciate that, thank you, it still doesn't change the fact that they will do anything—*anything*," he enunciated clearly, "to get to you and your clan women." He nodded slowly as her expression changed, "if there's a threat, you're inside—*locked* inside with lookouts." His resolve ended abruptly when she looked at him with an almost hurt expression in her eyes. "Help me keep you guys safe?"

She inhaled slowly, then nodded.

"Blair."

He turned to look at Calum leaning out the door of the little building. "It was a person."

"Bull shit." Blair started stomping over. "A person with *no* scent?" He paused and turned back to Kobie. He motioned with his head for her to come over.

Jesse stood there with Calum now.

"Does your little alcohol stunt purge the smell completely?" He shrugged, "is it a temporary stall technique or is it washed away forever?"

Kobie looked confused, "I checked it out thoroughly before using it, there's no scent forever." She shook her head, "I mean, if you miss a foot placement or something you touched, it's there, but once it's sprayed on it's gone."

Blair turned to see Calum standing there with his hands on his hips.

Jesse nodded when he looked at him. "Increase the patrols?"

"Yeah," Calum motioned to the back of the property, "every half hour, every other body out goes in a different direction. Nothing predictable." He turned slowly and looked all around them, then pointed, "find me some binoculars," he pointed to a hill that was higher than the landscaping around them. "Blair and I are going up there for an aerial look-see."

It surprised Blair he was taking him, but if Calum could teach him a few things that he'd need to keep these women safe, he'd take it.

Chapter Fifteen

Blair stared at the ceiling; he didn't know how long he'd been trying to fall asleep—but his internal clock told him it was too damn long. He should have passed out as soon as his head hit the pillow. Calum and he had not only gone to check on the hill to get a view of the area surrounding the property, but they'd run the outskirts and adjacent properties—twice, to check for any scents that shouldn't have been there. Then he'd come back and eaten enough for three people before walking, on two feet, the perimeter of the yard around the house.

So why wasn't he sleeping?

Right. He couldn't sleep because his brain and cat wouldn't shut up. He somehow needed to tell Kobie that she was his mate. Normally, he'd have no problem with that—or he hoped he wouldn't, but this was not normal. Not only had she just lost most of her clan, her father, and her home, but her brother might not make it either.

She was very perceptive, how hadn't she figured it out too? They'd been close enough in both forms during their trek up and over the mountain. Closing his eyes, he rubbed them. With everything happening in her little world right now, he was lucky she wasn't running around freaking right the fuck out.

Blowing out a breath, he rolled over and grabbed the pillow to squish it up more. He had to sleep, or he was going to end up running around freaking the fuck out tomorrow—or killing everything in sight.

"Blair."

He opened his eyes to see Daisie leaning over him. "What's wrong?" He blinked to try to focus.

"I can't find Kobie." She whispered.

He was awake now. "I'm coming. Wait outside."

As soon as the door closed, he flipped the blanket back and grabbed his jeans off the floor. He didn't even bother doing them up completely. Opening the door, he motioned for Daisie to go downstairs. "Did you tell the guys on watch?"

"I don't know them."

He didn't blame her, a few were even scary looking to him. "Okay. Did you check the *whole* house and yard?"

She nodded.

Reaching the bottom of the stairs, he touched her shoulder and then leaned down to talk to her. "Go knock on Calum's door and tell him, okay? Tell him I'm going to look."

She nodded. "Okay." She hugged him quickly. "Please find her." Turning away from him, she ran back up the stairs.

Blair went out the door and jogged over to the guardhouse.

When he opened the door, the one man in the room jolted like he'd been asleep. "Did you see Kobie go anywhere?" He motioned to his head, "pale blonde hair."

The guy shook his head.

Blair snarled, "check the tapes." He grabbed a radio off the table and went back out the door.

Going to the middle of the drive, he inhaled deeply and tried to catch her scent. If she used that damn alcohol to cover her tracks, he was going to—he didn't know what, but it wouldn't be pleasant.

Turning, he inhaled again. She'd gone this way. He picked up another scent as he started walking that way. He didn't recognize who it was. Blair's cat was on full alert and made him even more unsettled. Jogging, he headed in the direction her scent was going. The radio in his hand beeped softly. Stopping, he depressed the button, "Did you find anything on the cameras?"

"No. There's no movement since patrol an hour ago."

Shit. "Okay, check in with the other posts." He started jogging again. How had the cameras not caught her leaving? There had to be blind spots.

He kept running. Her scent was so strong now, a few times he thought he'd lost it, and was afraid she was gone from him, then he'd pick it up again. He was halfway to the back of the property when he picked up her cat's—she'd shifted. Why had she shifted? Stopping he turned slowly and inhaled, trying to sense any threats.

"Blair."

It was Calum on the radio. "I'm heading to the back." He told him quietly while watching and listening all around him. "She shifted."

"Is she alone?"

Blair blew out a quiet breath and tried to take in all the smells nearby, "I think so."

"What the hell is she doing?" Cal sounded as unhappy as Blair was starting to feel

"I don't know. Can you check the perimeter and see if anyone has been near here?"

"We already are. Keep us informed."

Blair knew that was the last of Cal using the radio unless they found something. He was just about to strip off his jeans when he realized he hadn't brought a pack. *Fuck.* He had nowhere to put the radio. *Shit.* Clipping it to his jeans, he started jogging toward the back. He scented the running water and was just about to radio and ask if the river was deep enough for a small craft to use it when Kobie stepped out of the trees. He stopped and stood there. She was wearing jean cut-off shorts and a halter top; both left a lot of glorious skin showing. In her hand were a string of fish and a makeshift spear out of a tree branch.

Turning her head, she shook her hair back from her face and smiled at him. "I needed to clear my head."

Blair felt his head moving. He was nodding, but words hadn't yet formed in his brain.

"Is everything all right, Blair?"

Fuck. He blinked. *No.* His brain reminded him. "You should have told someone where you were going." He remembered the radio and pulled it off his jeans to tell Cal to call off the search. "Found her. Everything is fine." That was a lie. Things were so far from fine right now. She'd scared the hell out of him and then reappears looking like some jungle goddess for fuck's sake.

"Sorry. I thought we had free roam of the land."

"You do, but you need to let someone know where you're going."

She lifted her hand with the fish in it, "hunting makes my head right."

He didn't care about the damn fish, not in any way. Okay, he did because she'd just caught a string of fish with a stick. Impressive. He couldn't stop looking at her. Her legs were long and toned—images of them wrapped around him popped into his head. His cat was assessing her as well and not helping him concentrate. Her body was toned, not sculpted, but curved in all the right ways. He had the urge to taste her skin.

She stopped walking and motioned behind her, "the river is so full of fish they practically jumped out for me."

He heard her, but his voice was paralyzed as he stared at the small tattoo of a black tiger resting on her skin just below the curve of her waist.

"Oh," she put her hand over it, "I had it done before my first shift so it wouldn't heal. I had no idea I'd be black when I got it."

That hadn't even crossed his mind. Then again, his mind was lost in images he needed to not be thinking right now. "It's nice." He finally said. Remembering how panicked he'd been a few moments before, he motioned back toward the house. "We should get back. Daisie woke me in a panic when she couldn't find you."

She started walking. He followed a few steps behind, which was a bigger mistake. He watched the sway of her hips and the hint of a firm ass peeking out from the bottom of the denim with each step. *Fuck.* Was all his brain could form. His cat wasn't happy, and it took a moment to think past his lust to understand why. She was going to walk back through the yard for all the guards to see that perfect fucking body.

"Kobie." It came out harder than he'd intended. Stopping, she turned and looked back at him. *How the fuck do I say this?* Closing the distance between them, he looked down at her.

She stood there, looking up at him. Her midnight blue eyes searched his face.

"There's something we need to talk about." He watched her lick those pouty lips and forgot what he needed to say. *Fuck it.* He cupped the back of her head and pulled her closer. Before she could say a word, he crushed her mouth with his. He'd expected resistance and hesitation, but she surprised him by returning his kiss with a matched urgency. Growling, he dropped the radio and lifted her up higher so he could deepen the kiss and taste more of her.

Boosting up on his body, she squeezed his waist between her knees. Blair's cat went crazy with the feel of skin on skin— he wanted Blair to bite her. Blair wanted to mark her, and that urge made him slow the kiss and then lift his mouth from hers.

"I haven't decided, Blair." She said breathlessly, her soft mouth brushing against his.

As her words registered, she slid down his body and bent down to pick up the fish. "You knew?" He looked down at her swollen mouth then at the fast rise and fall of her breasts. She didn't deny it. "How long?"

"Since I crossed that ditch." She said whispered and then started walking.

Blair was stunned. His cat was elated. She knew. That was one less issue. Shaking his head, Blair disagreed. Grabbing the radio, he caught up to her. "Why didn't you say something?"

He frowned and forced his gaze to stay on the ground in front of him. The perfume. "You used those perfumes to throw me off, didn't you?"

"Don't be too flattered, I always use them."

"You're not now." He licked his lips and wanted to groan. They tasted of her.

"I ran out." She confessed.

Lightly gripping her arm, he stopped her and looked down at her. "What do you mean you haven't decided? Decided what?" They were mates. It wasn't like you could pass on that and wait for the next one. There was no next one.

Heaving a loud sigh, she locked eyes with him. "I don't think now is a good time to get mated."

Blair raised one eyebrow and stared at her. "Schedule too full?"

She gave him a hard look. "You know what I mean. My clan is almost all gone. I don't know what happened to our Alpha, my brother is gravely injured..."

He couldn't argue with any of that. It made him feel like a jerk but was too stunned to dig past it and find compassion right now. "You can't put your cat on hold until it's a more convenient time." Her confession popped back into his head. "You should have told me, rather than let me think I'm losing my mind."

She jerked her arm out of his hold. "As I said, it's been a bad time." She started walking.

Blair ground his teeth together and watched the sway of her walk. Growling low, he caught up to her. "If you need to go for a walk, or a run, or whatever—from now on you tell someone." He stepped in front of her, she almost walked into him. "And that," he motioned up and down her, "is sexy as fuck and you look fucking amazing in it but you need to not be wearing shit like that in front of all the other guys."

She scowled up at him.

Blair shrugged and tried to give her a simple expression without the rage, "sorry, I can only be so understanding," he leaned down closer, "and my cat has *no* understanding. So, let's be clear, babe, you're mine—our cats both know it." He saw the understanding reach her eyes. Straightening, he backed away, "don't make me start killing good men." With a quick nod, he turned around and headed back to the yard. He needed to go for a fucking run. He needed to go kill something, anything. *What the hell was this bullshit?* She'd known since the moment they met and had hidden that from him? No wonder his head was a complete mess.

Calum met him by the guardhouse and gave him a curious look and then looked behind him. "Problem?"

Blair stopped and looked at Kobie stomping across the yard, the fish swinging as she went. "Nope. No problem at all." Blair said in a low tone.

Calum snorted. "Okay." He rubbed the back of his neck. "Gage said to call him when you got a minute."

Blair nodded his head slowly and then finally looked at him when the door to the house slammed and Kobie was out of sight. "Did he say if Coop was all right?"

Calum leaned against the fence. "He said something about a stubborn, ornery old man, so I'm going to say Cooper is recovering and not as fast as he'd like to."

Blair grinned. "That sounds about right."

"Kobie's brother will be here tomorrow."

Blair took a deep breath and nodded. Would that make things better or worse? He didn't know. "I need coffee." He stomped toward the house.

Kobie scowled at the jeans, then pulled them up. Who was he to dictate what she wore? And *why* was she listening to him and changing? Zipping them, she lifted her hand to her mouth and touched her lips. She'd never been kissed like *that* before. Heat moved through her as she thought about it. Sure, she'd been kissed before, but nothing the way he had. Licking her lips, she realized she could still taste him. Pressing them together, she paused. Her cat rubbed up against her. Kobie couldn't remember ever reacting that way to a kiss either. She'd needed to kiss him back the same way, not want, but *need.* Her cat repeated the motion. "Stop. I know what you want, you hussy." It felt like she had butterflies in her stomach now. That annoyed her because she knew her body and her cat agreed. Her mind, however, was not about to let her climb that tall sexy body of his without thinking it all through. And there was a lot to think about. She would not be one of those silent complacent mates—women, whatever. Nope, she'd spent her whole life proving she was good enough to be included and respected. Giving into hormonal urges was not on the list of things she had plans to do.

Chapter Sixteen

Calum came out with Shaelan and stood to the side as the van pulled in. Blair was ten feet from him but still felt the anger radiate from him as he cursed under his breath and stomped toward the van.

The door opened and instead of a medic getting out, it was Devin Addison. Why was the prince here? Blair closed his eyes and hoped it was a quick visit, just to drop off Kobie's brother. When Rayne climbed out next, he knew it wasn't. Now he understood why Calum was pissed. They already had nine females to protect from Tomas—and now the future king and queen of the entire shifter world were here.

"What the hell are you doing here?" Blair heard Calum, despite him saying it low and quiet.

"I wanted to meet the woman that saved the rest of her clan," Devin said, but there was no missing the smirk he was trying to hold in.

"Fine. Go home, we'll bring her there next week." Calum said bluntly.

Shaelan moved over and opened the back of the van to help get Kobie's brother out. Blair's nerves were zinging. He didn't know what to expect in her twin. He was the last male of their clan at this point, and Blair didn't want to have him feel like he was moving in on their territory and taking over. No shifter, male or female, would handle that well.

Kobie came running across the yard toward them. *Shit.* Moving quickly, Blair went over to help get the stretcher out. There was an IV pole with two bags hanging from it, a monitor with vitals blipping across it. He couldn't see most of his body, but if his bandaged head and battered face were any indications of what the rest of him looked like, Blair didn't want to see the rest of him.

"Jay?" Kobie leaned over the stretcher as it cleared the doors.

"He's sedated for the trip." The man told her.

Blair's cat didn't like him standing beside Kobie, stepping closer, he put his arm around her and pulled her against his side. "Let's let them get him inside, then you can sit with him."

Shaelan was reading through the folder that had been sitting on top of the sleeping man. Her brows furrowed, and Blair really hoped it wasn't for bad reasons.

Kobie was shaking but made no move to step away from him. Blair walked slowly behind them, all while keeping Kobie steady. The man on the stretcher resembled her in that their hair was the same color, but there were too many stitches and bruises to tell beyond that. Actually, now that he was seeing him, he was shocked they'd transported him at all.

He glanced over at Calum, his expression matched Blair's feelings.

Blair pulled Kobie to the side of the kitchen as they moved her brother into the room right off it.

Rayne came over, with an amused expression she noted Blair was still holding Kobie. A gentle smile appeared on her face, then she inclined her head to Kobie, "I'm Rayne, Devin's mate."

Kobie stiffened, then inclined her head and kept it down until Rayne touched it softly. Kobie looked at her, "thank you for escorting my brother here."

Rayne glanced over at Devin for a second, "Devin was

hoping to talk to him, but that may have to wait for a few days."

Blair rubbed his hand over his hair but didn't say a word. They were staying a few days? *Shit*. He glanced to Calum, who had also heard them, and motioned to the man that had just come from the guardhouse.

He spoke to him quietly, but Blair caught the 'oh shit' look when he'd glanced at Devin and Rayne. With a nod, he rushed from the house. Security was about to be ramped up.

Blair wasn't sure if he'd slept the night before and he'd already patrolled twice today, and it was barely nine in the morning.

He checked again to see Kobie was sitting beside her brother. He'd only stirred once and then would go back to sleep since he'd arrived. The way the man looked; Blair was glad he was sleeping through the healing. It didn't matter what part of his body Kobie's brother would want to move, it was going to hurt. Eight broken bones, three fractures, multiple areas too bruised and swollen to be certain of injury, and stitches on five other areas of his body. All Shaelan had said on it was he was a strong man to have survived this far.

He looked at Kobie, she was speaking softly to her twin. He didn't want to hear what she was saying, but the expression on her face told him she was giving the man every reason to hang on and fight through it. The link between twins may be the reason he survived, Devin or Rayne had said that—he couldn't be sure because his head was too full of Kobie's distress at that point, but now he had to wonder if it was her will that had brought her brother this far.

Rubbing a hand over his chest, he nodded and decided he needed to get out of here and grab some air.

He made it three feet outside and spotted Devin on the phone. *Shit*. He was supposed to call Gage yesterday. *Fuck*. Pulling his phone out, he brought up the call list as he walked. He had no particular destination in mind, just hoped to be out of earshot of any shifters because this was going to be a hard conversation. For him mostly. He'd bailed on the team at the shop and took off to lick his wounds—if he hadn't, Cooper probably wouldn't be miserable and laid up in bed right now. He also wouldn't have met Kobie...

He was just about to hang up after five rings when Gage barked a hello into the phone.

"Bad time?"

"No. Yes, give me a second." He heard the phone hitting what could only be one of the tool trays. "Noah, you push from that side."

Blair closed his eyes and tried to picture what they were doing.

"Stupid, son of a..." There was a loud clanging sound of something large and metal hitting the floor. Gage was laughing. "After you pick Noah up, Jake, go give Gary a hand."

"Hello."

Blair smirked, "they jammed the conveyer return again."

Gage chuckled, "second time this week." He cleared his throat, "have you been avoiding me?"

Blair shook his head like the man could see him from there and started walking again, "no, not on purpose, it's just been a fucking adventure here."

"Yeah, got a text from Calum saying Devin showed up yesterday. He's not impressed."

Blair looked back toward the house. "Yeah, he's even less impressed that Devin won't stay in the house."

"We're doing well here, Noah is back, plus we have Kelsey wreaking havoc and making everyone look bad in the shop now—you're needed there, especially now that Calum has to shadow Dev."

Blair stared at the ground at his feet, he hadn't even thought of that in days. He continued to stand there; hearing Kelsey was in the shop hadn't hurt like it would have a week ago either. Shaking his head, "some of the guys they have as guards here aren't very good at it."

"How's that? Did you tell Calum? I'm sure he could get

Dev to pull some from somewhere else…”

“No. I’ve got it covered. I know we’re spread thin right now.” He clenched his jaw recalling, “Kobie strolled right past the entire watch. I almost had a heart attack,” he shrugged, “I thought Tomas’ guys had found us.”

“Everything all right?”

“Yeah—she went fishing, or more accurately caught a half dozen trout with a spear—to clear her head…”

Gage started laughing. “It makes sense now.”

“What does?”

“Cal said you were having female issues or troubles or something,” Gage chuckled again, “I thought he meant because you were running herd on nine females, but it’s one, isn’t it?”

Blair blew out a breath and rubbed between his eyes with his thumb, “yeah. Kobie is mine and I don’t know what the fuck to do with that.”

“Your mate?”

“Yeah.”

“So the charming Blair Elden is having trouble with the woman that is his mate.” He could hear something running in the background, then fading as Gage must have walked outside. “What am I missing?”

Blair closed his eyes and tried to figure out how to say it. “She hasn’t decided yet.”

“Decided what?”

“Fuck if I know.” He cringed at his tone, which was close to whining.

“Is this the one that led the women to safety?”

Blair nodded, then remembered he was on the phone. “Yeah.”

“Is she Alpha?”

Another nod, “yeah.

“I heard her father is likely gone and her brother may not pull through.”

Blair sat down and stared across the field, “we haven’t heard anything about the rest of the men that went with them.”

"Sounds like she has a lot going on right now."

He was hoping for wisdom. If anyone knew how to cope with a mate that wasn't yours yet, it was Gage. "Yes, it's a huge emotional bizarre around here." He cleared his throat, "two of the women's husbands that stayed behind to watch over the clan—the women found them dead. Daisie is nine and her father went with the Alpha. Annamarie and Nichelle are close to their first cycle and their mothers are missing, fathers probably dead…"

"You sound pretty attached, Blair."

Blair opened his mouth and then closed it. "I am. I think I was the second Daisie came out of the trees looking like the bravest kid I'd ever seen." He paused, searching if he felt any remorse. When he found none, he continued, "I killed those two that tried to take Daisie, Gage—didn't even pause after."

"Are they all going back to Devin's camp?"

Blair blinked; he'd never asked. "I don't know."

"I won't lie, I need you here. Your part of this team and family, but—" he heard a door close and recognized the sound of the air compressor on the other side of the office door in the shop, "I was thinking about it last night and I have a thought, maybe I'll run it by Dev and see what he thinks."

Blair got up, "like what?"

"You know that abandoned place ten miles from here, the one set way back off the road?"

Nodding, Blair started walking toward the house, his cat was nagging him that they needed to check on Kobie. "Yeah, the property needs some work, but the house is huge and in good…" he stopped, "it's big enough to house all of them and a few more."

"Right. Dad was looking at acquiring it—it's a good chunk of land to roam. It would be a fast sale, I'm pretty sure the owners jumped ship."

Blair nodded and picked up the pace. "The team could help watch it when we're not working."

"We have the equipment to fence the whole fucking thing if we wanted to."

"I have a lot saved…"

"I'm sure the Alliance can help, save your money for now."

Blair stopped and put his hand on his hip and stared at the house. "I'd feel better with them close. Gage, I gotta be honest here, I'm a fucking mess right now…"

"I get it. You stay put, keep them *all* safe."

Blair jolted, he couldn't believe he'd forgotten, "how's Coop?"

"Miserable and bitching to get out of the bed, but Shaelan said the longer we keep him off that leg the faster it would heal."

Blair huffed out a quick breath, "good luck there."

"Exactly. Three more weeks of it. We may have to use the chains by next week to keep him down."

He grinned. "I'm not sure when I'll be back…"

"Just take care of them, Blair."

"I plan on it." He was going to say bye, then remembered, "Gage, did you know I have a brother?"

There was a long silence, "yeah, I asked Dad about that other clan a few years back."

"Calum told me—everything."

"It fits."

"What does?"

"I always thought your cat was pure Alpha warrior, then Dad confirmed it."

Blair was blown away that Gage had known and never told him. "I need to help the Alliance put a stop to Tomas', Gage— my own fucking family is responsible…"

"We're your family, Blair—those nine you rescued are your family now too, not that clan you came from."

He used the hard tone, the one that told Blair's cat to listen up. "I'm a fucking mess, boss."

Gage laughed, "you should have seen Calum acting like a lovesick puppy, *that* was a fucking mess."

As if he'd heard him, Calum came out of the house and started walking in his direction. "I want details some time."

"I look forward to sharing that story every year for the rest of his life." He heard voices in the background. "I have to go before Noah knocks down the shop trying to get that rig out of here."

"Shit. Go." The line went quiet. Jamming the phone in his pocket he started walking, then stopped. He had a place for the girls to go. Jake and Gary would help, he was sure Noah would too. Hell, he'd probably be better at it than the rest of them, considering what he'd lived through. He started walking again when his cat prompted him to go check on Kobie. Five feet later, he stopped. How did he tell Kobie about the property? His cat not so gently prodded him again. *Slow your roll for a second. Fuck.*

"Your head is going to explode if you keep thinking that hard."

Blair jolted and looked up to see Calum standing a few feet from him. "I was just talking to Gage."

Concern filled Calum's face. "Everything all right?"

"Uh, yeah," Blair blew out a breath, he felt better about some things, yet more tense with others, "he had an idea for," he waved his hand toward the house, "the girls."

"Oh? Don't tell me he's going to train them all in the shop." He smirked.

"Ha, no, well maybe some later, but for a place for them to live." He blew out a breath, "going home is off the table for them, and from what Rayne was telling Jesse the camp is getting pretty crowded."

"What's his plan."

Blair realized he'd been rambling and that was not something you did with Calum. "You remember that big place down the road from Ed's?"

Calum raised one eyebrow, "the one where I ran circles around you?"

Blair scowled, "Yeah, that one."

Calum was quiet for a moment, "it's a defensible location, with some work. Close to another clan of the same type."

Blair nodded, "I think so too, the house is huge too with those three little buildings…"

"Is he going to run it by Dev?"

"Yeah, he said he would." Blair crossed his arms over his chest, trying to ignore his cat once again.

"So why do you not look happy about that?"

Was it that obvious? "I don't know how to tell them."

Calum grinned, "tell the homeless women that they have a home to call their own? I don't know, Blair that's a tough ask."

He must have shown the shock on his face because Calum started laughing and then turned and walked away. "Wait until the Alliance approves it before you start sharing."

Get a handle on this, idiot, get your brain back in the game. As if on cue, his cat all but gouged his insides reminding him once more that they needed to check on their unclaimed mate.

Blair walked into the house. Rayne met him with an understanding look on her face. She motioned to the room Kobie's brother was in. Giving her a quick nod, he pushed the door open and went in. Kobie sat beside the bed in a chair, leaning forward onto the bed, with her face resting in her hands. His cat didn't react the way he'd intended when he brought the scent of an injured male into his body. He inhaled slowly, trying to settle his cat down.

Kobie lifted her head and looked at him.

Blair's heart thudded in his chest when he saw the forlorn expression on her face. That brought his cat back into line, fast. Going around the bed, he squatted down beside her and pulled her to the edge of the chair, and brought her head to rest on his shoulder. "You should go get some rest." He whispered into her hair.

She moved her head slightly. "I need him to open his eyes."

"His body needs rest, babe." She lifted her head and looked at him, "I'll stay with him if you like."

She shook her head, "I took a break a while ago and I can't," she motioned to the door, "go back out there until I have some answers."

The other women. He'd almost forgotten about their men. Nodding, he stood up slowly. "Do you want a coffee or something? Did you eat?"

She shook her head, "I'm not hungry."

Blair gave her a soft smile, "I know I don't have to remind you that you *have* to eat," he motioned to the door, "we have Annamarie for the dramatics around here, we don't need you having some emotional rant."

She grinned at him. "Okay, a tea, black, and something light."

He nodded and brushed the hair back from her face. "I'll be right back."

Going back out into the kitchen, he went to the fridge and opened it. It was stocked. Closing it, he opened a cupboard and looked in it. "Cups." He pulled out two. He kept moving along the cupboards until he found the dishes he needed. Turning slowly, he noticed the sliding door on the other side of the room. He went over and opened it, "pantry." Flicking the light on, he perused what was on the shelves and finally found the tea. "Kettle." Grabbing the tea, he went back out and then spotted it on the counter beside the coffeepot. Turning he went back in and grabbed the coffee. "Okay, now we're getting somewhere." He flipped off the light and slid the door closed, then turned to see both Calum and Devin standing there watching him.

"Are you talking to yourself?" Devin smirked.

Blair motioned around the kitchen. "Just trying to get the lay of the land in here."

The men moved to the table and sat down.

"Jayden awake yet?"

It took Blair a moment to realize that Jay was Jayden. He shook his head and then glanced at Calum, "Shaelan say when he should be?"

Calum shrugged, "when his body was ready."

Blair paused for a moment, "that's not helpful." He glanced at the door that Kobie was on the other side of. "The others are hoping for answers."

"As are we," Devin said quietly.

Daisie came running into the kitchen, she gave Calum and

Devin a cautious look, then smiled at Blair. "Can I help?"

Blair set the tea and coffee on the counter. "No thanks, honey, but you can tell your mom I'm putting a pot of coffee on in case she wants one."

Daisie stood there for a moment. "She's with Mika right now. Mika is crying again."

Blair set the kettle down and squatted in front of her. "You know those flowers by the side of the house?"

She nodded.

"I think Mika would like it if you picked *one* and took it to her."

"Do you think that will make her feel better?"

Blair nodded, "it can't hurt, right?"

Daisie nodded and then turned to leave. Before Blair could stand up again, she launched herself at him and hugged him tightly. "Thanks, Blair, Mom says it's good you're here and I think she's right." Spinning, she took off out the door.

Blowing out a breath, Blair stood back up. He needed a moment before he looked at the other men. Turning back to the sink, he filled the kettle and then plugged it in. Setting up the coffee maker, he flipped it on then turned and leaned back against the counter. "Did Gage call you?" He looked at Devin.

Devin nodded. "It's a good idea. I'll tell Dad about it later when I talk to him."

Blair glanced to Calum, then nodded and went over to the fridge. Opening it, he grabbed one of the four cartons of eggs and set it on the stove. Leaning in, he pulled out some cheese, then closed the door. "I'd like to have something good to tell them." He glanced to see both men nodding.

Reaching up, he pulled a frying pan off the hook on the wall and set it on the stove. Pausing, he opened the fridge again and grabbed the margarine.

"Your very domestic."

Blair spun to see Franki standing in the door smiling at him. He grinned at her, then motioned to the stove, "eggs are the only thing I make well," he shrugged, "it's easier to shift and go eat something."

She laughed quietly, "I agree, but don't tell the girls. They keep trying to teach me how to bake."

"Baking is always appreciated." He leaned over and pulled the bowl closer, so he could get the eggs started.

"I heard there was coffee?"

Blair motioned to the corner. "Help yourself." He beat the eggs with the fork and poured them into the pan. "How's Mika?"

Franki paused with the cup in her hand, "she and Waylan were only together for a year, so it's tough, you know, without kids to hold you together."

Blair nodded, even though he didn't know.

"Daisie confessed the flower was your idea." She smiled at him.

Blair lifted his hands in an innocent gesture. "The flower was my distraction, so she wouldn't ask about her dad again."

Franki filled the cup and then got out another one, "we're all hoping Jay can tell us what happened to Robbie."

Blair stirred the eggs around and then started opening drawers looking for a shredder for the cheese.

"We're still searching for any of the others," Devin said quietly.

Franki looked over at him. "Have you found any of them?"

Devin shook his head, "it's my understanding that Jay was alone, no evidence of the others."

Franki looked at the floor for a moment and then turned and picked up the cups. "Any answers will be better than what we have now."

"You'll get them," Calum said in a low tone, "one way or another."

"Thank you." She gave them both a somber look and then turned to Blair, "there's no shredder." She smiled at his dramatic look and walked back outside.

Blair blew out a breath and then busied himself with cutting the cheese into small chunks and tossing them in the pan with the eggs. No one said anything again until he was putting the eggs onto two plates and pouring the tea into a cup. Pausing, he turned back to look at the prince, "I want to help."

Devin gave him a confused look.

Blair motioned around him, "once we get the girls settled, I want to help bring Tomas down." He glanced at Calum briefly, "it's only right that I do."

"No one blames you for any of it, Blair," Devin told him.

"I know," he tapped his chest, "but it feels like I need to." Reaching up, he pulled a tray off the fridge and put the two plates and cups on it, "I owe it to my mother to do the right thing."

Devin nodded, "I'll let dad know he has another warrior if needed."

Blair clenched his jaw together, trying to fight the fury that was filling him just thinking about his *own* brother doing this to other shifters. Nodding, he went over and pushed the door open to go back to Kobie.

She was standing looking out the window.

"I'm afraid the only thing I cook well is eggs."

Turning, she gave him a gentle look, "that's fine, thank you."

He set the tray on the dresser and then held out her cup of tea.

Taking it, she looked back out the window, "Rayne seems really nice."

Blair picked up his cup and then went over and glanced through the glass to see Rayne and Daisie laughing about something. "Yeah, she's what the clans need right now."

Blowing on the tea, she went over and sat down. "They're not what I expected." He held out her plate. "The prince and princess."

Blair shrugged, "they're hands-on." He jerked his chin at the plate, so she'd eat. "Devin has a huge campground, and it's now set up as a refuge for those we rescue from Tomas."

"Are there many?"

He watched her take a bite before answering. "More every day."

"Good."

Picking up his plate, he stood there leaning against the dresser, eating and watching her. She was only eating to humor him, he got that, but at least she *was* eating. "I was thinking we could take Daisie and Kasia to the river later, let them go for a swim."

Kobie gave him a surprised look. "They would *love* that. It would give Torrey and Cortney a break too."

"I'll talk to Cal and see if he and Shaelan want to come, then we don't have to drag guards along."

"Okay." She raised the fork and then stopped and looked at him again, "thank you."

Blair set the dishes in the rack to dry, and then went back in to persuade her to come outside and go blow off some steam at the river. As he opened the door, he heard talking. Pushing it open, he looked to see her brother was awake and she was sitting on the bed, leaning over him.

"Here he is," Kobie looked over at Blair, a relieved expression on her face, "this is Blair."

Blair moved over close to the bed, so Jayden didn't have to move around a lot to look at him. He was met with an expression he didn't expect. He looked angry. Probably in a lot of pain. "How are you feeling?" He motioned to the door, "I can go get the healer…"

"Not yet." His voice was weak. "Thank you, for getting them here."

Kobie must have filled in some details of how they got where they were. "Of course."

The fragile man looked back at his sister. "Where's Huntley, Waylan, and Mace? Are they outside, I need to talk to them."

Kobie leaned back from him and shook her head slowly. "We found them. That's when I gathered everyone together and we went to Fish's."

"They were on our land?"

Kobie nodded.

"Fuck." With slow movements, he reached over and touched his sisters' hand. "Dad's gone too, Kobe."

Kobie nodded, "I figured as much." She wiped her cheek with her free hand and Blair had to struggle to stand there and not invade their little family moment to comfort her.

Shaelan came in the door and then stopped and smiled. "It's good to see you awake." She gave him a pleasant smile. "I'd like to check on a few things before Devin and Calum come in here to talk, is that all right?"

Jay looked at Blair, then at his sister. "Devin Addison is here?"

Kobie nodded. "He came with you."

"I'd like to talk to him." He said in a weak voice.

Kobie leaned down and kissed his forehead. "I'm just going to take Daisie and Kasia to the river for a swim, then I'll be back."

"I'll be here." He said with a half-smile.

Chapter Seventeen

Blair looked around the yard, she wasn't there. Giving his head a shake, he turned and went around into the house. He had to meet Calum at the guards' house and here he was seeking out Kobie—again, all because he hadn't laid eyes on her in an hour. Standing in the kitchen, he listened to see if he could hear anyone in the house. He heard the water running, maybe she was in the shower. Closing his eyes, he dropped his head forward, picturing her in the shower was not going to get him to the guardhouse any faster.

"Blair."

He spun around to see the door to the room Jay was in was open. He went in quickly. "Do you need something?" He looked at the broken man laying in the bed.

"No." His voice was so rough like it hurt to talk. "Close the door."

Blair gave him a curious look, but closed the door, then continued to stand in front of it.

"I wanted to talk," he licked his lips, "to you alone."

Every word he said looked like it hurt to say, so Blair moved closer to the bed so he wouldn't feel like he needed to speak louder.

"When we were," Jay closed his eyes for a second, then looked back at him, "ambushed," he paused again and took a few breaths.

Blair was hurting just watching him. "Hey, if it's not important, it can wait until later when you're feeling better."

The battered man moved his head from side to side slowly, "it can't wait."

Blair nodded and squatted down beside the bed. "Okay, take your time."

"One of the others, a white cat," his words were broken, but he watched for Blair to nod to let him know he understood, "when he shifted back," Jay closed his eyes again and took some slow breaths. "He thought I was gone and didn't see him."

Blair looked at the door wondering if he should go get Devin or Calum or anyone other than him.

"He was older, but," he stopped until Blair looked back at him, "he looked a lot like you."

Fuck. Blair squeezed his eyes shut for a second. Opening them, he hoped he conveyed anything other than the anger coursing through him. "That was probably the brother I've never met." He stood up, unable to stay still. "I just found out I have one not even a week ago."

"You don't know your brother?" Jay watched him, a painful look on his face.

Blair shook his head, "I was sent to live with another clan when I was two." Putting his hands on his hips, he took a deep breath and tried to breathe away the emotion flooding him. "You have my word. I will find him."

The silence was heavy as they continued to look at each other.

"Don't tell Kobie." Jay finally said.

Blair shook his head, not that he was agreeing with him, but more because secrets were going to be the end of him someday. "I have to go meet Devin and Calum. Do you need anything before I go?"

Jay closed his eyes. "No. Kobe is in the shower. She'll be

back soon."

"All right," Blair watched him for a second, "get some rest." He wasn't sure if he'd fallen asleep or just didn't want to see his face a moment longer, so he opened the door and silently walked out of the room.

Stepping out of the house, he took a deep breath. His brother was there when Kobie's father was killed. *Fuck. Shit just keeps getting worse.* Clenching and unclenching his jaw for a moment, he tried to get his head under control. Inhaling deeply, he lifted his head and looked at the clear sky. *Meeting, then long run.* Nodding, he blew out his breath and lowered his head. He looked back up, Daisie sitting in the large tree in the center of the yard. That's just what he needed, her to fall and get hurt. He started toward her when she gave him a wide-eyed look and pointed.

Turning, he looked where she pointed and didn't see anything. Walking faster, he went around the corner of the house and then he saw what she was so anxious about. Across the yard on the other side of the fence was Annamarie and one of the guards. Blair didn't know his name, he was a wolf shifter, so he hadn't really given him a second look as wolves weren't a problem for the girls. Or shouldn't have been a problem. Apparently, he was wrong.

He started moving faster. From what he could tell, the wolf had Annamarie cornered and she was not wanting whatever he was offering. His cat wanted blood as they watched him grab her wrist and pull her back. Blair growled low and hopped the fence.

"Annamarie." He kept moving, noting the scared look on her face.

The guard turned and kept her behind him. He looked Blair up and down. "We're fine." He told Blair and shifted to the side when Annamarie tried to walk around him.

"It doesn't look fine from here." Blair didn't look away from him.

"We were just going to have some fun." The guy shrugged.

"Annamarie, go," Blair said, his tone low.

He watched her dart in the other direction and go over the fence before turning back to the wolf in front of him. "What are you doing?" He lifted his hands and was honestly going to try and give the man a chance to explain. One chance, despite his angry cat ripping his insides apart.

"How is it any of your business?" The guy spat back at him and rolled his shoulders.

Fucking idiot. Blair didn't know if that was his thought or his cats, but the movement was aggressive, and they both knew that. "Do you know what this clan has been through?" It really wasn't a question. Blair took one step and the guy lunged for him. Lifting his arm, Blair smashed his forearm into his face. Grabbing the back of his hair, Blair held his head up and leaned down. "She has no family left. She's not even old enough to have had her first change." He growled and shook his arm, so the guy's head was jerked around.

Blair's cat was disappointed the man didn't fight back but just stood there holding his face and dripping blood all over the ground. Dragging him along with him, he started for the fence and then spotted Calum and Devin standing there with one of the other guards.

Blair gave him a shove when he was almost to the fence. He looked at Devin. "This is one of yours." He gave Calum a quick look, "Which way did she go?"

Calum pointed toward the back of the property. Then he scowled at the man on the ground.

Blair nodded his thanks and hopped over the fence. As he ran, he spotted her red shirt on the other side of a big tree.

Reaching it, he looked around it to see her sitting on the ground crying. Kneeling, he pulled her into his arms. "Are you okay? Did he hurt you?"

"I'm okay," she sobbed. "I'm sorry."

He held her and waited until she settled before speaking again. Leaning back, he lifted her chin and wiped the tears from her cheek. "I need you to listen to me, okay?" He wasn't sure what to say, but he somehow needed to get through to her.

She nodded.

"You're a very pretty girl and you don't need to flirt with guys to get them to notice, okay?"

She nodded again.

"How old are you?"

"Almost twenty."

Blair nodded, even though he was feeling like he was ancient compared to her when he really wasn't that much older than her. "Soon, you are going to go through so many changes—and you're going to love how you are after them," he offered her an earnest smile, "I know it's hard to be around all the rest of the clan that can shift and feel like it's taking forever for you to." It was true, he's been the most impatient out of all the guys. "Just be patient and enjoy who you are, okay?"

Annamarie sniffed and wiped her face. "I miss them so much."

He didn't ask who, he knew none of her family were left. "I know, honey. You have so many around you that want to help you, just let them." He gave her a questioning look.

"I'll try."

Smiling, he stood up and held out his hand to her, "if you could cut back on the drama a bit too, I'd appreciate it." He winked at her. "All of this is new to me." He looked down at her, "I'm used to being around a bunch of guys. You need to break me in gently here."

She giggled, "I'll try."

"Okay." Blair put his arm around her and turned to walk back to the house. He stopped, Kobie was standing ten feet away from them, her hair was dripping wet. He didn't need to know how she knew what was happening, Daisie stood beside her.

Annamarie wrapped her arms around him and squeezed him tight for a second and then ran to Kobie.

Kobie hugged her. Over her head, she gave him a small nod and then turned and started walking back toward the house. Blair pointed to Daisie and then to the spot in front of him.

With a scared look, she came over and stood there.

"First, thank you." He smiled down at her.

Daisie nodded.

"And please be careful climbing the trees," Blair bent down and motioned to his back. She climbed up onto his back, "I don't think I could handle a broken Daisie."

She laughed, "I'm *very* careful. Mom says I'm part monkey. Can that happen? Can a cat be part monkey?" She leaned forward and rested her face on his shoulder. "I think you can do *anything*, Blair."

"Let's not try." He stopped at the back of the house and bent his knees so she could get down. "Now, do me a favor and run and see if there's any coffee left."

"You drink a lot of coffee." She gave him a hard look. "Mom says too much will stunt your growth." She looked him up and down. "Are you done growing?"

Blair smirked, "as far as I know."

She gave him a careful look, "okay, I'll go check."

He watched her run around the corner. Putting his hands on his hips, he blew out a breath. He really needed to go for a run.

"How's your day going?"

Blair's heart jumped in his chest. He turned to see Calum standing. "Just fucking peachy so far."

Calum smirked. "Seems to be an adventure a minute."

Blair took a deep breath, trying to settle his pulse back down. "Oh, it's even better than you know." He glanced around and saw a few of the women were within hearing distance. "I'll tell you in a bit." He said to Calum's curious look.

They walked into the small building. Jesse was standing in front of the screens, checking the cameras.

Devin motioned to his phone, "Dad had to take another call, so we're on hold."

Calum perched on the edge of the table and gave Blair a look, "what else?"

Both Jesse and Devin turned to look at Blair.

Blowing out a breath, he rubbed a hand over his hair. "Jay

saw an older man that looks like me when they were ambushed. He's a white tiger when he shifts."

"Your brother," Calum said in a quiet tone.

Blair nodded, "I think so."

"He was involved when their Alpha died?" Jesse swore softly.

Blair's chest hurt when he heard it out loud. "Yeah."

"Does anyone else know?" Jesse inquired quietly.

Shaking his head, Blair blew out a breath again. "No. He said not to tell Kobie either."

"That would be very bad," Devin said, giving Calum a look.

"As mates go, yes." Calum agreed.

"Your brother Lindon was involved in killing Damar?"

It startled all of the men when the voice came over the phone. Shepard Addison, the King of the Shifter Alliance had been listening.

Blair nodded, "Yes, sir, that's what Jayden said."

"Kobie is his twin, the Alpha's daughter," he paused for a second, "and your mate, Blair?"

Nodding again, Blair stared at the phone. "Yes."

"That may simplify things." Devin's father stated, to which Devin gave the phone a wide-eyed look.

"How does *that* simplify anything?" Devin asked.

"I'll get to that in a moment." Shepard said, "first, I approve of the idea to use that other property near Ed for this broken clan."

Blair glanced at Calum, who looked almost as relieved as he felt.

"What does Shaelan say about Jayden's recovery?"

Everyone turned to look at Calum.

"It's going to be a long one, there is still no guarantee he'll be able to shift afterward," Calum said with a somber expression.

"It's a miracle he's even alive." The king said in a soft tone, "they intended him to be dead along with his father—leaving no male in the Alpha family alive is the pattern."

Jesse turned from the screens, "Jayden says he knows for

sure six of the men were taken and not killed. He's not sure about the other seven."

"What possessed them to take fifteen of their men and go after them on their own, I don't know but we're communicating with *all* clans with missing members to let them know to contact us before taking action. The team down there aren't due to report in for another day, so I don't have anything to add to the information on their men right now." Shepard cleared his throat, "the recovery is going to be too long for Jayden to be an active Alpha, will his sister take the lead?"

All eyes turned to Blair, "I don't know." Other than that one time she mentioned it, he hadn't given it a lot of thought. There had been too many other things occupying his mind.

"The only way to have them stay on the new land long term is if they have an Alpha or merge with another clan. Clans without ruling leaders are not given the Alliance's protection. I haven't spoken to Ed about this yet, but as you know, Blair, your clan already has its hands full with many females."

Blair huffed out a breath, "yeah."

"Once you and Kobie are mated, you could take the Alpha roll."

Moving just his eyes, Blair looked at Calum and then to Devin, they were both smirking. "Uh…"

"She hasn't decided yet," Calum said with a grin.

"Decided?"

Calum leaned closer to the phone, "*if* she wants a mate."

"Oh," the sound he made sounded like a chuckled to Blair, "I see." Shepard's tone was softer. "Well, son, I suggest you get her deciding. We are *expediting* the sale of the land and I'm sending a renovation team to that property and we're hoping to have transportation set up in two days."

Blair's eyes couldn't have gotten any bigger as he stared at the phone. He jerked his head and looked at Calum.

Calum mouthed, 'yes, thank you,' and nodded his head.

"Yes," Blair said too loud, "thank you—sir." He broke out in a nervous sweat without warning.

Shepard chuckled openly for a moment. "Now, I need a few

words with my son and Calum."

Jesse nodded and looked at Blair, motioning to the door.

"Thank you," Blair mumbled again and followed Jesse outside.

Once outside, he bent forward and leaned on his knees.

Jesse laughed, "that moved a little fast."

Lifting his head, he looked up at him. "You think, huh?"

"So, what are you going to do?" Jesse was smirking.

Blair straightened up, "I, uh, shit," he looked around the yard, "I guess I need to talk to the clan," he swore softly, "and Kobie."

"Can I listen in on that conversation?"

Blair glared at him.

"I mean, what are you going to say? So, the king says we have to mate and I'm taking over your clan?" He shrugged, "oh, and by the way, my brother works with Tomas' organization."

Blair opened his mouth and then closed it. "I don't even know."

Calum and Devin came out and looked at him.

"Figured you'd still be standing here," Calum smirked.

Blair lifted his hands and then let them smack on his legs. He motioned to the house, "I don't know what to do first."

Calum looked at Devin then back to Blair, "our Prince knows too well what happens if you don't tell your mate everything."

Devin nodded, then shook his head, "it's not good. Tell her everything—beforehand."

Calum jerked his head toward the house as if to say, 'off you go'.

Blair nodded, "everything, all right." He started walking toward the house, with each step getting slower. *How the fuck do I start? Tell her the worst first? Shit.* He spun on his heel and pulled his phone out and started walking away from the house.

Calum, Devin, and Jesse stood there grinning at him.

He lifted his phone in the air and waved it around.

"Gage?" Calum called out.

"Coop," Blair said, not caring if they could hear or not.

"How's your vacation going?" That is how Cooper answered the phone.

Blair hissed out a breath. "It's going."

"Gage shared some bits with me."

He sounded fine, that made Blair feel better. "Which bits?" He pictured Coop laying there propped up in bed with his hat on.

"The trip, the females, the trouble, and your mate."

Blair nodded and then closed his eyes. "There's been some recent developments."

"I figured by the tone of your voice."

"How are you feeling?" Blair was stalling.

"I'm fine. You didn't call to talk about my leg, what's going on?"

Blair stopped beside the same tree Annamarie had earlier. Sitting down, he leaned back against it. "You know about my family and clan?"

"I do."

He shrugged, "I figured you probably did." He glanced at the field and wished for a run, like a long, long one. "You know how badly injured this clans' last male is."

"Yeah, Gage told me that too. How's he doing?"

Blair rubbed his thumb between his eyes, "they don't even know if he'll ever be able to shift again. He's," he paused before saying out loud for the first time, "my mate's twin brother, they're the last of the Alpha family."

"That's a mess."

Blair snorted, "that's not even the worst of this fucking mess, Coop."

"I won't know until you tell me, and if you don't tell me, I can't help straighten your head out."

Blair blew out a breath, "okay, so my brother was there when their Alpha-my-mates-father," he said slowly, "was killed. Her twin put two and two together and asked if we were related…"

"Well, shit."

"Right. She doesn't know—but I have to tell her about my original clan and *all* of it…"

"You definitely should at that."

"She hasn't decided if she wants to be mated, Coop. What the fuck do I do with that?" He knew it was all going to spew out of his mouth like a dam had just broken, but he couldn't stop. "The king has approved her clan to move to that big property down the road. It was Gage's idea. I think it's a good one. *But* they can't stay unless they have an Alpha or merge with Ed's clan—and the last thing Ed needs is *nine* more females," he shook his head, "I'm pretty sure Kobie doesn't want to be the Alpha and her brother may never be capable of it again—so the king says I should be, and I don't even know, Coop." His teeth clicked together as he stopped talking abruptly.

"Just hold on two shakes while I process all that," Cooper said thoughtfully.

Blair nodded and forced air back into his body.

"That is a lot. Here I was thinking you, our pretty boy was having cold feet about finding his mate."

Blair rolled his eyes, "I wished that was the only thing happening here."

"Yeah, I get that now." Cooper paused, Blair pictured him taking off his hat and rubbing his hand over his brush cut vigorously, which was Cooper's thinking move. "Okay, let's try this, take a deep breath, close your eyes and answer me one question."

Blair sat forward, "okay." He waited for the question.

"I said close your damn eyes."

He had no idea how Cooper knew he was staring straight ahead, but he took a deep breath, closed his eyes, and breathed it out.

"How do you feel about them—the whole lot of them?" Cooper asked softly.

Blair didn't even hesitate. "I would die for any fucking one of them, Coop. Strongest women and kids I've ever seen."

"That's your answer, kid."

Blair's eyes popped open, he scowled at the ground. "How's that my answer?"

"Sounds like you're what they need, Blair, so go fight for them."

Blair got up slowly. "So what you're saying is tell Kobie everything, and lay it out for the rest of the clan?"

"That sounds about right."

"Fuck, Coop, this is going to suck." Blair hissed out a breath.

"Of course, it is. Anything worth having is fucking hard to get." Cooper chuckled. "And, Blair?"

"Yeah?" He held his breath waiting for some clue on how to go about it.

"I look forward to meeting them. I'll even stand watch over them for you when you're busy."

A lump formed in Blair's throat. "I know you will, thanks. And Coop? Try to behave just a bit for Beth."

Cooper laughed, "that's not going to happen. Now stop stalling and go get it done."

Blair ignored the looks Calum and Jesse gave him as he walked past them and went into the house. He went straight to where he knew Kobie would be, beside Jay's bed. "Kobie?" He stood at the door, "you have a few minutes?"

Jay gave her a slight nod. "I'm going to try to sleep before Shaelan comes and stabs me again."

Kobie nodded and got up. "You better try harder to eat that soup or Rayne is going to pour it in you."

Blair led her outside and kept walking.

She walked alongside him without saying a word until they reached the end of the fenced-in area. "This must be pretty serious if we're moving out of hearing distance."

"It's complicated." That was all he could manage. His mind was processing a hundred different ways to start this. He didn't stop until he was back at the same tree he'd just left. He motioned to the ground, "Might as well grab a seat, this will take a minute."

She gave him a cautious look. "Okay," she said slowly, "one thing first, though."

He was just about to ask what that was when she stretched up and kissed him on the mouth, lingering for a second. "Thank you."

He glanced at her, "for what?" His cat, even knowing why they had brought her out here wanted a real taste. He jammed his hands in his pockets so he wouldn't touch her.

"What you did for Annamarie."

He bobbed his head, "that's kind of part of what I wanted to talk to you about—after I talk to you about some other stuff. Not just Annamarie—" Oh yeah, this was going brilliantly. He shook his head, "I wished you hadn't kissed me—" He almost choked on his tongue fixing that when she looked hurt. "Not that," he touched her shoulder, "I don't want you to kiss me," he tilted his head, "I do. It's just now—" Dropping his hand, he closed his eyes and took a deep breath before looking at her again, "any time I'm near you I can't focus so…"

Kobie smirked, "okay, I get it." She motioned to the ground, "sit down and behave so you can focus." Sitting down, she clasped her hands in her lap.

"Yes." He wanted to sigh in relief and would have if he didn't know what he had to do next. He sat down, keeping several feet between them. "Okay." He watched her looking at him. "I don't even know where to start this."

"At the beginning?" She offered with a serious look on her face.

He nodded, "yeah. Okay." He blew out a breath, "my clan, the one I'm with now, isn't the clan I was born into." Blair didn't even want to blink; he wanted to watch her eyes and see every reaction she had. Needed to, his cat prodded. This was as important to his animal side as it was to him. "My mother sent me to live with Ed's clan when I was two."

A compassionate look appeared in her eyes, so he continued while it was there. "I just found out all of this," he motioned between them, "when we met up with Calum on that mountain."

"You never asked before?"

He shook his head, "I wanted to know but didn't, you know what I mean?"

She nodded.

"My father was the Alpha and was killed," he frowned, "I believe it was orchestrated by his own people—because my mother sent me away to keep me safe after that."

She put her hand over her mouth, "that's awful, Blair."

He nodded slowly, then touched his chest, "I don't *feel* it, I was two, so it just doesn't register."

"That's probably a good thing." She said softly.

He hoped, really, really hoped that compassion in her voice didn't change. "Yeah, so," he swallowed because his mouth suddenly dried out, "Calum told me my clan—or the rest of *that* clan had agreed to work with Alberto Tomas, and that's why they killed my father because he was trying to move them away to stop it from happening."

Her expression changed, but she didn't look appalled—yet.

"He told me I have an older brother."

She sucked in a breath, "your brother killed your father to become Alpha and help those horrible people?"

Pausing he considered her words, they weren't against him, so he kept going. "I guess that's what happened." He shook his head, "I don't remember a brother, and I don't remember my mother either."

Her expression changed to one of those ones that women made when they went 'aww'.

"Your brother told me that *mine* was among those that ambushed them. I wanted you to know that." The last word was barely a whisper. Blair watched what he'd said register, and the emotions went through her eyes. It was only a few seconds, but it may as well have been a year before she spoke again.

"I can't blame you for what a brother you didn't even know you had, has done." She finally looked at him once more, "or for a traitorous clan you're not part of."

He wanted to jump up and down and cheer, but his cat was

still silent, so that reminded him he wasn't finished yet. "I'm going to find him." She sat straighter. "My brother. One day, somehow. I'll find him and it won't be for a family reunion." He clarified.

She nodded but offered him no comment.

He sat there, trying to figure out how to tell her the next part. If he knew anything about women, they didn't like to feel forced into anything.

"There's more?"

He tilted his head, "not to that part, but there is more."

"Okay, tell me."

Nodding, he studied her for a moment. "There's a huge property close to my Alpha's property that I want to move you guys to." She raised her eyebrows. "Devin's father approved the plan," he needed to make it sound amazing, "it's huge with amazing terrain for runs. Total privacy. Big house, with a few smaller ones some of my team from work could stay at to help watch over the girls." Her expression was guarded, making it hard to tell what she was thinking.

"You're selling this pretty hard, what's the catch?"

Rubbing his hand over his hair, he looked at the ground before meeting her look again. "To stay there permanently, your clan has to either merge with another—" he shrugged, "we don't know if Ed is willing yet, we already have a problem with more women than males…"

"What's the or? You said either."

He nodded his head slowly, "or your clan needs a new Alpha of their own." As he finished the last word, it was like every insect and bird in the vicinity paused. The silence was harsh.

"My brother can't be, can he?"

Blair shook his head, "the healers don't know if he's ever going to fully recover or—shift again." He said it quietly, afraid that she may not have thought of that yet.

"And that leaves me as the last option in the Alpha family."

Blair nodded slowly, stiffly.

Kobie shook her head, "I don't want it." She shook her

head again, "I can help, but I'm a hunter, I train the young ones. I'm not a leader."

He wanted to object. That was exactly what she had done, hold her clan together and lead them to safety. If his cat could kick him, Blair knew this was when it would have. "The king has another idea."

Her eyes went wide. "Please don't tell me he's going to bring in some old Alpha shifter or something."

"No." Blair cleared his throat, "he knows we're mates…" When her head snapped back so she was looking at him, he tried to look innocent, "I didn't tell him."

"Calum?"

He nodded.

"Does he notice *everything*?"

Blair had no issues with letting Calum take the fall if it saved his hide. "I think that's why he's so good at what he does."

She stood up and all he could think was 'oh shit, here we go'. He got up slowly.

"So," she waved her hand around in the air, "what? We're supposed to be mated, post-haste, so you can be the Alpha and we can live on this *awesome* land?"

Okay, when said that way it sounded like shit, he realized. "I don't know." He'd watched Ed use that line on Beth when she was on the warpath from time to time, and it always saved his ass.

"Did you tell the king I wasn't ready?" Her tone was higher pitched.

"I did." He nodded.

She huffed out a breath and studied him. "Good. Because I'm not."

Waves of hostility were pouring off her now, his cat prodded him to fix it. Blair would have gladly if he had any idea how to.

She pointed a finger at him. "And don't you go getting any ideas that you'll just claim me." She stomped away.

Blair raised his hands. "Kobie," she was pacing the other way, "look at me." He used a serious tone to get her attention.

She turned back to him, he put his hands down. "I would never even consider such a thing." He spoke slowly, enunciating each syllable for her. "Nothing happens unless you consent," he motioned toward the house, "Calum, Devin, hell all the guys back home would cut my balls off if I ever considered such a thing."

She stood there, unmoving for a few seconds. "Good. I'm happy to hear the rest of your clan is as upstanding as you are." She blew out a breath, "what are the women like in your clan?"

Blair froze. Of all the questions to ask him, why did she have to ask that one?

"What?" She stepped closer, with her hands on her hips, watching him.

Blair closed his eyes and swore every cuss word he knew inside his head before he opened them. "There's nothing wrong with the women." He said quietly. "But, uh, full disclosure…"

Kobie gave him that look. That look that women got when men did stupid shit.

"Everything I said about Kelsey and Layna was the truth…"

"But?"

Blair reached for his cat, who he was pretty sure now sat with his back to him, disowning him. "Before I knew Gage was Kelsey's mate—I fell in love with her." He shrugged, "we were kids." Was that a viable reason? "Nothing ever happened between us, but," he waved his hand around, "it might be tense when we're together because I haven't seen her since she accepted Gage." Kobie didn't move. He didn't know what that meant. Her expression was unreadable. He couldn't sense a damn thing. *Fuck.*

"How do you feel about her now?"

That was a question. He realized he hadn't thought of it. "I," he frowned, "haven't even thought about her like *that* since I saw you." He sucked in a breath and held it. Again, with the unreadable expression. Could he get a small break?

"Layna?"

Blair bit his tongue, needing to feel the pain of it for a second. He wasn't into pain, but he may need to be after this. Why hadn't he just breezed over her question? "Because we have so many unmated females in the clan—" he cleared his throat, "and there are no other clans of tigers close by when some of the women's cycles…"

She held up her hand, fingers wide, so there was no mistaking what the signal meant. "You run around servicing women in heat?"

He opened his mouth, then closed it. "What? No. There are no *women*." His cat was back and threatened to rip his insides apart if he mentioned the summer when he was eighteen. "Layna—a few times, that's it." He stepped closer and stopped with one look from her, "look, you've had your cycle, right?" Was that a question he should ask? Too late now.

She glared at him.

Taking that as a yes, he lifted one hand slowly, "then you know how bad it can get," he paused, "unless you've found some oil or herb shit that helps with that?"

Kobie did not look amused.

"Okay, s-so then you know." He nodded, hoping she agreed. He watched the emotions come and go on her face and had no idea whether any of them were for or against him. When had he become such a screw-up with women? "What do you want me to do, Kobie?" He put his hand on his chest, "just tell me what you need."

She took a deep breath and glanced at the house. "How long can we live in this new place without an Alpha?"

"I'm sure it won't be a problem for a while—after everything you've been through."

Kobie looked at him, a hard look on her face. "You're going to tell the king, first, thank you for allowing us this new start and *then* you're going to tell him I have *not* consented to be mated and will not be rushed." She bobbed her head and started walking. "I'm going to get everyone and meet in Jay's room, then you can tell them about our new home." She kept walking without even glancing back at him.

Blair blew out a breath. He had no idea where he stood right now. None what-so-ever. Turning, he followed her, keeping a good distance between them. He knew one thing, he owed Gage a huge apology for pushing him with Kelsey all the time. This mate shit was not easy.

As he crossed the yard, he spotted Devin walking toward Kobie. When he glanced over at him, Blair shook his head to tell him to stay clear of her.

Kobie spun around suddenly and marched right back to Blair. She scowled up and him and then poked him in the chest. "Thank you for being truthful and not a complete asshole *male* that doesn't tell the little *woman* important details." She stabbed him again, "I've had enough of that to last the rest of my life." She huffed out a breath and stomped over to the house.

After she went into the house, Calum came over with Devin.

"Went that well?" Calum asked.

Blair frowned, "I don't really know, but all of you guys are assholes right now for forcing this on her."

Devin gave him a startled look. "I didn't…"

Blair backed toward the house, "your father, you, Calum, and any other male that's involved in making decisions."

Calum smirked. "So, it went well."

Blair rolled his eyes, then jerked his chin toward the door. "Now I get to tell all of them." He stopped, "Oh, and I have to tell your father thank you for the new start and she will *not* be rushed."

Devin crossed his arms over his chest. "I'll relay that for you."

"Blair?" Kobie opened the door.

Blair mouthed 'thank you' to Devin and then turned. "Let me grab a coffee and I'll be in." He told her as he stepped inside.

Chapter Eighteen

Carrying the coffee, he really didn't need, but *had* needed to stall for a moment, he stepped into the room. It wasn't a large room and now, with nine people crowded around the bed, it felt like there wasn't enough room to breathe.

"What's going on?" Jay asked in a quiet voice.

"Blair has something to tell us," Kobie said but didn't make eye contact with him when she said it.

Everyone looked at him. Was spontaneous stage fright a thing? Because something was happening he'd never felt before. His chest was tight, his heart was racing, he had to work to keep his breathing under control and he wasn't sure, but it felt like his fricken cat was pacing inside him. Clearing his throat, he bent down and set his cup on the side table. "I spoke to the King of the Alliance a while ago," he glanced around at the hopeful faces watching his every breath, "he's approved moving all of you to a property not far from where my clan is." He cleared his throat again, "it's a huge property, a great big house, more than big enough for everyone." He stopped there and looked around, trying to gauge the opinions.

"Will we be safe there?" Daisie asked.

He gave her a reassuring smile, "yes," he looked down at

Jay, "it's easily defendable, easy to patrol." He was being as respectful as he could to the only male left in this clan, the one that if he hadn't been in the state, he was in would for all purposes already be the Alpha. "And my clan is close by, you'll always have help."

Jay looked at him for a moment, then moved his eyes and looked at his sister.

"How will we support the clan? We left everything we had behind." Torrey hugged Kasia against her side.

"The Alliance can afford to help, so don't worry about that right now. Details like that can be sorted out later on." He knew it was the truth. He'd find a way to get what they needed.

"When are we moving to it?" Nichelle kept her voice quiet, respecting the seriousness of the conversation.

"A few days from now." He glanced at Jay, his expression was hard to read because he was still watching his sister. Blair was willing to bet that he sensed the trouble their earlier conversation has stirred up.

"There's a catch," Kobie said quietly.

"No Alpha," Jay said in a small voice.

Blair nodded, "it's not an issue right now, with everything you've been through."

"But it will be?" Cortney was sitting beside the bed with Daisie in her lap.

"It's part of the Alliance's pact that no clan is left without a leader." He looked to see Jay was looking at him now. "For everyone's safety."

"It makes sense," Franki said. "You can't have clans out there running amok and doing whatever, they could endanger all shifters."

Blair gave her an appreciative look for saying that.

"I can't be Alpha," Jay said slowly. A few of the women gasped at that. Jay turned and looked at Mika for a second, "I can't lead when I can't even move, Mika."

She blew out a scant breath and nodded briefly.

"So what happens then?" Annamarie asked, looking only to Blair.

"There are a few options." He said slowly and looked at Kobie, trying to get a sense of how much he was to share. "Merging with another clan, but no specifics have been figured out regarding that."

Torrey looked at Kobie, she shook her head.

"Kobie has never been after a leader's position," Jay said to the room.

Daisie jumped up from her mother's lap. "Blair can do it." She looked very excited. "He got us here." She nodded, "he helped Annamarie, *and*," she looked at Jay, "he let me ride on his back up the mountain when I was tired."

Blair rubbed his hand along the side of his jaw as he looked around at the others. "No decisions have to be made right now." He finally said as ten pairs of eyes studied him with great scrutiny, "I just wanted you to know that you have a safe place to call home."

"Thank you," Jay said and then glanced at Kobie again. "I'm quite tired."

Those sitting stood up.

Blair wasn't sure if he really was or if he was throwing him a little help in a crazy-tense situation. Picking up his cup, he backed out of the room and went out into the kitchen.

Annamarie came out and looked at him. "I agree with Daisie." She gave him a serious smile, no flirtation at all. With that, she walked outside.

Nichelle came out and smiled at him. "Thanks, for looking out for us."

Blair lifted his cup to her, but couldn't think of a thing to say that didn't sound boastful.

Daisie and Kasia came out and darted out the door. Right behind them was Cortney. She paused by the door. "Any word?"

He knew what she was asking. "The king still has a team down there looking into it. He's hopeful they'll have some answers in the next few days."

She nodded and then looked over her shoulder checking on the others. She came over quickly, "do you know if they were all…" she broke off, tears in her eyes.

"All they know right now is, they took six unharmed." He didn't know if it was unharmed, but he couldn't bring himself to say six were alive.

Cortney inhaled loudly through her nose and then nodded. "Okay, that's more than I had. Thank you." She touched his arm briefly and then went outside.

The others came out, Kobie was last.

"Blair, Jay wants a second with you."

Setting his cup down, he went over to the door.

"He needs to sleep." She whispered as he went by her.

He nodded and went in and closed the door.

"I couldn't back you," Jay said quickly, "in front of my sister—not with the waves of anxiety coming off her."

Blair nodded, "I get that." And he did. That same sister was pissed at him right now, so he understood that her brother would know all about his sister's wrath.

"But I do." He whispered. "The girls have been telling me things you've done."

Blair tucked his hands in his pockets, unsure if he was meant to say something or not.

"When Daisie was taken," Jay gave him a look that said he'd understood those two were no longer among the living, "what you did for Annamarie earlier." Jay moved his head slowly like he was trying to nod, but it was just too much effort to follow through. "They've lost all their menfolk, Blair," his voice cracked with emotion, "they need a strong one to get them through."

"I'm not going anywhere." He said, meaning it completely.

"I know," Jay looked at him again, "but you have to convince my sister that you are what she needs." His voice was getting quieter and quieter, "just," he coughed breathlessly, "if you're one of the Alliance's warriors, make sure you're on the same page with her and her with that."

Blair nodded, even though Jay had closed his eyes again. "Get some rest."

"Yeah."

She'd done it. Avoided Blair for the rest of the day. Her mood sucked for it, her cat was pissed right off with her, but she'd managed it. Kobie just needed time to think, she needed to figure out how she felt *without* the mating draw involved. She couldn't think when she was around him, or saw him, or scented him. Opening the door quietly, she peeked inside.

"I'm awake," Jay said with a hoarse voice.

"I wasn't sure." She went in and closed the door.

"When we get to that new place, can I get a room with a view?" He gave her a bored look.

Kobie looked at the ceiling, "that's not entertaining enough?"

He snorted, then groaned because it hurt. "I'd just like to see outside."

Kobie sat down. She understood. Honestly, she didn't know if she could cope with not being able to be outside for long. "We'll get you a bed with wheels and I can roll you outside."

"That works." He turned his head and looked at her. "How are you doing?"

She opened her mouth and then closed it. "I don't even know."

"Have you talked to Blair today?"

Shaking her head, she got up and went over to the window and looked out it. "I needed some space."

"You needed to analyze and try to figure out a way to work around him. He's your mate, Kobie, I'm injured, not fucking blind." Her brother stated in a flat tone. "I've never seen you watch someone the way you do him. And he *only* sees you."

Kobie shrugged, "it's just a lot, Jay."

"You are probably the only shifter in history that doesn't want a mate." He chastised. "Fate decides this shit, Kobe, not you."

"I know."

"So, is he ugly to you?"

She felt her cat brush against her at that question. "No."

"Is he white with black or black with white?"

Kobie inhaled slowly, "white with black."

"Your opposite." He stated.

"I suppose." She shrugged, but still didn't turn around and look at him.

"Is he forcing the issue with you? The mating?"

She hugged her waist, "no, he's been very respectful of giving me time."

"He doesn't strike me as dense."

Finally, she turned around and gaped at her brother, "why would you even think that?"

Jay smirked, "I'm just trying to figure out what the problem is." He tried to shift positions and then winced in pain.

Kobie went over and helped him move and stuffed a pillow under his shoulders, so his head wasn't at an uncomfortable angle. She sat on the bed in case he needed more help.

He took a moment to catch his breath and then nodded, "everyone else comes in here going on and on about him and you're treating him like he's the plague of the earth."

Kobie snorted. "Exaggerate much?"

"What's going on in that head of yours, Kobe, really?" He rested a shaking hand on her leg.

"He told me about his real clan." She picked at the blanket beside him.

"He wasn't raised with them."

She shook her head. "No, his mother sent him away when he was two when his father was killed." She looked at him. "His father was the Alpha." His eyes widened. "He told me about his brother."

"He did?" He licked his lips, and then motioned to the water beside the bed. "I told him not to."

Taking the glass, she held it out to him. "Why would you do that?"

He rolled his eyes, "because I *know* you and didn't want him to give you ammunition to use against him."

She stuck out her tongue at him, then sobered. "I can't hold that against him. He doesn't even remember any of them."

"Okay, so what are you holding against him?"

"He was in love with someone else's mate." She blurted out.

Jay was quiet for a moment, "well, he's alive, so I'm guessing nothing happened there."

She knew that. Blair was too honorable to move on someone's mate. "He goes and helps girls when they're in their cycle."

Jay smirked, "and how is *that* bad? You've said it yourself, it's the worst fucking uncontrollable thing you've ever experienced." He blinked a few times, "so he's evil because he won't let someone suffer that?" He opened his eyes wide, "unless you tell me it's like *all* the women in his clan," he smirked, "then he's just my fucking hero."

"Uh, you are so gross." She snarled at him, "and I can't even smack you right now."

"Look, as your older brother, I need you to hear me out…"

"You're like six minutes older than me, you dork." She sighed, purposely being dramatic.

"Just listen," he gave her a serious look, "you're trying to find reasons because you think you need to be alone to be the best you. I think he'll let you be who you need to be."

Kobie sat there, some of that was true, but she wasn't going to admit it out loud.

"Give him a chance, Kobie." He cleared his throat, "we're going to be on his turf tomorrow. *If* there's something truly wrong with the guy, it will come out where he's most comfortable."

She drew in a breath slowly and weighed his words. "Okay." Leaning over, she kissed his forehead, "now get some sleep. You look awful."

"Yeah? I feel pretty fucking awful too."

Getting up, she smiled down at him. "I'm glad I got you back. You, dork."

He smiled and closed his eyes.

Going outside, she turned to look around, she wasn't sure

what to do. She wanted to go for a run but didn't like asking permission to do things.

"Hey."

She turned to see Rayne and Shaelan walking toward her.

Rayne motioned to the guardhouse. "We just got the thumbs up from the powers that be that we could go for a run."

"You should come along." Shaelan smiled at her.

Kobie nodded, "I was just working up the courage to go beg for that."

Rayne laughed. "I don't ask. I get to tell." She nodded slowly.

Turning, Kobie saw Calum and Devin standing beside the small building.

Rayne motioned between the three of them, "girls run only, guys, sorry." She blew a kiss to her mate.

Blair came out of the building. He stopped and looked Kobie up and down. "What's going on?" He glanced at Calum.

"The girls are going for a run," Devin told him in a tense voice.

Blair looked at him for a moment, then to Kobie. "You know the boundaries, make sure they stay in them."

Kobie smiled, "you know it." She saluted them and started walking toward the back of the property.

Shaelan and Rayne caught up to her.

"What magic was that, and how do you do it?" Rayne asked. "I have to use pouty lips and bat my eyes at Devin to get a few minutes alone."

"Cal doesn't argue, but I can see the words going through his head when I ask," Shaelan said.

Kobie shrugged, "I'm a hunter and tracker, so I guess the time we spent in the mountain he understands I'm good at it."

"Show us some of this hunter stuff." Shaelan grinned, "going for a run without him trailing me, is a never before happened thing."

"My only run without Devin involved escaping our captors and tearing through a forest with Kelsey after she climbed the trees as a tiger to see which way to go."

"You were taken? By those people of that Tomas guy?" Kobie undid her shirt as they walked.

Rayne nodded as she shrugged out of her jacket. "We had to climb a cliff and hide there until the men found us." She smiled at Kobie, "if it wasn't for Blair, I don't think they *would* have found us."

"I still can't believe she climbed the tree in tiger form." Shaelan asked, "that's got to be hard. She's really big when she shifts."

Rayne nodded, "I don't know the first thing about a tree, in any form, so it was that or wandering in circles forever."

Turning, Kobie checked they were far enough they could strip down.

Rayne touched her arm. "Blair is one of the good ones, in case you need any testimonies." She smiled and then stepped over to the tree and took off her top.

Shaelan pulled the tie out of her hair. "I don't really know Blair, but I know Calum thinks highly of him and that says a lot." She nodded, "I've never met a man with rock steady morals like Cal's."

Kobie nodded, not having any words to say to any of that. "I think I just need time." She pulled her shirt over her head. "So much has happened, I can't even process."

"Of course you do." Rayne slid her slacks off and folded them neatly, adding them to her shirt on the ground. "No one expects you to decide right now."

Shaelan smirked, "as someone who has been through the weirdest life, ever, I agree, take all the time you need. Do what you need to do."

Calum paced to the center of the yard again and stood there.

Blair turned to see Devin watching in that same direction.

"You two need to tone it down—the tense vibes are suffocating me."

Devin turned to look at him, "why aren't you freaking out?"

He motioned in the direction the women had gone. "Were you placating her with what you said?"

Blair grinned. "Nope. If they run into any trouble, Kobie will get them back here."

Calum blew out a breath, "he's right, she *is* good in a bush."

Blair nodded, "I think you should go against her when we get them back to that property."

Frowning, Calum rubbed the back of his neck for a second. "I think I'll pass on that." He shrugged, "I have a rep to protect, and if she beat me…"

"I would broadcast it to the whole fucking planet," Devin said.

Calum motioned to Devin. "That."

"Fair enough, but you two need to get back in here and go over the routes with me." Blair opened the door.

Devin looked back at the trees.

"If you're standing there pacing when they come back, they will not be happy." He motioned in the door, "and we have screens in here from the cameras all over the bush."

"Fuck." Calum shook his head and went through the doorway. "Why didn't you remind us of that sooner?"

Blair chuckled, "and here I was going to ask you guys for advice on wooing a mate."

Devin laughed out loud. "Don't look at me, I botched that up completely."

"He did." Calum went over and leaned on the table, checking the screens. "And I'm no help either, I was chained to a wall, literally, when I marked Shaelan without intending to."

Blair frowned and looked from one to the other. "Shit. You guys are no help."

Devin leaned over Calum's shoulder to look.

"There's something you don't see every day," Calum said, sounding amused.

Blair went over and looked.

"I don't think I've ever seen a black tiger before," Devin said quietly.

"I was referring to a black tiger, blonde wolf, and midnight black jag running through the bush together." Calum looked at Devin for a second, then back to the screen.

"They're moving so fast the camera can't keep up in spots," Devin said quietly.

Blair didn't care about speeds or anything other than watching the sexy black tiger doing what she loved. He watched her pause and then nudge Shaelan, so she'd go in another direction.

"She is keeping them within the boundaries," Devin said.

Blair smiled and crossed his arms over his chest. His heart felt like it was going to burst as he watched her look out for the other two women blowing off steam.

Jesse came in carrying a mug and looking like he just woke up. "How's the planning going?" He stopped and looked at the table and then at the screens. "Are you spying on your mates?"

Devin snorted, "yes."

Backing away from the screens, Blair turned and motioned to the table. "The other route wasn't going to work. Too many populated areas and delays in construction zones.

Jesse glanced at the other two men not paying attention. "Okay, let me ingest some of this and bring up some routes on my laptop. We need fast, smooth for Jay's sake, and the fewer stops and traffic cams, the better."

"I think we should split them up." Blair crossed his arms and looked at the papers scattered across the table.

That got Calum's attention. "Like a few vehicles instead of all of them in one?" he shrugged, "Jay is going to have to travel in a separate one."

Blair nodded, "Yeah, we'll all stay connected through the phones, and if there's any trouble we can split off and still be in touch to know what's happening." He jerked his chin toward the door, "that van will be like a beacon if that car that followed us before was one of Tomas'."

Devin turned and leaned on the desk. "Rayne and I could ride with Jay and one guard."

Calum rubbed his hand along his jaw as he thought. "It's a

good plan. He motioned to Jesse, himself, and then to Blair, "there's three of us to drive, we could take three each."

Jesse nodded, "I like the idea of breaking off if anything goes down. I was nervous as shit hauling all of them in one vehicle."

"Yeah, it was too tense to breathe," Blair admitted.

"Okay," Devin motioned to the door, "go find Cale and see which vehicles here will work for that," he smirked at Calum, "you're not going to squish three people in your back seat, are you?"

Calum scowled at him, "No, but you better get my car sent to Gage's without a scratch on it."

"Fine." Devin smiled again then looked back at Blair, "make sure Cale gases them all up too."

Blair nodded and went to find Cale. He was the only guard whose name he knew. He liked his quiet style too, he always stood back and observed, he was good with that. Glancing to check if the women were back yet, he rubbed his hand over his hair. Maybe he'd see if Cale wanted to come to help him keep a watch on the girls until they got some defenses hammered out. His cat wasn't too happy with that, which confirmed the other man was a cat shifter and likely tiger variety, or he wouldn't be tensing up inside him right now. "We need the help, so suck it up." He said out loud.

Chapter Nineteen

The drive ended up being a little over four hours, with two bathroom stops added to the agenda. Blair spent most of the trip worrying about—everything. He had no idea what the state this house was in, he just hoped it would be livable until it was fixed up. He couldn't remember how long it had been empty— that alone told him he could have a lot of repairs over the next few months. Winter in their area tended to arrive earlier than the rest of the province, so it could be even less than that.

His cat was no help the entire drive, not with Kobie sitting in the passenger's seat and being so close to him. If it hadn't been for Daisie's chatter in the back seat, Blair may have lost his mind completely or done something stupid, like confessing more things to the woman beside him.

He didn't know who Daisie had grilled, but she knew more about the Alliance and the politics of the clans than he did now. There were two hundred clans in North America and an unknown amount around the world. Also, Devin's father didn't have to run all of them personally, Daisie had informed the adults in the car because he had ambassadors in other countries that took care of everything.

The only thing she said that he knew, was all clans looked

out for one another no matter if you had fur, hair, or other stuff.

He wasn't sure what the 'other stuff' was, but trying to figure it out had distracted his brain from worrying and his cat from jumping out of his body onto his mate beside him. He needed to ask more questions about the clans and Alliance, he decided once they got through all of this.

"I am so over long trips." Rayne's unamused voice broke the call's silence.

Blair hit the mute button on his phone. "Five more minutes." He informed everyone. Then his nerves hit him, making him tenser. Five minutes and hopefully he pulled in to see a habitable home. He pointed down the dirt road as they went by. "That's where my Alpha lives and we work."

"I haven't seen a house in twenty minutes," Cortney said quickly.

Blair glanced at her in the mirror. "That's the way we like it."

She smiled, even though it didn't reach her eyes. "I suppose it makes going for a run easier."

Blair nodded. "Just have to be careful of the bog areas."

She gave him a quick, curious look and then turned to look back out the window.

Blair pulled into the long drive. "We're here." He glanced at Kobie, who had been silent most of the ride. "It's going to need some work, but it's a safe place to live." He slowed as he crested the small hill and saw three trucks he recognized. He grinned. "Looks like you get to meet some of my clan that I work with." He shrugged one shoulder, "most of them are like brothers. We've been together since we were kids."

Kobie turned, and he could be sure, but it looked like she was scared. Blair reached over and squeezed her hand, then winked at her, trying to assure her it was all good.

Parking beside Jake's truck, he got out and stretched.

As the other cars pulled in, Jake and Gary came out of the house. Paint was splattered all over their clothes and faces. Blair hadn't realized until this moment how much he'd missed them.

The women and girls got out of the vehicles, and all stood together in a little cluster beside the van that Jay was in. Blair's heart ached for them, having left their entire lives behind. He'd be damned if he would let anything happen to them again.

Blair's cat was on edge with other men near their mate. Mentally shaking it off, he went over to Jake.

Gary turned and looked up at the roof. "Noah, come down. Beth will be back soon, and we'll need a hand."

Blair looked up to see Noah crawling like a crab down the roof to the ladder.

Jake grinned, "he's not good with a paintbrush."

"Or a hammer," Gary added.

"Who's running the shop if you guys are here?"

Jake wiped his hands on a rag. "Ed and Gage have it covered. Kels is with Coop—who is demanding one of us big assholes carry him to a truck and bring him over here to supervise."

Gary nodded, "Beth left early this morning to pick up some groceries and things for the kitchen." He shook his head, "she's been barking orders and buying things for the last few days."

A lump formed in Blair's throat, "I can't thank you—"

"Fuck that." Jake glared at him. "We need your ass back at the shop before the fall hits and everything comes in for repairs and painting."

Nodding, Blair glanced over to see Kobie watching. "All right, come meet the girls."

"Brave son of a bitch." Jake mumbled under his breath.

The van door flew open, and Rayne jumped out looking frazzled. "I think we need to start flying everywhere." She flipped the hair back off her shoulder and watched her mate get out and stretch.

Jake and Gary bowed their heads to him.

Devin waved them off and then looked from one to the other. "How much did you get done?"

"Five rooms upstairs and the lower one for," Jake motioned

to the van. "They'll have to double up until we get some more ready."

Gary pointed to the closest of the small buildings. "We got that one all cleaned up."

Devin nodded his head and looked at Blair. "The crew Dad sent are doing the fencing and setting up alarms along the property edge, so Gage volunteered his guys to get the house ready."

Blair glanced over to see the emotional expression on some of the women's faces. "I appreciate it." He said to no one in particular.

"We'll stay and lend a hand for a few days." Calum put his arm around Shaelan, "Shae wants to keep an eye on Jay for a while."

"I can help paint too," Shaelan said, then covered a yawn. "I don't travel well," she smirked.

Kobie stepped away from the girls and held Blair's look.

He motioned to her, "I guess I should introduce everyone." He went over and stopped beside her because his cat demanded it. "This is Kobie," he winked at her and then placed his hand on the back of her neck. To all the shifters it was an obvious display that would let all the males present know she was off-limits.

Keeping his hand resting there, he motioned to the women, one at a time. "Franki, Mika."

Mika inclined her head.

Franki smiled, "I'm good with a hammer and saw."

Jake tapped his chest, "I'm Jake. We will put those skills to use."

Blair gave him an appreciative look. "This is Torrey and her daughter Kasia."

Torrey pulled Kasia to stand in front of her.

"I can help paint," Kasia said.

"We have a lot of trim to do." Jake gave her a thumbs up.

Blair pointed to Nichelle, then Annamarie. "Here we have Nichelle," he glanced at Jake, "who will set you straight with a verbal lashing like you have never heard."

Jake placed his hand over his heart and patted it. "She's on my team for all future disagreements."

Nichelle grinned at him.

"And this is Annamarie." He watched her smile and turned to see it was Gary she was looking at.

"And what's your name?" She all but purred at Gary.

"Annamarie," Blair warned softly.

Huffing out a breath, she glanced at him. "Sorry, but he *is* cute." She added quietly.

Jake chuckled as Gary's face went red. "His name is Gary," he told her, then grinned at the blushing man.

Clearing his throat, Blair motioned to the remaining two, "This is Cortney and her sunshine, Daisie." He winked at Daisie.

Cortney nodded, "thank you for all the work you're doing. We'll pitch in wherever we can."

Daisie walked away from her mother and over to Noah, who was standing off to the side. She held out her hand. "Hi. I'm Daisie, what's your name?"

Noah hesitated for a moment and then took her hand. "Noah."

Daisie nodded, then turned his hand over. "You should be very careful when using tools. That's what my mom used to tell my dad."

Noah tilted his head, "good advice. I'll keep it in mind."

"Can we get a hand moving Jay inside?" Devin watched Shaelan get out of the van after checking him over.

Noah, Jake, and Gary went over and took a corner of the stretcher. Jake looked down at Jay and did a terrible job of keeping the shock off his face when he saw him. Glancing over at Blair briefly, one look conveyed his thoughts, and 'holy fuck' summed it up.

"We did a room downstairs with lots of windows." Jake gave Jay a quick smile, "there's a small patio just outside it for when you're feeling better too."

Blair couldn't hear if Jay replied.

"Let's all move inside," Rayne suggested. "We'll need to get a list going on what needs to be picked up." She went over and held the door open for the men.

Blair stood there with Devin and watched everyone go inside. "I appreciate all the Alliance is doing," Blair told him while trying to keep his emotions on a tight leash.

Jesse finally got out of the car, he was looking at his phone. With a shrug to Devin, he lifted his hands. "I have to bail. I'm needed elsewhere."

"You just don't want to paint," Devin said.

Jesse smirked, "with the size of this place, there will be painting left to do when I get back this way."

"Take care," Blair told him with a nod. "Call if you ever need backup."

Jesse saluted and turned back to the car.

Cale closed up the van and came over. As he did, he pulled his thick curly red hair behind his head with an elastic. He grinned. "This place is the epitome of private."

Blair nodded. "That's the only way to have it."

"I *had* that." Devin mused. "Now my campground is full of people in every direction I look."

Blair watched Rayne run out the door to the van and grab her purse. "But your mate is happy."

Devin nodded as he tracked her with his eyes until she was back in the house. As the door closed, he looked at Cale. "If you want to stay here, Dad says that's fine. Blair is going to need all the help he can get."

Cale nodded and looked around. He pointed to the small building down the driveway. "I was going to claim that and stay there if that's okay. I just need a bed." He glanced at the house, "my cat is afraid of staying in a house with nine females."

Devin laughed.

As if cued, there was the sound of high-pitched squabbling between Nichelle and Annamarie carried through the emptiness of the house.

"Yeah," Blair rubbed his hand over his hair and started for the door to find out what the problem was. He didn't even get the door closed before a horn honked outside. Looking back, he saw Beth climbing out of her SUV.

Jake and Gary pushed past him; both had haunted looks on their faces. Her arrival was a good excuse for them to get away from having to see how broken Jay was.

Beth started toward him. In her usual fast walk. He loved that woman, she was the only mother he'd ever known. She was a tiny thing, but he'd learned the hard way to never piss her off.

She smoothed back her wavy, red hair, which was now streaked with grey highlights, and then stopped in front of him.

He smiled down at her.

"Glad you're home, Blair." She patted him on the chest.

"It's good to be back, Beth."

She bobbed her head a few times, "okay enough chitchat, we have a lot to do."

Kobie, Franki, and Mika were standing in the kitchen when they went in.

"Hi, I'm Beth," she grinned, "from the clan next door." She pointed over her shoulder, "the boys are carrying everything in. I bought some groceries and all the dishes and things for the kitchen."

She smiled at Franki. "I need sizes and then I'll go out and grab some clothes. I only bought towels and linens this trip." She looked over at Blair, "I gave Shep an earful—expecting an entire house to be set up in two days. It's ridiculous." She looked back at the women, "I spoke with Irene this morning and as soon as possible, they're sending some people to pack up all of your homes and ship everything here." Beth paused again to smile at Cortney and Daisie as they came in. "Shep is working with some Fish man to sell the houses and get some accounts set up for you."

She nodded and smiled at Torrey, Kasia, and Nichelle when they appeared in the doorway. "Hi, I'm Beth—the Alpha's mate in Blair's clan." She bobbed her head. "What else? Oh, Blair," she didn't even look to see if he was paying attention, "there's a phone in one of these bags. You get it set up with all of our numbers in case they need something. We have three cars and a van being certified for you. Do you all drive? Beth waved her hand around, "it doesn't matter, Cooper can teach anyone to drive."

Jake and Gary came in and set down some bags.

"Now, more furniture will be here," she glanced at her watch, "Oh, it's late now," she shook her head, "I'll call and rattle them about it in a minute."

Blair grinned, knowing how rattled they'd be once she was done with them.

"Don't worry about dinner. Ed and I will be over and bring some once the shop is closed up for the day." She looked over at Blair, "and I believe Gage and Kelsey are going to bring Cooper over to meet everyone later too."

Clasping her hands in front of her, she turned back and surveyed the women standing there. Before anyone could speak, she waved a hand at Blair, "well, get to putting this away."

Blair took the bags from Jake and went over to the counter.

"I have a list started." Rayne came in, "Oh, good you're back," she smiled at Beth, "we need to go over this and see what you've already taken care of."

Beth nodded and started for the door, "everyone, I need sizes and preferences, so once this is all sorted, come and tell me." She nodded again and went into the other room with Rayne.

Devin came in carrying more bags. "I think she bought a grocery store." He mumbled.

"Is that your mom?" Daisie looked up at Blair.

He smiled, "only one I've ever known."

Daisie smiled back at him, "I like her, she's happy."

Jake snorted, "and that's the way you want her to stay."

Daisie watched her mother emptying a bag onto the counter and then darted over when she spotted cookies.

Setting the bags down on the counter beside Kobie, he gave her a questioning look. "Are you okay?"

She looked up at him and his heart jerked in his chest to see those deep blue eyes swimming in unshed tears.

"They're doing so much." She whispered.

He checked to see that everyone else was occupied, then took her hand, "come here." He headed for the first door in sight. Opening the door, it surprised him to see it was a small bathroom. Leaving the door open, he pulled her in and then turned and perched on the counter's edge, so they were the same height.

The tears were now trickling down her cheeks. "Oh, babe," he pulled her to stand between his legs and gently wiped them off, "don't do that. My heart will shatter if you cry."

She sniffled, "I just—I didn't expect…"

He leaned forward and kissed her mouth softly. "This is how my clan, my family is. They know you all mean a lot to me, so they're going to look out for you just as much as I am." He frowned when she didn't look happy about that. "What?"

Casting her eyes down, her lashes shielded them and so couldn't see what she was thinking.

"I wanted you to be a big jerk once you got home."

Blair grinned, "sorry to disappoint you, babe. What you see is what you get."

When she looked back at him, the expression in her eyes had changed. His cat nudged him as if he didn't recognize a heated look when he saw it. She was playing with the material of his shirt on his chest and just that slight contact had his blood simmering. Touching her chin with just a fingertip, he leaned closer. His cat was practically chanting inside him and it was distracting as fuck.

"Oh, there you are."

They both turned to see Beth standing in the doorway, smiling at them.

"Kobie was feeling a little overwhelmed."

Beth's expression changed to that understanding motherly look. "You poor, dear." She tsked. "You've endured so much." She gave her a soft smile. "You are so brave," the smile widened, "and absolutely gorgeous."

Before Kobie could say a thing, Beth pulled her into her arms and hugged her. Grasping her arms, she leaned back.

"Don't you let him step out of line, you hear? You have my blessing to give him a wallop upside the head if he does."

Blair couldn't see Kobie's face, but she nodded.

"You are a sweetheart." Beth whispered, "and you can trust that all my boys are the best catches in any clan. I raised them up right. There's none of that he-man stuff in our clan. If you want to drive a rig and have your nails hot pink, then that's what you do." She released her and looked at him. "Gage wants to know if he should toss your belongings and bed in the truck when he comes over."

Kobie watched him, waiting for him to reply.

He nodded, "yeah, I'll bunk out in that building they cleaned out.

"Okay, then. I'll tell him to bring your dresser and things over." She smiled at Kobie and then was gone in the other direction.

Kobie smirked at him. "How do you keep up with her?"

Blair shrugged, "You don't." When she went to leave, he blocked her with his arm and turned her to face him. "Not so fast." Holding her eyes with his, he leaned down and kissed her lightly on the mouth. It wasn't nearly the kiss he wanted, but he wasn't going to push the issue. "That will have to do for now." He straightened and grinned down at her.

"Do you have to be so damn charming all the time?"

Blair chuckled, "It's built-in, babe. I can't turn it off." Taking her hand, he pulled her out of the room and went down the hallway. "Come, show me who's called dibs where."

Chapter Twenty

Calum leaned against the house and looked to the end of the driveway again.

Blair wasn't even sure if he was breathing as he watched the truck come up the drive.

"You're going to have an aneurism if you don't stop."

Glancing at him, Blair blew out a breath. "It's just…"

Kobie came out of the house and straight for him. She grinned, "Ed is so laid back compared to Beth."

Calum chuckled, "that's a good thing, imagine if they were both wound tight."

Even Blair had to grin at that.

"I'm going to see what Shae is doing." Calum walked away after giving Blair a 'good luck' look.

"Is that her?" Kobie asked quietly.

Blair nodded, "Yeah, Kelsey."

"How do you feel about seeing her?"

He looked down at her, and then sighed, "I don't know how to explain it. We were like best friends, did a lot together, but," he shrugged.

"Things have changed." She offered.

He looked back toward the house. Annamarie and Nichelle

154

were in each other's face again as they waved their hands around. Blair nodded slowly as he looked back at Kobie, "in *so* many ways." He grinned, "most good, I think," he put his hands on his hips and gave his head a quick shake, "we have to get Annamarie and Nichelle in different rooms."

Kobie tucked her hands in her jeans. "Beth bought them both the same pair of shoes."

Blair cringed, "In her defense, she's only ever had one girl to look after, the rest of us were boys and we didn't care if our shoes were the same." The lights from the truck crested the small knoll in the drive.

"Do you want me to," she motioned to the house.

There was no hesitation in his answer, "no. I want you here." She gave him a small nod, "it's just I was," he glanced at the ground, then back to her, "a bit of a dick the last time I saw—everyone…"

Kobie put her hand on his arm and gave him an understanding look, "with everything they're doing for us, for you, I think you're forgiven."

Putting his hand over hers, he closed his eyes for a second, "I…"

"You want to stop lollygagging and give me a hand?"

Cooper bellowed from the truck.

Blair turned to see Gage holding him in his arms while Kelsey grabbed a wheelchair. He rushed over and opened the chair, and set it in front of Gage.

"Thanks." Gage grinned, "he's a stocky guy.

Cooper settled in the chair, with Kelsey lifting his leg gently and placing it on the footrest. "Are you saying I'm fat?" He grinned up at Gage.

"No, just that you're a lot heavier than you look." Gage rubbed his jaw.

"Or you're just getting weak." Cooper took off his hat and rubbed his hand over his nearly bald head. Placing it back on his head, he looked up at Blair. "You look good. Running around the country has done you good."

Blair rolled his eyes, "you make it sound like I was on

vacation."

"Whatever you call it, it did you good." Cooper glanced over at Kobie, who hadn't moved. "Well, get me over there, I want to meet the gal that's messed you up good."

Gage chuckled as he put his arm around Kelsey.

Kelsey smiled at him, it was the same smile she'd always given him, he realized. At that moment, he understood it would never have changed or been more. "I think it was the entire clan of females that messed him up." She grinned wide, "he's smooth with one or two, but nine?" She looked up at Gage, "I think that's a challenge for any man."

Gage jolted. "I can barely manage one, thank you."

Blair grinned and looked over at Kobie. She had no idea what was going on but still smiled back at him. Grabbing the handles on the chair, he started pushing Coop over, "Annamarie wants to learn how to drive, Coop, Nichelle, and Kasia too."

Cooper nodded, "that's good, we'll teach them all."

Blair stopped in front of Kobie and then stepped to stand beside the chair. "Kobie, this is Cooper, Gage, and Kelsey." He motioned to each of them.

Kobie smiled down at Cooper, "it's a pleasure to meet you." She inclined her head but made no move to extend her hand.

Blair's cat was glad for that. Rubbing a hand down over his chest, he nodded. "Coop's going to teach Annamarie to drive." He gave her a big smile.

A surprised looked appeared on her face, "oh, I wish you luck with that."

Coop looked from one to the other, "bit high strung, is she?"

"A bit," Kobie said trying not to laugh. She nodded to Gage, then Kelsey, "hi."

Kelsey pulled away from Gage and held out her hand. "I can't say how happy I am to meet you." She gave Blair a sideways glance, "I've been surrounded by men *all* my life. Now there are women. Finally."

Kobie shook her hand. "I get it. I've spent my whole life

proving I'm just as good, if not better than them, only to be shoved to the side to let the *men* take over."

Kelsey made an unpleasant noise. "Men." She mumbled, "come, introduce me to the rest. I have big plans for you ladies at the shop."

They walked away without so much as a backward look.

"What just happened?" Blair asked quietly.

Cooper was chuckling. "This may get interesting around here."

"Shit," Gage said under his breath.

"Well, I need to meet Calum's Shaelan." Cooper said looking up at Blair, "all I'm hearing is Shaelan said this, Shaelan said that."

"Shaelan is right here." Shaelan stepped out of the door and smiled at him as she walked over.

"Good. What's this about me staying in bed another two weeks?"

Shaelan stopped in front of him and looked down at his wrapped leg. "Well, if you'd let me put a light casting on it, maybe we could get you over at the shop, in the chair—supervising." She smirked at Blair.

Copper motioned to the house. "Let's get this cast on. I'm going to lose my mind if I have to look at those walls a minute more."

Shaelan went behind the chair and started pushing him to the house. She glanced back at Blair, "give me a hand lifting the chair inside."

Gage and Blair jolted and went over to help.

Gage shoved the mattress, forcing Blair to move. "Relax, they'll come back. She's probably just showing Kelsey the house."

Blair backed in through the doorway. "It's not that." He leaned it against the wall and then looked around. Single room, small bathroom. Shaking his head, he followed Gage out. It wasn't like he was going to be spending a lot of time in it. There was a house to finish, and he had to work.

Leaning on the truck, Gage grinned at him. "You've looked at the house at least twenty times in two minutes.

Blair scowled at him and motioned with his head to get in the truck to get the dresser. "I knew they'd meet, obviously…"

"Weren't they supposed to?" Gage dropped the dresser, almost ripping Blair's shoulder out of the socket. "You told her?"

Dropping his head forward, Blair rested it on the end of the dresser. "Yeah. I didn't intend to, but then it just—" he looked at him, "came out."

Gage wiped his hand over his face and then looked at him. "Why? I mean, did you want to make it awkward."

Blair lifted the dresser again. "That's not even the worst thing I told her." He shuffled backward until Gage had his feet on the ground.

"What could be worse than that?"

Blair turned his head to watch where he was going as he backed up, but mostly so he wouldn't be looking at the other man. "I may have mentioned Layna."

Gage shoved the dresser, causing Blair's shoulder to slam against the wall. "Dear God, tell me you only told her about Layna."

Snarling at him, as his shoulder throbbed, he gave a jerk of his chin. "I'm not a complete idiot.

Gage snorted and set his end down. "Could have fooled me." Wiping a hand over his face again, he shook his head, "did you not learn anything watching me suffer?"

Blair lifted both arms out from his body and held his hands in the air, "that's why I did—because secrets come back and bite you on the ass."

"Do I want to know?" Calum stood in the doorway holding a box.

Gage motioned to Blair, "he's an idiot, making things harder on himself. He told her damn near everything."

Calum nodded, "I know." He looked over his shoulder, "Devin and I think Cooper told him to."

Blair went over and took the box from him and set it on the dresser. He turned back to Gage, "you procrastinate, and I'll be truthful, okay? I'm not fucking it up."

"What does pro-cras-tinate mean?" Daisie was now standing beside Blair. "Mom says I do that when it's time to go to bed."

Blair blew out a breath, "it means avoiding doing something you know you have to do."

She nodded slowly, "oh, I do that." She pointed at him, "and you said a bad word again."

Gage grinned.

"I did." Blair motioned to go back outside, "I guess I forgot."

Daisie turned and looked at Gage, "Kelsey says stop being men and come in and eat." She frowned, "can you do that? Stop being a boy?"

Gage laughed, "it would probably keep me out of trouble if I could."

Blair rested his hand on her shoulder as they walked to the house.

"Being a boy sounds hard. I'm glad I'm a girl."

Gage laughed and looked at Blair. His look wasn't hard to read at all, he was thankful it was Blair's problem to deal with all the females he'd brought home.

Chapter Twenty-One

Stepping out of his tiny house, Blair rubbed a hand over his face and yawned. He was going to have to get a coffee maker for in there. He was used to it being within reach as soon as his eyes focused in the morning. Especially if he was going to keep having these long restless nights.

Closing the door, he looked around to see Cale running toward the front of the house, to where Gage, Devin, and Calum stood. None of them looked happy. Something was going on. "So much for coffee." He mumbled and hurried to find out what was going on.

Devin was waving a hand around as Calum scowled and looked out toward the road.

"What have I missed?" Blair stifled another yawn.

"Dev's parents have decided to visit."

"What?" Coffee or not, that woke him up. "Here, now?" He looked at Calum, who mirrored his thoughts. They had enough issues keeping the women safe.

"They're flying in, Devin said, looking around. "We'll land them over at Ed's."

"Shit." Blair looked around, he knew how many guards traveled with Shepard Addison.

"They can stay at our house," Gage motioned to the small building Blair had just come from, "we'll put the guards up in the bunkhouse."

Blair nodded, still trying to process. "Why now?" He turned to see Kobie coming out of the house and forgot he'd asked a question. She was wearing low riding jeans with a black and white patterned halter top on. It covered most of her waist, he was thankful for that with the men here, but it left all of her shoulders and neck bare. He wanted to go over and lick that skin. She smiled at him and his heart started pounding. She was wearing makeup and it only enhanced how fucking gorgeous she was.

As she got closer, she held out a cup to him. He hadn't even seen it.

He took it, unable to find his voice to speak. Taking a sip, he burned his tongue and didn't care. It was probably the best coffee he'd ever tasted.

"What's happening?" She looked only at him. "Rayne is in there on the phone with Beth making a shopping list that sounds like it will feed an army."

"My parents are coming," Devin said, in an unamused tone.

Kobie's dark eyes went wide, "The king and queen are coming? Here? Now?"

"Yes." Calum looked at Blair, an expression he couldn't read on his face.

She put a hand over her throat, drawing Blair's attention back to it. "I guess I better go try to tidy up, if that's possible with paint cans and ladders all over the place." She smiled up at Blair and then walked away.

Blair took another sip of the coffee, watching her walk away, momentarily mesmerized.

"We need to…"

Blair held up his hand to pause whoever was talking and darted after her, spilling hot coffee all over his wrist. "Hey," he touched her bare shoulder and his cat rolled against him, prodding him to mark that soft skin. "Thanks." She turned and gave him a soft look, those eyes, was all he could think. "For the coffee." He added in case she was having as much trouble thinking as he was.

Kobie smiled slowly. He wanted to nibble on that bottom lip of hers. "You," she placed a hand against his chest, "need to focus on whatever needs doing before royalty is on our doorstep."

He inhaled, taking her scent into his body. No perfumes, no oils, just the intoxicating scent that was her, "you look fucking amazing," he said in a whisper.

She smiled, a playful look in her eyes. "Thank you."

Blair nodded slowly, his eyes moving all over her face. *Just fucking amazing.*

"Blair?" She whispered.

He watched her mouth as she said his name. "Yeah?"

"Kiss me and then go do whatever it is you have to do."

His gaze darted back to her eyes. A man could get lost in those eyes. Holding the cup out of the way, he leaned down and grasped the back of her head, and pulled her closer. He wanted to devour her, his cat wanted more, but instead, he kissed her gently, slowly, tasting her mouth, coaxing her to kiss him back. When she did, he still controlled himself and kept it soft and sensual. Lifting his head slowly, he looked down to see her eyes had a sexy, longing look in them. He smiled and kissed her briefly. "Go in the house so I can focus. You're killing me here."

Backing away, she touched her mouth and gave him a heated look. "Let me know when you want breakfast." She said in a breathless voice and then went back into the house.

Blair waited until she closed the door and then blew out a breath.

"All better now? Can we focus on how the hell we're keeping Dev's parents safe?" Calum said loudly.

Blair turned his head, his body following slowly, and went back toward them. Nodding, he took a quick sip, "what were you saying?"

Gage grinned, Devin shook his head. Even Calum looked amused, despite the serious issues they needed to talk about.

"Tell me I didn't look that dopey over Rayne," Devin said quietly.

"You were worse," Calum said.

Devin scowled at him, "you were an idiot with Shaelan."

Calum rubbed a hand over his chest. "Completely different circumstances."

Blair smiled, "we're all idiots when it comes to them." He lifted his cup, "now how the hell are we keeping, nine coveted females, and the entire royal family safe?"

Blair stood beside the house and watched the helicopter fly overhead, then disappear as it landed at Ed's.

"I'm nervous as fuck." Cale came up beside him.

"Gage said the vans of guards arrived an hour ago." Blair crossed his arms and looked up at the sky. It was getting darker.

"They must have been on the road before we were told they were coming." Cale followed where Blair was looking. "This storm is going to hit hard."

Blair nodded, "yeah. Because this isn't enough of a challenge." He motioned to the house, "having the whole royal family here and then twenty people trapped in an unfinished, partially furnished house."

"What's my priority here?" Cale scratched the side of his head, "I'm here to watch over this clan, but when royals are here…"

"They'll bring about ten of their own guards," Blair glanced back at the house, "you just keep doing what you've been doing and patrolling and keeping an eye on the girls." He blew out a breath, "they're getting better at not wandering away…"

"They're getting annoyed with shadows at their every move," Cale said quietly.

Blair nodded, "I know, but it's either that or stay in the house. I'll remind them."

"Thanks. I thought Franki was going to take a bite out of me last night for trailing her on a run."

Blair laughed, "would you rather be assigned to the girls that can't shift yet?"

Cale's eyes widened, "I think that might be worse. Those four are going to be a force, mother nature won't even challenge."

Blair nodded. "And they're all ours."

Cale turned to watch the vans come up the drive. "I'm definitely on their side in any battle, fight, or squabble."

Blair felt pride move through him.

Kobie looked around the yard. There were so many guards. She didn't know how many, but was glad some had stayed over at Ed's with Irene, the Queen of all shifters—she still couldn't believe she'd met her. Turning, she watched Gage, Blair, and Devin come back with huge grins on their faces.

Calum eyed them, "what's going on?"

Gage shrugged, "we just thought a little fun has been earned."

"Fun?" Calum frowned.

"Yeah, you remember fun, don't you?" Devin glanced at Gage. "Was he ever fun?"

"I can't remember," Gage smirked.

"What have you guys done?" Kelsey looked from one to the other.

Blair motioned to the back of the property. "We hid something out there and want to see who finds it first."

Calum looked over at his mate, then back to them. "Again? How many times do I have to make you guys look bad?"

Devin crossed his arms over his chest and grinned, "oh, we're not participating."

Blair turned and smiled at Kobie, "best tracker and hunter against the all-mighty Calum."

Calum's eyebrows both went up as he looked at them.

Kobie shrugged, "what are the rules?" She could use a little fun right now.

Gage was still smiling. "You both leave on two feet, once you reach the stake you can shift, and whoever brings back the hidden object wins."

She looked at Calum, then back to Gage, "what's the object?"

"A rabbit fur," Calum said in an annoyed tone.

Kobie stood there for a moment, "how old is it?"

"A few days since it was cleaned., Blair confirmed, looking at Cooper.

"It's not dried out?" She asked.

Cooper shook his head, "No, it's still good and rank." He tipped his head to her.

Kobie shrugged, "okay then. Any other rules I need to know about?"

Gage and Blair exchanged a look. "Nope." Gage crossed his arms and smiled at Calum, "you in?"

Calum stood looking at them for a long silent moment, then gave her a quick smile. "I'm in."

"This is going to be interesting." Shepard stood in the doorway.

Devin glared at him. "Stay inside."

His father stepped out the door and looked around at the number of people and guards standing there. "If they can get to me through all of you, then we've failed on many levels."

Kelsey and Rayne came over to Kobie.

"Kick his ass," Kelsey mouthed, then smiled.

"Can we carry our packs?" Kobie asked.

Daisie ran out the door with hers in her hand and gave it to Blair, who started walking toward her with a big grin on his face.

Kelsey leaned closer, "Blair is the only one that found the hide at the same time Calum did, but Calum runs faster."

Kobie nodded, "yeah he's got the speed I don't have."

Rayne looked over at Devin, "he's even faster than Dev's wolf."

"Okay," Kobie took off her jacket and handed it to Rayne, "so outmaneuver him is what you're saying."

Kobie bent down and pulled off her shoes as Blair reached her.

"You got this, babe." He looked over at Calum where Gage

and Shaelan were whispering to him, "use those amazing skills of yours and ignore him. He'll try to send you on a wild goose chase and then run like the wind in the right direction."

Kobie took the pack from him, "why would I follow a male when I can scent things for myself?"

Rayne and Kelsey glanced at Blair and then smiled.

"Good luck, we believe in you," Rayne said and took Kelsey's elbow and went over to stand with the others.

Kobie looked up at Blair, "I hope I don't screw this up."

Leaning down, he brushed a light kiss over her mouth. "I believe in you." He smiled at her.

She held his pale eyes, her heart pounding in her chest, "that means a lot, Blair. I've spent half my life trying to prove to men that I was useful to the clan."

"Babe, you don't have to prove that here." He motioned with his head to where Kelsey and Rayne had gone, "Kelsey's been making us look incompetent for years." He grinned.

"I doubt that, but thank you." He continued to stand there and look at her. His expression was gentle, his eyes flicking to her mouth, then back to her eyes. Kobie's insides tightened, "stop distracting me." She hissed.

"I'm not doing anything." He answered honestly.

Kobie rubbed her hand over his chest and then gave him a little push. "You don't need to." With that, she turned around and walked over to where Calum stood.

He inclined his head to her and motioned to start walking.

She did. "You didn't know this was coming?"

Calum shook his head, "no."

"You don't seem happy about it." She glanced at him but kept walking.

Huffing out a breath, he held her look for a moment, "I almost hope you beat me."

That surprised her. "You do?"

He nodded, "yeah, then you can be challenged constantly every time there's a group of shifters together."

Kobie laughed quietly, "what clans have you beaten?"

"All that has challenged me."

That didn't tell her much about which type of shifters he had beaten in the past.

"Blair is the only one that came close." He told her quietly.

Looking around for the stake they were supposed to be going to. "That doesn't surprise me. Everyone only has good things to say about him."

He looked down at her while he walked, "is that a bad thing?"

Kobie shook her head, "no, I just feel like everyone is trying to sell him to me."

"Maybe they just want to see him happy and you're what's going to make him happy." He said quietly, and then pointed to the red stake in the ground. "Who knows, maybe you'd end up being happy too."

Kobie paused and looked at him, she hadn't thought of that. Having someone that believed in her and trusted her had been something she'd been looking for since she was little. She frowned at Calum, "that's cheating, distracting me right before this."

Calum pulled his shirt over his head, "if you're as good as I've been told, nothing will distract you from the task at hand." He grinned, "nothing." He turned his back to her.

Blowing out a breath, Kobie stood there. When he started to take off his pants, she turned her back to him and pulled her shirt over her head. Inhaling slowly, she scented all around. From this point, she could pick up Blair, Gage, and Devin's scent. They were smart, doing this right after a rain when all the scents of nature were amplified and enhanced.

She pulled off her jeans and stuffed them in the pack and put it over her head. They'd be smarter than that, making sure their scents crossed all over this area. Find the pelt, she thought as she shifted fast.

Kobie had found four places the men's scents crossed paths, and twice where Calum had followed them. She paused and looked up. Would they have put it in a tree? That would hardly be fair, but she wasn't putting anything past them. She was near the furthest border of the property by this time. She could make out the decaying smell of the pelt, but the fresh rain was messing with her picking the exact location. Stopping, she inhaled slowly and processed everything that came back to her.

Rage moved through her, and she froze. That scent. She would never forget it. The last time she smelled it was on the bodies of their loved ones when she'd found them dead. Spinning, she inhaled again. She had to find Calum—had to warn him.

Catching a hint of his cat's scent, she took off in that direction, paying no heed to any obstacle that was in her way. As she ran, she filtered through the other scents, trying to see if there were any others in this area that were out of place or didn't belong to one of the clans that had been out here.

Spotting Calum, she leaped over a small ditch and then changed direction to cut him off before she lost him again. She moved fast and silent as she jumped over a downed tree and then took a quick right. This should put her right in his path.

When she could smell him closer, she crouched down and debated if she should just leap on him. If she ran for him, he may think she was just looking for the pelt and trying to weigh lay him. Too late to decide, she made out his dark fur on the other side of the ferns growing. Bounding over them, she landed in front of him—later she'd do a victory cheer that she'd been able to startle him as he crouched down, his ears lying flat. Straightening, she bumped her head into his shoulder and then turned and visibly showed him she was scenting the area. She emitted a low yowl so he would hopefully understand.

She looked back to him, he was standing straight again, sniffing the air.

Calum shook his head, then moved over to bump against her and then turned to look in the house's direction.

Kobie took off. She hoped like hell he'd been telling her to go get backup because that's exactly what she was planning on doing. Bounding over a mucky area, she caught the scent of the pelt. Later, she told herself she'd come to get the prize and win that. Right now, she needed to get help and get all those she loved hidden away safely.

She jumped over the fence and heard cheering as everyone thought she was bringing the pelt back.

Blair stepped out of the small crowd when she was almost to them. "Something's wrong."

Kobie slid to a stop in front of him, then went back to the corner of the house and looked out in the direction she knew Calum to be, then growled for all to hear.

"Fuck." Blair ran over and stood with his back to all the other shifters. He inhaled slowly. Then glanced down at her. "Someone's out there."

"Shit." Gage was already pulling his shirt over his head. "Kelsey, you get the women in the house and lock all the doors."

Devin started to take off his shirt when Gage shook his head, "You're staying, watch over your dad and kill anything that comes near the house."

Devin didn't look happy but turned back to usher the others to the house.

"Cale," Blair called out as he kicked off his boots, "you get on that roof with a loaded rifle."

Kobie watched Cale run for the truck.

"Noah, you're with us. Jake, you and Gary stand guard here." Gage said quickly, then unzipped his jeans.

"Take us to him, babe," Blair said as he pulled down his jeans.

Kobie turned and waited until three tigers were standing beside her instead of three naked men. The size of Noah momentarily shocked her, then shook it off and took off in the direction she'd come. She didn't plan to run straight for Calum. The odor of the intruders wasn't leading toward him. There were two scents now, possibly three, the rain was covering their presence like it had the pelt.

Skidding to a halt, she turned to see the men had no problems keeping up with her. She lifted her chin and inhaled slowly, then made a slow movement with her head to show them the directions she was picking up scents.

Noah didn't wait for any further instruction, he bound off in the direction she'd started with.

Gage went to their left, leaving her and Blair to go down the center.

Calum was straight ahead, and she wasn't sure if he was stalking them or waiting for backup. They were smart, she had to give them that, they weren't sticking together to make it easy to be found.

Blair kept pace with her and didn't even hesitate when she'd deviate around something in their path, he was letting her lead, and not making it more work for him to stay with her. She respected that he wasn't trying to send her back to the house now that they knew what they were looking for. Their cats were in synch with each other. That was something she'd had to work for before, even with her own twin.

The scent of blood filled the air, Kobie stopped quickly and listened to pinpoint a direction. She could barely make the sounds of frenzied movement, but it was enough to show them where to go. Twisting, she turned and ran in that direction as fast as she could. They couldn't kill these men, despite her cat thinking they should, they might have information about the rest of her clan, and that had to be her main objective.

Clearing a small grouping of trees, Blair and Kobie came to a fast stop to see a naked Calum standing there with a naked, bleeding man on the ground. Around the man's neck was a thick leather collar. That would prevent him from being able to shift. Kobie didn't even care that Calum was naked. With some cord in his hand, he zipped the pack back up and motioned to a tree. "I'm going to tie him to that." He dragged the man by his arm to the tree, then looked at Kobie. "You can bring the guys here for him after we get the other two."

Kobie made a soft prusten to let him know she would before moving closer to look at the man. She didn't recognize him, nor his scent. He wasn't one of the men that had killed her clan members. She snuffed at him, then turned away.

Calum was back in cat form. He swung his head and looked at her, then looked to their right.

Kobie inhaled and checked to confirm the other two scents of their intruders were both in that direction. She didn't wait to see what they were planning on doing, just took off running. She needed to get to them before Noah or Gage killed the one that had killed her clan members.

No animals were making a sound with this many predators present. It wasn't hard to find the other two, the sounds of fighting traveled easily in the quiet bush. As Kobie burst through the foliage, her heart pounded when she saw a body on the ground. She trotted over to it and inhaled. It wasn't the one that had been on their land back home. Turning, she saw the flash of orange through the trees and took off toward it.

Calum and Blair were already there, circling with Gage as Noah took on a large tiger. He couldn't kill him, she relayed to her cat, so she'd ignore the scent of blood. When Noah pinned him to the ground, his teeth clamped under the other cat's jaw, Kobie sprung in that direction and flew at him. She hit Noah hard, causing him to release the other animal. Scrambling to her feet, she stood over the injured animal and growled low, ears flat.

"We need him alive," Blair said loudly from behind her.

Kobie stared at the tiger and hissed at him, demanding he shift.

His animal cried out in pain and ended with a man screeching as he finally lay there on the ground in skin and not fur.

"I got him." Calum was there, wrapping his shirt around the man's bleeding neck. He glanced behind them. "Noah, go get help and bring that body back to the house."

Kobie looked to see Noah take off into the trees.

"Blair, Kobie, go get that other guy," Calum said.

Gage, wearing his jeans again, walked over and squatted down beside Calum. "I got this one." He glanced at Calum, "you go find out how the fuck they got on this land without us knowing."

Calum stood up. "It might take a while. I'm going to have to go around the entire perimeter, that team of Dev's missed something."

Blair came over to Kobie and rubbed along her side, giving her a gentle nudge. They had to track back and get that one that was tied to a tree.

Bumping her head against him, she turned and took off back into the trees.

Chapter Twenty-Two

When they got back, Kobie assessed quickly what was happening. The tailgate of one of the trucks was down, a barefoot was visible. Beside the truck, Shaelan and Devin leaned over someone. Kobie picked up the pace, despite the stones cutting into her feet. Shaelan had to keep that man alive.

Devin stood up and nodded. "Run in and grab an IV bag from Jay's supplies." He told Rayne. "He's going to pull through."

Kobie huffed out a breath, letting her shoulders slump forward.

Blair walked by her, half carrying, half dragging the other man, and then just let go when he was near the truck. The man slid to the ground and just lay there. "His side might need a patch, Shaelan."

Standing up, Shaelan glanced at him. "Okay, just let me get the IV going here."

Devin moved back to stand beside his father, where they spoke quietly. Seeing them reminded her. She walked over and dropped the mud-covered pelt beside their feet.

"Oh," Devin looked at it then, pointed his finger at her while grinning at Calum.

Calum frowned. "Did you find it on the way back?"

Kobie shrugged, "No, it was in the muddy bog right near where I met up with you," she jerked her head at the man lying on the ground, "before all this. I found it when I came back for help but wasn't stopping to get it then."

Gage was grinning from ear to ear now and nodding his head as he looked at Calum.

"Shit, I knew it was right around there," he spun and looked at Blair, "in the mud? That's a new low."

Blair shrugged, "I was only making it fair for you, my man," he reached over and pulled Kobie to stand beside him, "my girl can scent things through perfumes, oils, and god damned ointment, so leaving it out in the open would have made you lose in a heartbeat."

Calum laughed, then turned to look at Kobie and bowed to her, his arms spread out from his body. When he stood up, he pointed at her, "you have a job any time you want it." He scoffed, "having someone else come out to help me track people down that is *good* at it," he looked at Gage, "would be more than welcome."

Shepard started clapping. "While they're cleaning this up," he motioned to the men on the ground, "and taking them over to Ed's shop," he pointed to Calum, Blair, Devin, and Noah, "we're having a discussion." He smiled at me, "and Kobie has just earned her place at the table."

Frowning, Kobie looked around. Everyone was looking at her. Her clan, Blair's clan, and every other person there.

Shepard motioned to the door, "shall we use the kitchen here?"

She realized he was asking permission to use her home. Her *home*. Then jolted and nodded, "Absolutely."

Curious glances were being exchanged as the five men sat down at the table. Kobie's heart was racing, she didn't know what this was about. Giving herself a few minutes to stall, she grabbed some bottles of water and put them on the table and then opened the cupboards and pulled out a bag of jerky and a package of cookies and added them to the table. All of them needed to replenish. She slid into the nearest empty chair, "sorry, it's the best I have on short notice."

The men were already helping themselves.

"Food is food," Blair said and winked at her.

Taking a bottle of water, she opened it and took a sip.

"As far as I can tell, they left a tree overhanging the border." Calum turned to Shepard, "it's easy enough to climb, stay off the camera's and not trip any alarms."

Devin picked up his phone, "I'll send Jake and Cale back to cut anything away."

Kobie was trying not to crush the bottle of water in her hands.

"No need to look nervous," Shepard told her.

She nodded. Kobie was sitting at her table with the king, the prince, and one of their top warriors, of course, she should look nervous. She continued to watch Shepard as he glanced around the table at the others. He was a big man, it was hard to believe he shifted into a wolf. How big was his wolf? She wondered. There was no mistaking Devin was related to him, they had the same streaked brown hair. Only the King had some grey in there too and combed his neat whereas Devin's just did what it wanted.

Blair's hand touched her knee under the table, and she almost jumped, only remembering at the last second they weren't alone, she didn't want to look like a skittish fool. Turning her head, she looked at him to see a reassuring expression on his face. He could feel how nervous she was, which meant the rest of the men probably could too.

"Are you going to tell us *why* we're here, Dad?" Devin grabbed a cookie and took a bite.

"I am. I was just pausing to look at my new team." His father gave him a look, "minus you, of course, you're more like the coach and not going to be doing the work."

Devin raised an eyebrow and looked at his father and then turned to Calum, "you know what this is about."

Calum nodded, and then took a drink.

"Jesse is also part of this and a few others, but you here," he motioned around the table, "are the start. I need outstanding fighters, trackers, and," he looked at Calum, "ones that can think on the move."

Calum sat back and crossed his arms over his chest. "You know I'm in, Shep, but," he looked at Blair and then at Kobie, "they need to have some serious discussions."

"How do you mean?" Blair frowned.

"*One* of you will be Alpha of this clan," Shep said quietly. "You need to decide if Alpha and mate are both going to be going to help the Alliance and stop Tomas, or if one stays behind."

Kobie leaned on the table. "I'm not sure what we're talking about." She didn't want to be the dumb female, but they were talking around something and she needed clarification.

Shep motioned to Noah, "Noah was a captive of Tomas' for fifteen years. Between his knowledge and Rayne's we have a list of addresses and places we know people are being held," he paused and glanced at his phone.

Kobie studied Noah for a second and then turned to Blair, who nodded.

"Sorry about that," Shepard put the phone back down, "Jesse is just keeping me up to date on a few things." He cleared his throat. "Within the next week or two, we're going to liberate as many captives as we can."

Kobie's sped up. She clasped Blair's hand under the table.

"Keep in mind this isn't something that can be done in animal form. A lot of these locations are in cities," the King leaned forward, a serious expression on his face, "can you track just as well on two legs? With all the other scents and distractions?"

"I don't know," Kobie said quietly.

Calum made a weird noise. "You found the damn pelt when we had intruders and still remembered where it was afterward."

"I can still track, but I've never tried in a city." Kobie blew out a breath, "I'm willing to try."

"It could prove useful if we lose sight of some of Tomas'

associates." Shep nodded his head slowly and then looked at Blair, "we need another warrior like you, Blair."

Blair lifted his chin. "You know I'll help."

Nodding in a thoughtful way, he glanced at Kobie before speaking to him again, "and you're okay with your mate being involved?"

Blair looked at Kobie, she couldn't make out what he was thinking with his expression, then he looked away saying nothing. It was starting to feel like a hundred discussions she had with her father. She was good enough for sport, but when things turned serious, it was best to let the men handle it. *Where did that get you, Dad?*

"That's up to Kobie. She's my mate. I'm not her ruler and I don't give her orders." He shrugged, "I'll lead the clan if that's what they want, but she's beside me, not behind me."

Devin and Calum exchanged a quick look.

Kobie looked at Blair and met his gaze. He wasn't just saying it, he meant it. She could not only see it, but she could feel the emotion coming off him. Later, she'd work through the shock she was feeling. Right now, all eyes were on her waiting, for her to say something. "I want to find my people," she said to him before turning back to the King, "I want to free others and," she turned back to Blair, "I want to help Blair find his brother, bring him to justice for what he did to Blair's and my family."

Blair inclined his head to her.

"Okay. Then you need to pick a second family in the clan— it's my understanding the last of your father's choices went with him."

Kobie nodded, "they took his wife and daughter earlier this year."

"Sir," Blair waited for him to look over, "I trust in Gage and Jake and the guys to watch over the others if we're not here." He cleared his throat, "the girls need to heal more than they need to be worrying about taking over in case anything happened."

Shep sat there for a moment thinking that over, then

nodded and looked at Kobie, "you're all right with that?"

Kobie nodded. A week ago she would have said hell no, but now that she knew Blair's clan and how they were, she could think of no one better to look after everything if something happened. She got stuck for a second, they were *asking* her, not telling her. "I agree with him, yes."

Blair squeezed her knee gently, with an emotional expression was in his eyes when he looked at her.

Devin's father looked at his phone again. "I'm glad we settled that," he lifted the phone, "Jesse has just informed me they have found a few of your men."

"Found?" She couldn't bring herself to say alive.

He nodded, "yes two that weren't captured."

Kobie sat on the edge of the chair.

"They're in rough shape, but not like your brother." He stood up. "I'm going to call and get more details." He turned and walked out of the room.

Kobie stood up and put her hand over her mouth. "Oh my god." There were tears in her eyes. She wanted it to be Robbie, Daisie's dad but wanted it to be others just as much.

Blair gave Devin a look and then stood up and pulled her closer.

"I'll go see if we have names." Devin got up.

Blair nodded but didn't take his eyes off her.

"I'm going outside to patrol. Let me know if we're needed for more discussion." Noah walked by them.

Kobie's heart was beating so fast she was having trouble breathing. She held Blair's look, trying to stay calm.

"I'm going to check on Shae, she's in with Jay." Calum left quietly.

"Hey," Blair touched her shoulders gently, "breath, this is good news."

Kobie nodded, "I just…" She couldn't voice it. How could she want it more for one than another? "I need it to be Robbie, for Daisie." A tear rolled down her cheek. "But then there's Annamarie, Nichelle, and Franki." Blair pulled her against his chest. He didn't try offering her words that would make it okay to hope for one and not another. There were four from what was left of her clan that had no answers, that waited on news of a relative. Grasping his shirt, she pushed her face into the scent that was unadulterated Blair. Inhaling it, she searched for calm. Even her cat didn't know what to do. He was right there, his scent inside them, but clan members' families mattered too. Blair just stood there, running his hand up and down her back, the motion was soothing, comforting, but she noticed it was his scent that helped her keep it together.

"Dev will find out, babe." He whispered against the top of her head.

She nodded, not able to say anything, she just needed to touch him, inhale the warm scent of his skin. It felt like hours were crawling by.

Someone cleared their throat. Kobie lifted her head and looked over to see Devin standing in the door to the living room area. She straightened but continued to cling to Blair.

"Niles and Robbie," Devin said softly.

Kobie nodded. A tear ran down her cheek.

Blair held her shoulders and leaned down. "Niles?"

Kobie swiped at more tears. "Nichelle's uncle." She said in a voice shaking so much, she wasn't sure he'd understood.

"Okay." He nodded and kissed the top of her head.

"This is stupid. It's good news." She leaned her face into him again.

"It is." He hugged her. "Just hold on to hope that more will be found or rescued." He leaned away again, "we're part of that rescue team, babe." He offered her an understanding smile, "we'll find as many as we can."

Daisie came running into the kitchen and stopped. She gave Kobie a wary look, then frowned at Blair. "Did you make Kobie cry?"

Blair hugged Kobie against his side, "no, sweetie, I didn't." He cleared his throat. "Can you go round up your mom and Nichelle for me?"

She looked at Kobie again.

"It's a happy cry." Kobie lied.

Daisie frowned even more, "there's happy crying?" She slumped her shoulders and turned to the door. "There's *so* many kinds of crying."

Blair went to step away, Kobie grabbed the back of his jeans. "Please stay."

He smiled down at her. "I was just going to grab you a Kleenex." He made a scoffing noise, then pulled his t-shirt up and wiped her cheeks gently. He kissed the top of her head, "so they don't freak out and beat me thinking I made you cry."

She had to smile at that. "They wouldn't beat you."

He raised both eyebrows and looked down at her. "I would put nothing past the group of you."

"You wanted us?"

Kobie turned to see Cortney and Nichelle standing in the door with Daisie right beside them.

"She was crying," Daisie said.

Kobie smiled at her briefly. "I was." Taking a deep breath, she inhaled slowly. "They've found Robbie and Niles." She waved her hand in the other room. "They're in rough shape, Devin's father is getting more details now."

Cortney hugged Daisie against her side, her hand over her mouth. "Any of the others?"

Kobie shook her head. "Not yet, but they're still searching."

Nichelle looked from Cortney to Kobie, then back. "Uncle Niles is alive?"

Cortney nodded.

Nichelle turned to Blair, "are they coming here?"

"I'm sure they will as soon as possible."

Nichelle nodded her head quickly. "We need to get more rooms done." With that she spun around and went back outside.

Cortney looked at the door. "I'll go make sure she's okay." She gave Kobie a quick look, "let me know when you know more."

Kobie nodded. She held her breath until they went out after Nichelle. Blowing it out, she looked up at Blair. "I need to go for a run."

He searched her face for a moment. "Do you want me to come along?"

"I just need some time to process." She whispered.

Leaning down, he kissed her mouth softly. "I'll tell the guards to give you some space," he straightened up, "any hint of anything off, you hightail it back here."

She nodded, even though it wasn't a question. "Thank you." She rubbed her hand over his chest. "For everything," she motioned to the table, "you shocked me by some things you said."

Blair shrugged one shoulder, "I meant them. Where things go from here is your choice." He looked at her for a moment, "everything."

Stretching up, she pecked his cheek, then turned and went outside.

Chapter Twenty-Three

Blair watched the three vans pull out of the drive before turning back to the shop. The last twenty-four hours had been rocky. Devin finally convinced his father to leave by agreeing to go with him. The two men were recovered enough to transport and were being taken back to the Alliance headquarters for questioning. Blair didn't even know where that was and didn't think he wanted to.

Kobie's clan was a roller coaster of emotions right now, with two men found, but no news of the rest. She'd gone for her run yesterday and then spent the rest of the time avoiding him. He scowled, he wasn't used to that at all, a female avoiding him. Then again, they'd had an awful moment, where harsh words were spoken when she came back.

He looked at the big excavator parked in the yard and smiled at it. A task he could focus on to get out of his head. He had missed this. Turning, he looked at Gary as he walked out of the shop, "does it run?"

Gary grinned, "non-stop, that's the problem."

Blair tilted his head and looked back at the machine, "a challenge."

"Kelsey tried something yesterday and ended up tossing a

wrench at it and walking away." Gary shrugged and walked around the corner of the shed to whatever piece of equipment was there.

Blair grinned and put his hands on his hips and looked at it. "We're going to communicate, you and I," he motioned between the machine and himself, "I need a win today." He started walking toward it, then bent down and picked up the wrench sitting on the ground. "I've got enough situations and problems to keep me occupied—so let's work together on this." Setting the tool tray on the bumper, he climbed up to open up the engine hood.

"Kelsey's good with an engine, so you have secrets…" he mumbled as he started going over obvious things, but he wanted to cover all his bases. He hadn't been exaggerating, he had enough to occupy his brain, he needed the distraction. This is exactly why he'd volunteered to come over and lend a hand and left Jake at the house painting more rooms with several women 'helping' him. He grinned, they helped, but it was like having a meeting with four bosses present and no workers. Everyone had their idea of how it should be done. Maybe it was cruel to leave him there to sort it out, but he needed to *do* something.

Kobie had been sitting in with her brother since finding out that Robbie and Niles had been found. It was going to take days to get them here. There just wasn't enough of the Alliance team freed up right now to go escort them here. Jesse was headed that way, but even then, he'd been told Niles wasn't up to the long trip just yet. No one was sharing why and that upset Kobie, and all the women of the clan. Daisie had been oddly quiet since finding out about her dad, but Cortney was now energized and she wanted to get the whole damn house done—in an hour, or so it felt.

Blair blew out a breath and leaned over the engine looking at it, but not really seeing it. He'd had words with Kobie, she wanted to *go* get the men. Not even an hour after him saying he didn't give her orders; he had basically ordered her to stay put because she was *not* going.

"Need a hand?"

Blair looked to see Noah standing there, looking up at him. He shook his head, "I don't know yet."

Noah smirked, "I thought with all the mumbling you were doing, you were struggling."

Blair straightened up and leaned back. "Oh, I'm struggling all right, but it has nothing to do with this," he motioned to the engine.

"It's been a hell of a ride for you, huh?"

Blair smirked, seemed like Noah had developed a sense of humor since he'd been away. "It's been a hell of something, that's for sure."

Noah looked over to see Gary waving a hand for an assist. "Well, when you're done riding out the storm, just know I'm behind you one hundred percent of the way."

"Thanks." He'd already figured out that Noah was fond of Daisie and would be her protector forever after, but it was good to hear it. "I just have to survive the damn storm."

Backing up a step or two, Noah bobbed his head, "it takes a brave man to fill that place, but I think you've got it."

Blair watched him walk over to Gary. Did he? Have it? Damned if he knew. He wasn't even sure which storm Noah was referring to. The disagreement with Kobie didn't bother him as much as other things—well, his own behavior pissed him off, he didn't enjoy going all territorial jerk on her. He wasn't even sure the upset women were an issue. He was starting to think he was the issue.

Seriously, none of that was something he could fix, even if he knew how. Those that had lost loved ones, well, he wasn't God, he couldn't soothe that. The ones that had no answers, he couldn't do a damn thing about either. He frowned at the engine and paused for a second. "Won't stop. There's got to be something jamming, gummed up, or broken off—" He leaned down further to look more.

Jay had accepted him, for that he was thankful. If her twin was against him, Blair knew that would have been a problem as far as Kobie and him ever getting together. Blowing out a breath, he gave his head a slight shake, best not to think about that at all.

Now two more males from the clan were coming back. Blair didn't know how he felt about that. He was happy they were, happy for their family that was waiting, but was he going to butt heads with them? He *had* gotten their women this far, so surely that counted for something.

He pushed against the valve, if he had been gone, regardless of the reason, and came back to some strange man taking over, how would he feel? He scowled at the engine; he probably wouldn't be too accepting. Hanging over the edge, he grabbed a screwdriver, "maybe you just need some attention, huh? A little adjusting." He grinned. With his luck lately, the chances of this excavator tossing something at him he didn't understand were high. He pushed against the valve again. Seemed to be a little smoother. "Okay, let's see how you like that."

Sitting up, he turned to climb down and saw Kobie standing on the ground, grinning up at him. He'd been so lost in his head, she'd managed to sneak up on him. His heart picked up, "Is everything okay?"

She nodded, "at the house, yes, I just needed to get out of there."

Swinging his leg over the engine casing, he sat on the edge of the bumper, "painting going that well?"

She smirked, "your friends may regret offering to help. Cortney is on a mission."

Pointing the screwdriver in the direction of the house, he nodded, "and that's why I'm over here today." He frowned, "I like to think that makes me a smart man and not a coward."

Kobie tucked her hands into her jeans, "we both may be cowards." She looked at the machine he sat on. "What is this and what are you doing to it?"

"This," he looked from one end of it to the other, "is an excavator and she doesn't want to stop once she's started."

Kobie raised an eyebrow, "she?"

Blair shrugged, "this one is because she's a mystery." He

smirked. Pointing to the cab, he gave her a hopeful look, "want to give me a hand?"

"I know nothing about things like this."

Jumping, down, he held out his hand. "You don't need to. I just need someone to turn it off and on when I say."

"If it gives me an excuse to avoid the house, okay." She took his hand and then let him lift her up to the first step. Climbing up, she looked in the cab. "There's a lot of switches and gearshifts, and far too many things to hit in here." Kobie glanced over her shoulder at him, "are you sure you trust me with this?"

Blair grinned, "I trust you—and I won't be near anything that can crush me."

"Good to know." Careful to not touch or hit anything, she climbed in and sat in the seat. It was more comfortable than most furniture she'd sat in. She inhaled, and smelled like sweaty man boots, she noted.

Blair leaned in, "okay," he flipped a switch and did something with a shifter, "when I say, just push that in and turn the key."

Kobie noted where he pointed. "Okay."

"Once we get it running properly, we'll take it out in the field and you can play with it."

She looked to where he pointed. The field looked like it had been dug, dragged, and buried hundreds of times. Did she want to play with this monster machine? "Okay, but I accept no blame if I break something."

"There is nothing you can do that one of us hasn't already done, trust me." He winked and then ducked back out of the cab and swung up to stand and lean over the huge motor that was open.

"Okay, start it." He said loud enough she heard.

She did and felt a little exhilarated when the machine was vibrating with the power of the motor. Keeping her hand on the key, she watched Blair as he leaned down in, almost dangling his body *in* the motor. She held her breath and watched him reach in and do something to it. She wouldn't even look under the hood of a car with it running and he was sticking his face and hands in a huge motor. Forcing herself to breathe, she hoped this was going to be an easy fix, so she didn't have to worry about him losing pieces of his body.

It may not have been the most intelligent move he'd made, confining the both of them in the small cab of the rig. She smelled fucking amazing. Like, he had to keep his mouth away from her so he wouldn't take a bite, kind of amazing. Each time she laughed, it made his cat side want to yowl in victory, that their mate was happy.

Kobie growled low in her throat when the rig hesitated in a deeper rut in the thoroughly dug-up field. He watched the look of determination appear on her face and his heartbeat kicked up a few notches. She was perfect.

"So," he leaned down closer and adjusted the throttle, so the tracks would dig in, "when I can arrange it," she paused and gave him her complete focus. *Those eyes. Fuck.* "I thought we could go do something—together." So much for the smooth Blair that was seemingly a thing of the past.

She grinned slowly, her eyes lighting up, and it hit him in the gut or more groin. "Are you asking me out on a date?"

Blair grinned, "yeah. Some time without work, escape, or two clans present."

Kobie laughed softly, "is that even a thing? Asking your mate for a date."

Blair leaned back away from her before he grabbed her and did something stupid and uncivilized. "I fucking hope it is." He snorted, "I don't plan on a marking, and then that's it, we're stuck in a daily grind deal."

She didn't mask the surprised look on her face fast enough. Her dark eyes locked with his. "Good and yes, some time with just the two of us would be great."

Blair nodded slowly, "I'll figure out how and when." He winked at her, "now get this rig out of this hole or I'll have to call Jake to pull us."

Her eyes went wide, "we're not doing that." She looked at the dash and pointed, "this one? Give it power, but not too much?"

He nodded.

With a determined expression, she leaned forward in the seat and maneuvered the rig, so it turned to gain better traction. Grinning at her expression, he turned to see the dirt kicking out beneath the tracks and spotted Noah running toward them, waving his hand. "Something's wrong." Blair reached over and throttled down the engine and shut off the rig. Opening the door, he hopped down and looked all around them. Nothing seemed out of place here.

"You need to get over to the house," Noah called out.

Kobie climbed down and stood beside Blair.

"What's going on?" Blair started toward him, a hundred different scenarios going through his mind. Had Tomas sent more? Was Jay okay? If Daisie fell out of a tree, he was going to freak out…

"Jake called, it's one of the girls," Noah stopped and took a deep breath to settle his breathing.

Blair's heart thudded in his chest.

Noah waved his hand beside his head, "the one with the red streaks…"

"Nichelle." Blair supplied quickly.

Noah nodded, "her first shift."

"Shit." Blair turned to look at Kobie, then held out his hand. They started jogging toward the shop. "Get two of the guys over there to run the perimeter, in case she runs wild." All he could think of was Kelsey's first shift. He'd never been so worried and scared, but proud all at the same time. How had he not sensed it this morning when he'd seen her? He scowled as he opened the door for Kobie to get in. Nichelle had been quiet and keeping to herself a lot the last few days. Blair assumed it was because her uncle was coming back and not in good shape. Still, someone should have noticed and told him.

"It's exhilarating and nerve-wracking each time," Kobie

said in a tense voice.

Blair only nodded; first shifts were always intense.

"It's too bad none of her family is here for her."

Blair eased off on the gas to keep the truck from drifting across the road as he turned out onto it. Reaching over, he squeezed her hand. "She's got the rest of us."

She was quiet until they pulled into the drive. "Maybe one of the older women will help."

Chapter Twenty-Four

Blair pulled the truck out of the way and opened the door. He looked at her. "As part of the Alpha family, she may need you to keep her cat form in line."

Kobie got out and then looked at him over the box of the truck. "I've never done this." She pulled her jacket off and hung it over the tailgate.

Blair took his shirt off and set it beside her jacket. "I'll be there." Taking her hand, he tugged it as they rushed to the back of the house. "Just stay out of reach." They met a worried Cortney and Daisie as they rounded the corner.

"Better hurry," Cortney said quietly.

Blair and Kobie both jogged down the path to the trees. Jake and Mika were there. Mika was talking to her quietly while Jake was pacing, looking like he wanted out of his skin. Blair gave him a nod, and Jake turned and walked into the trees.

Nichelle was leaning against a tree, hunched over and hugging her waist.

"She's fighting it." Blair released Kobie's hand and jogged over to her. "Don't fight it, hun." He said in as soft a tone as he could manage. The last thing she needed right now was her cat to be spooked.

Mika gave him a quick nod and went into the treed area.

"I'm scared, Blair." Nichelle moaned quietly.

"I know. The first time is hard—the not knowing." He squatted down so he could see her face. Kobie came up beside him. "You need to strip down and get down on your hands and knees, hun, it's easier for the first few." He pulled the laces loose on his boots. She gave him a quick look, he nodded. Blowing out a breath, she moved from the tree and grasped the hem of her shirt. "I know it's hard, but just relax and let your body take over, okay?" Standing slowly, he backed up a few steps, "don't fight it, just let it happen." He glanced at Kobie, "I'm going to shift, Kobie will be right here to talk you through it." Kobie nodded.

"Okay," Nichelle dropped her chin and panted out a few forced breaths. "Just—just stay here, Blair, please. Don't leave me."

Blair nodded, "I'm not going anywhere, hun. I'll step behind this tree, you strip down and get down on the ground, okay?" His heart felt like it was cracking at the scared tone in her voice.

She nodded quickly but said nothing.

He moved behind the tree and made fast work of getting out the rest of his clothes.

"You've got this, Nichelle…"

He listened to Kobie's soothing tone for a second and then shifted.

Giving Nichelle a wide berth, he walked out slowly so he didn't startle her.

She was on all fours and panting quickly, her breathing already changing to that of her cat and not a two-legged form.

"That's it, just let it happen." Kobie squatted down, out of paw's reach. She had stripped down as well. Blair took a moment to appreciate her nakedness, but even his cat accepted now was not the time for any lusting thoughts.

He made a soft prusten sound, hoping to bring her cat out faster. He remembered his first shift like it was yesterday. Even wanting it as much as he had, it still felt like it was taking forever. When he heard bones shifting and reforming, he crouched down on his belly, still far enough from her he wasn't a threat, but still close enough to spring into action if Nichelle lunged for Kobie.

Once the initial movements passed, a beautiful dark orange she-cat stood where the young woman had been. Blair noticed a few dark red streaks in her coat near her eyes and was momentarily surprised that her fake color had held through the shift.

He chuffed as Nichelle hesitated and stretched slowly. She was a fairly large female for one so young. Kobie stepped back, so Blair moved forward to be between the newly shifted cat and her so his mate could shift.

Nichelle stood at her full height now, her legs no longer shaking. She turned her head slowly, probably adjusting to how different things looked through the feline eyes. Turning back, she looked right at Blair. He paused and let her inhale to test out the marvel that was the scenting power of her cat form.

Giving her a friendly, quiet yowl, he walked over and stood almost nose to nose with her. She didn't hesitate, just moved to rub against his shoulder. It was the equivalent of a hug in this form. Kobie moved into view and Nichelle repeated the same move with her.

Turning, she looked into the wooded area. Blair bumped against her, telling her to take the new body for a test run. Before she moved, Mika came bounding toward them and did a playful crouch in front of the younger cat.

Nichelle yowled and then paused at sound of her own voice. Without further prelude, she twisted and took off running into the trees.

Blair followed behind Kobie and Mika, hoping only that she wasn't as fast as Kelsey was her first run. When she made a quick turn and started in a different direction, that hope died. She was fast and just as agile as the more seasoned cats trying to keep up with her. It was standard to let those on their first shift have free run and to just follow and keep them out of trouble, but with the current threats, they couldn't give her too much freedom.

Five minutes later, she made another abrupt turn and increased speed. The moment of pride faded when he realized she was heading toward the river. Blair increased his speed. He knew she loved the water and swam like a fish, but learning to tread water with paws and heavy wet fur was a whole other thing. Hopefully, she'd turn and head to the narrow, shallow part and just splash around in it.

He glanced to see Noah running hell-bent in the same direction.

Kobie called out in hopes she slowed, but Nichelle was having none of it.

Jake came running out from the trees on his other side, he zagged in front of Blair, probably hoping to cut her off and get her to change directions.

Blair felt short-lived pride again as the first-time shifter evaded his experienced friend and the redirection he was trying to do. The pride was replaced with panic when he heard the loud splash. Nichelle had taken a flying leap and landed in the deepest part of the rushing water.

Jake and Noah skidded to a halt on the edge of the water. Neither was fond of water in any form.

Blair, having learned the hard way, during one of his attempts to win against Calum, bound past them and right into the water. He pushed off with his back legs toward the struggling she-cat. She was holding her own, mostly, keeping her head above water. Swimming during a first shift was a guaranteed method of hitting exhaustion, fast.

Kobie appeared on the other side of the water. He wasn't sure how she'd gotten there that quick, but he was glad for it, it gave him a direction to take Nichelle.

When he was a foot away from her, she noticed him and stopped flailing around. Using a powerful stroke, he nudged her side, so she'd turn and head toward Kobie.

The first thing they were discussing once they got back was what you *shouldn't* attempt to do in your first few shifts. With more girls in the clan to go through it, he needed to establish some sort of rules.

She panicked again and went under. Blair let his body sink below the surface and went under her chest to lift her above the water again.

Yeah, a sit-down with all the new and upcoming shifters was *definitely* happening.

Using all his strength, he shoved her toward his mate.

No trees. No water or cliffs...

He hit the bottom and practically lifted her in the air to make sure she was in shallow enough water she could touch the river floor.

Would it be poor leadership if he built a fenced run for new shifters? Probably. He'd have to think about that some more.

Climbing up the muddy slope, he shook, spraying water in all directions.

Noah and Jake came tearing along the bank, side by side. Mika was right behind them.

Blair shook again, then finally looked at Nichelle. She didn't look frantic or phased at all. With a hushed chuff, an apology he interpreted, she watched him.

He took two strides toward her when her head snapped to look to her right.

A rabbit was about to have the fastest run of its short-lived life. Without pause, Nichelle took off after it.

Blair was pretty sure he heard Jake moan as the adults spread out to keep her from doing anything else that aged them through terror on her first-ever run.

Stepping out from behind the tree, Blair glanced over to see Nichelle standing with Annamarie and Kasia. She was smiling and talking excitedly.

Jake came across the yard to him. His expression wasn't as happy as the others. "No more first shift watch for me." He said when he was closer. With his hands on his hips, he studied the younger girls for a moment. "At least with females." He gave Blair a hard look, "what is with females and their first shift? Guys, they shift and run around scaring everything," he shrugged, "or eat it."

Blair chuckled, "she did good."

"She's fast," Jake grumbled. "Felt like I was ancient and trying to keep up. I think we need to go for actual runs again. Patrol isn't much of a work-out."

Blair shrugged, "that's a little hard to pull off right now."

Noah came over to them. "She's got guts." He mumbled. "I don't even like running through a puddle." Crossing his arms over his chest, he studied the women all gathering. "You're going to have one hell of a pack to contend with once they all shift."

Blair smirked. It was true. If Kobie worked with all of them, hunting and tracking, not to mention speed, they would be a clan no one would mess with. "I think we need to establish some basics with the girls."

Jake snorted. "Good luck with that."

Nichelle turned around and spotted Blair, and ran toward him. He barely had time to brace himself when she launched herself at him.

She squeezed him tight, then jumped back. "That was—" she grinned, "I can't even describe it." She sobered quickly. "Sorry about the water…"

Blair rubbed his hand down her arm, "it's okay, we should have discussed things before your shift," he frowned, "why didn't you tell me?"

She blew out a breath, "I didn't know what was happening," she waved a hand around, "and with everything else I didn't want to bug," she looked over at Torrey, "anyone." She shrugged, "I thought it was because Uncle Niles was alive, you know?"

Leaning down, so he could make eye contact with her, he spoke in a soft tone. "I don't care what's going on or isn't, you can *always* talk to me, got it?"

She nodded, then inhaled deeply and put her hand on her stomach. "I can't believe I ate a bunny." She smirked.

"I can't believe how quickly you caught it." He chuckled

and then noticed the forlorn expression on Annamarie's face. "Go in and grab a protein bar. You need to eat often and never let your body run on empty until you can control the shifts more."

"Okay." She backed up a step and then paused, "thanks, Blair. I was really freaking out until you got there."

He winked at her. "You did great."

She smiled and then spun around and jogged to the house.

Pulling his shirt over his head, he walked over toward Annamarie. "Are you okay?"

She huffed out a breath, "Yeah, fine."

"Feeling gypped?"

She gave him a surprised look. "How did you know?"

Blair grinned and motioned for them to move away from the others. He rubbed a hand over his chest, "I remember when one of the others shifted first, and I was still on two feet."

"I just thought—I'm oldest..."

"Age has nothing to do with it." He stopped and looked down at her, "each cat is different, comes out when it's their time, not yours."

She nodded, even though the disappointed look was still in her eyes. "I guess."

He grinned, "Being older when the first-time hits will help you be more in control."

"Yeah?"

Blair chuckled, "Gary shifted young, younger than Nichelle and he was so out of control..."

Her eyes lit with humor. "Really? Think he'd mind if I asked him about it?"

Blair raised an eyebrow at her, "just keep the flirting out of it and I'm sure he'll be fine talking about it."

She blew out a breath. "He's really cute..."

"And you're off-limits."

"I am?"

He nodded, "yeah, I have enough going on right now, I can't even fathom any of you girls dating at this point." He blew out a loud exaggerated breath, "so please, just…"

"I'll behave. For now." She whispered, "but I need to get out of the house before I lose my mind."

"Deal. I'll see if Beth wants a shopping partner."

Her eyes went wide. "Really? That would be amazing."

Blair put his arm around her shoulder and started to walk back, "go celebrate with Nichelle."

"Did she really jump into the river?"

He glanced down at her, "yes and that's a bad thing for a first shift."

"But you saved her?"

Blair nodded, not saying anything.

"Of course you did. You've saved us all." She hugged him briefly and then walked over to where Franki was standing with Kobie.

Rubbing his hand over his hair, he dropped his hands to his hips and stood there looking at them.

"Busy day?"

Blair glanced to see Calum standing there. "Yeah."

"You did good, wrangling her."

Blair snorted, "Which one?"

"Both. All." Calum smirked, "I don't think females are anything like men when they first shift."

Rubbing his temples, Blair blew out a breath. "Nope. Nothing similar. Kelsey climbed a tree, Nichelle went for a swim…"

"Shae took down the corrupt Alpha in her clan."

That made Blair pause, "really?"

Calum nodded slowly, "I was all set to fight him, and she struts through the crowd and takes him down the first time in her cat body."

"Damn." Blair looked back at the females grouping together and reveling in Nichelle's first shift, "and I still have more to get through."

Calum chuckled, "Noah said you dove in the water and hauled her out," he gave Blair a serious look, "you've got this,

Blair. You'll be the best Alpha they need."

"You think?" He turned and tracked Kobie with his eyes, "if I can ever get a moment with my mate, that might be closer to happening."

Shaelan was walking toward them. "Too bad there are no pink shacks here."

Calum chuckled.

"Pink what?" Blair looked from one to the other.

"Long story." Calum hugged Shae against his side, "short version is you'll never get closer to being mated if you don't get her away from the clan of women she feels obligated to watch over."

"We were sort of discussing that when Noah came running to tell us about Nichelle," he motioned to where all the women were listening to Kobie, then turned his head slowly and looked at Calum, "how do I manage that?"

Before Calum could answer, Gage's truck came up the drive. Blair went to go over when Kelsey hopped out of the driver's door.

"Problem?" Shaelan asked quietly.

Blair studied Kelsey for a moment. "No." He noticed her carrying something. "A pack." He grinned, feeling some relief that it wasn't something urgent. "She's bringing Nichelle a run pack." He blew out a breath. "I hadn't even thought of that."

Shaelan grinned up at him. "Good thing you have women around to cover what you forget."

"Nine of 'em," Calum said with a big grin then guided Shae toward the others.

"Yeah. Nine of 'em." Blair said under his breath. "I am so far out of my league here." He blew out a breath and followed them over.

Chapter Twenty-Five

Blair lay there, looking at the ceiling in his little space. He should get up and was working toward it. Nichelle had wanted to go for a run three more times yesterday and he'd insisted on escorting her each time. Then Kobie wanted to, so he'd gone with her too. At least his cat couldn't grumble he wasn't getting out enough. Blair rubbed his hand over his face. He needed to think about things for the women to do. Once the house was fully painted, they'd start going stir crazy. Sitting up, he stared at the wall. At least he was thinking ahead on some things.

Getting up, he grabbed a clean pair of jeans and shoved his legs into them. As he was doing them up, a soft knock sounded.

Opening the door, he looked down to see Daisie standing there.

"I need to talk to you." She said in a serious tone. She held out a cup. "I brought you coffee."

He smirked and took it. "Thank you." He took a sip and then leaned against the door jam. "What do we need to talk about?"

She looked over her shoulder and then back at him. "I want a dog—or a puppy, but maybe a dog because they don't pee all over." She nodded, her expression more serious than he'd ever seen it.

He hadn't seen that coming. "Well," setting the cup down, he went over and got a t-shirt out of the drawer and pulled it over his head, "it's rare for our kind to have pets." He drawled, not sure how to tell her no without breaking her heart. "Did any of your clan have pets before you came here?"

She shook her head.

"There's a reason for that, hun." He picked up the cup and motioned for them to go outside. "Dogs aren't fond of large cats and because we're…"

"Large cats they don't like us." She gave him a sad look.

"I wouldn't say they don't like us, but they're afraid of us and…"

"Oh. I can't make a dog live where it's scared." She said and looked at the ground.

"Something like that." Blowing out a breath, he reached down and tipped her chin up, "but Bruce has some other animals on the farm. We can go there sometime."

"We can?"

He nodded, hoping that was the end of the problem. He wondered for a second if problems came before coffee every day or if it was just the situation lately.

"Are you leaving when my daddy comes home?" She blurted out quickly.

Blair wondered if that was the whole reason for her visit this morning, she'd probably known the answer about the dog. "No." Squatting down, he ignored the coffee he splashed on his wrist. "I'm not going anywhere."

She fell against him, wrapping her arms around his neck and squeezing. Blair wore the whole cup of coffee as it hit his leg before landing on the ground. Putting his arm around her, he held her close. "You're stuck with me, kid."

Releasing his neck, she nodded. A single tear rolling down her cheek shattered his heart instantly.

"Good." She backed up and looked at the cup on the ground. "You need more coffee." Picking up the cup, she ran toward the house.

He sat down and looked at his soaked leg.

A soft chuckle had him turn to see Kobie standing there leaning against the side of the little building.

"She knows why no dogs."

Blair wiped at the wet leg of his jeans. "I figured." He got up slowly and looked down at his jeans again. Deciding he'd live with the wet material, he motioned to the house.

"All Nichelle can talk about is how you dove in and saved her." She looked amused.

"That reminds me, I thought we could talk with the other girls about things not to do during the first few shifts."

"We?" She pushed away from the wall and started for the house.

Blair nodded, "yeah, I thought it would be easier if you were there…"

"Afraid of laying down the law with the girls?" She smirked up at him.

Blair rubbed a hand over his jaw, "that obvious?"

Kobie nodded, still looking amused.

"I don't want to order them around…"

"Look," she stopped and put a hand on his arm, "right now they think you walk on water. It might be the best time to get through to them." She sobered, "because once that wears off the road is going to be bumpy."

Blair shook his head slowly, "I have *no* idea what I'm doing here."

She patted his chest, "not to worry, I will let you know if you step out of line."

He reached over and played with the hair hanging over her shoulder, "yeah? Going to keep me in line?"

"You know it." She smiled up at him.

"I'll hold you to that." He whispered.

"Oh good, you're up."

They turned to see Calum standing at the door, holding his phone and a cup.

"I'll go get you that coffee." Stretching up, she kissed him on the mouth so briefly she was walking away before it registered.

Blowing out a breath, Blair held up his hand and motioned to the building he briefly slept in. "Stand guard for me?" He started walking.

"For what? Calum followed.

"So I can use the bathroom before my bladder explodes."

Calum chuckled. "It's bound to get easier."

Blair paused in the door. "Is it? I don't think so. I think it's going to be a matter of me adjusting and running with it than it ever settling down."

He held his hand up to prevent Calum from speaking and took a sip of the coffee. Closing his eyes, he savored it. "Okay," he looked at him, "now you can speak."

With a grin, Calum leaned back against the truck. "Devin called before I was even awake."

"Lucky you." He joked.

"Yeah," Calum shrugged, "goes with the job." He glanced to see Kobie go back into the house. "Robbie and Niles are being transported tomorrow. They should arrive just before dusk."

"Jesse bringing them?"

Calum shook his head, "no, he's still trying to track down some clans that the Alliance hasn't been able to reach in a long time."

"Is there a lot of them like that?" Blair took another drink, hoping the hot liquid worked fast.

"More than initially thought." Calum's expression was harder. "After the shit show with Shae's clan, they went back over the records and found many had just faded out, no news from them in years." He cleared his throat, "not as long as with Shae's, but long enough to raise some alarms."

"Shit."

"Yeah. I don't know all the details, but Jesse is a good one to go searching."

Blair couldn't argue with that, Jesse seemed like he was as

capable as Calum, only with more diplomacy. "Okay. How are Robbie and Niles doing?"

"Shae spoke to him and got the full medical run down." He took a quick drink. "They're not as bad as Jay, but it's still going to be recovery time."

"I've been thinking of transferring Cale to this clan if he agrees." He rubbed his hand over his hair, "I'm not sure how that works, but we need a few more males to lend a hand."

"I'll talk to Devin about it."

Blair dropped the tailgate and sat down. "Okay, tell me how bad they are." His nerves were getting the best of him, wondering how these two clan males were going to feel about him taking over their clan. *His clan.* They were his clan now, regardless of what anyone thought.

"Robbie is the better of the two, his neck area—I don't know the anatomy terminology, but Shae made a motion up her throat when she said it," he shrugged, "it was sliced open, but healing well enough." Calum motioned across his hip to his back, "he was cut up pretty bad there too."

"No chance to shift and heal it?"

Calum shook his head, "it was too deep. He can't shift until it heals more."

"Shit. Okay."

"There are a few more things, but non-life-threatening." He blew out a breath, "Niles on the other hand is a lot worse off. Broken arm, collarbone, a few ribs, and his ankle."

"Holy fuck." Blair wanted to beat on something. The fact that other shifters could do this to one another pissed him right off. "They're both going to be on the mend for a while."

Calum nodded. "Yeah." He glanced at Cale as he came up from his small house. "Shae and I will stay until they're more recovered."

"I appreciate it," Blair said, still unable to digest what had happened to them. "So, do we know if they got away or were left for dead?"

"I don't have the details yet. Devin wants us to do a conference call with Shep and a few others that are key in the

Alliance." He rolled his shoulders. "I'll set it up for later today."

Blair nodded. "Yeah. I'd like to know as much as I can about it."

"The team sent in found fresh graves."

Blair's heart felt like it was beating in his throat now. "Kobie's father?"

"They're still working to identify who was buried there." He straightened away from the truck. "Unless more show up, I figure there's at least six dead."

Blair nodded, "I'm hoping with more details we'll find out there are more alive and not in captivity."

Calum raised his cup to mock a toast. "I'll drink to that." He jerked his head toward Cale, "find out if he's good with a transfer and let me know."

Blair nodded, "will do."

Cale stopped when he reached him and then he looked around. "Quiet today?" He grinned.

"So far." Blair took a quick sip. "They are transporting the two clansmen here tomorrow night."

Cale nodded, "that's a good thing." He cleared his throat, "maybe it will settle down some of the women."

Blair smirked, "I doubt it." He stood up, "they will not be able to shift for a while," he paused at the look the other man gave him, "it's not as bad as with Jay, but it's still long recoveries."

He nodded slowly, "that's good though, that they *will* be able to shift." He huffed out a breath, "I don't know what I'd do if I could never shift again or had to wait…"

"Yeah." Bair agreed, "that's my own personal nightmare."

"For sure."

"Listen," Blair gave him a serious look, "I wanted to talk to you about something."

Cale gave him a wary look.

"I know I asked you to stick around and help out."

"Happy to do it."

He liked that about the man, he spoke his mind with few

words. "I appreciate it, really." Blair wasn't sure how to ask him. "I was thinking maybe you'd consider transferring to this clan, as your own." He shrugged, "to be honest, I have no idea how that works, but you're a good fit and able males are something this clan sorely needs."

Cale gave him a sober look and then nodded. "I've noticed the lack of testosterone."

Blair chuckled, "hard not to."

"I'll be straight with you, Blair." Cale pulled his thick hair back and put it in a quick man-bun. "I was hoping to stay."

"You were?"

Cale motioned to the house and then Blair's cup. "I need coffee." They started walking. "Yeah, my clan has no available females left and so far, only boys seem to be born."

"Oh shit." Blair looked at him. "That's…"

"*Way* too much testosterone." Cale nodded. "It's one of the reasons I joined up with the Alliance, so I could travel around, take in some sights, and help." He stopped, "so if I join this clan, I'm not renouncing my own family, right?"

Blair opened his mouth and then closed it again. "I don't know, but we'll get the details."

Cale shrugged, "okay, and just so you know, I have no issues with you as an Alpha." He smirked, "I'll back you up any day."

It felt like Blair's heart expanded. "Thanks. I appreciate it. Now I just have to figure out how to tell the two men of this clan I took over while they were gone."

Cale stood there for a second. "I'll back you up, chief."

Grinning, Blair motioned to the door, "food and coffee first."

"Agreed."

Chapter Twenty-Six

Blair looked in the room to see it was empty. The smell of fresh paint assaulted his sensitive nose. He couldn't believe they had this one finished, too. Going over, he opened the window and then continued his search for Kobie. Since telling the women that their men would be home in a day's time, it had been chaos.

Before Cale and he could digest their breakfast, the women already had a plan of action. Furniture lists, room assignments, who was doing what. He'd gone out on patrol with Cale and since coming back, he hadn't been able to catch up to his mate. Pausing at the top of the stairs, he listened again. He could hear her but had checked the whole upstairs. He took two steps down the stairs and then looked to see the drop-down steps weren't closed all the way. The attic. Why hadn't he thought of that? Why would he think she'd be in the attic?

Going over, he reached up and pulled it down. Climbing up, he stopped when his head was in the room. Sure enough, Cortney and Kobie stood there in the dust-filled space, with their hands on their hips.

"Oh good, this saves us hunting you down," Cortney said with a smile.

Moving up so he was in the room, he looked around. It was a large space with a big round window. From what he could tell, it had never been used for anything, or even completed if the empty electrical outlets were any sign.

"What do you think?" Kobie asked, an excited look on her face.

"About?" He didn't know what he was being asked.

"This." Kobie motioned around the room, "finishing this to be the Alpha's room."

Blair was surprised, he hadn't thought that far ahead with anything. Of course, the Alpha needed space in the clan house. He paused before speaking when he realized they were talking about this being his room. "It's big." He nodded slowly, he looked at the hatch going down. "The stairs could be moved over so they're permanent stairs."

Kobie nodded, "that's what I was wondering—if that was possible."

Blair put his hands on his hips and looked around. "It's not finished, so moving them won't be too hard..."

"So, you like it?" Cortney asked.

"Sure."

"I hope you weren't planning to live in that little shed," Kobie said.

"To be honest, I haven't thought that far ahead." He shrugged, "but it makes sense. To use the smaller buildings for guards, guests, or maybe unmated males."

Kobie nodded, "*or* unmated females."

"That too." He smirked, realizing she was holding true to her word and keeping him on the right path. "We could put up a few more later on if needed."

"I think that's a good idea," Cortney said.

"Before I get sidetracked," Blair looked from one to the other, hoping to gauge their reactions, "I've asked Cale to transfer his allegiance to this clan."

Cortney nodded slowly, "I think that's a great idea." She gave him a small smile. "The men will need to recover, and fresh faces will improve spirits within the clan."

"I agree." Kobie gave him a soft look. "He's a good fit. The girls all get along with him."

"Yeah, he's easy-going, I think we need that," he smiled, "I need that." He went over and rubbed the dust off the glass and looked out the window. The view was a nice clear one of the front of the property, a perfect spot to see if anyone was coming or going. He'd work on accepting this was meant for the Alpha, or him, later. "How are we with the arrangements for the men?" He turned back around to see Cortney writing in that little notebook she carried around.

"Material list." She mumbled.

"I think we're set," Kobie told him. "Jay said it's okay to move Niles in with him for now, so he doesn't have to navigate the stairs," she shrugged, "and the room is plenty big enough."

Cortney looked up from her notes, "we have the rooms done. Daisie and Kasia want to bunk in together, so that simplifies." She tucked the notebook in her back pocket. "We have two empty rooms left over."

Blair grinned. "I knew this place was huge, but never dreamed how large it was."

"I don't know what the original builders planned, but I'm glad they left." Cortney blew out a breath, "okay, tea, and then back to work."

"Beth and Annamarie went to pick up some clothes and other supplies," Kobie told him as she went down the stairs.

"Furniture will be here in an hour," Cortney added, following Kobie.

Blair looked around the space again and then nodded to himself. Everything seemed to be sorted, except him getting a few moments alone with Kobie. He was almost ready to kidnap her, almost. Maybe he could just pick her up and take off in the truck with her for a few uninterrupted moments. Pulling out his phone, he looked at the time. So much for that, he had to go over to Gage's for the conference call with Devin.

Jake and Gary went over to watch over the clan while they

were at Gage's. Blair brought Cale, wanting him to start taking a more active role in the clan.

They walked into the kitchen to see Calum, Noah, Ed, and Gage standing there. Coop was hovering in the doorway leading to the rest of the house. Blair shrugged it off, it's not like he could get up and walk out of earshot. Coop knew when to speak and when not to, so I doubted anyone minded him being there.

Blair motioned to Cale, "Cale has agreed to transfer to the clan and I want him to take a more active role," he glanced at Ed, out of habit him being his Alpha, "especially with the recovery the other men are going through."

Ed nodded.

"That's your call, Blair." Coop said quietly, "no one can question a decision you make for that clan. You are the Alpha."

Blair's heart was lodged in his throat as he looked from Ed to Gage, both nodded, confirming once more that he was truly the new Alpha of the Sorum clan. "Okay."

"That work for you, Dev?" Calum asked and looked at the phone on the table.

"I have no problem with that," Devin said clearly.

Blair didn't know the call was already started.

"I'm in complete agreement as well." There was no mistaking Shepard Addison's voice.

Ed grinned, "you always lurk in on calls unannounced, Shep?"

The King of all shifters chuckled, "that's how I find out the best information, Ed."

Calum grinned but said nothing. "Let's get this started. We have furniture to haul upstairs shortly."

"Calum filled me in earlier, Blair," Shepard said in an amiable tone, "you've got things well in hand, son. I knew you were the right one for the job."

Blair swallowed the snort he was going to make. "I'm doing my best, sir."

"I have faith you will succeed."

"Okay, to expedite this, we have a few things to cover,"

Devin interrupted before his father could say anymore.

Blair was glad for the interruption. All the talk about him being Alpha made him more uncomfortable than he wished to share with anyone.

"Did you find out anything from those two?" Calum asked without preamble.

"We did," Shepard said abruptly. "Some details with locations and such, but there's something else."

The line was silent for a moment. The men in the room looked from each other to the phone.

"Robbie confirmed it, I went and spoke with them this morning."

"Confirm what?" Calum asked.

"Lindon," Shep paused, and Calum looked at Blair, "was with the party that attacked your mate's clan, Blair."

"I knew this, sir. Jay said we resemble each other." Blair's throat felt tight as the emotion, the fury threatened to choke him.

"Yes, it seems your brother is looking for one particular clan member."

"Are they coming for Jay?" Calum leaned on the table and glared at the phone.

"No," Devin answered. "He seems quite interested in obtaining the *black cat*."

Every sound in the room was muted out as the blood rushed through Blair's veins. He inhaled slowly, trying to stop from reacting.

"Kobie?" Gage asked softly.

"That's our take," Devin answered.

"Does he want her because she's the last of the Alpha family?" Ed crossed his arms and scowled at the phone. "He probably thinks Jayden is dead."

"He doesn't want her dead if that's what you're asking," Shepard said in a low tone.

Blair backed away from the table. His adrenalin was right there matching his rage now. His brother wanted his mate. Putting his hands on his head, he gave Gage a quick 'I'm fine' look and took one deep breath after the other to keep his cat from bursting free. "He wants to take over the clan." He said through clenched teeth. "Claiming Kobie would assure him control of all the females of the clan."

Calum's quick look confirmed he was thinking the same thing.

"That's our belief as well," Shepard stated quietly.

Blair nodded to no one in particular. Taking another deep breath, he blew it out and dropped his hands down. "Do we have a location for him?" His cat went still inside him, waiting for an answer.

"We're narrowing it down now."

Blair nodded again. "Let me know when you do."

"We will, Blair," Devin said, "but before you go rushing anywhere, you need to get things in place with the clan. Also, we're sending someone there for weapons training."

Blair stared at the phone but remained silent.

"Calum and Cale have both been through it." Devin informed him, "sometimes shifting isn't a possibility."

"All those on my new team will have it," Shepard told him.

Blair nodded. "That's fine, but I won't need a weapon when I find my brother." His tone was full of venom, and he knew it but couldn't help it.

"Is there anything else?" Gage asked while eyeing Blair.

Blair was grateful he recognized he needed to see Kobie, now, and assure his cat she was okay.

"One thing," Devin said quickly. "We had a call from Fischer."

Blair looked down at the floor without seeing it.

"Tomas' people are still circling the area looking for any returning clan members." Devin paused for a moment. "He asked if they should stay or go to their cabin."

"For their safety, we advised they go to the cabin."

"Which leaves us with no eyes in the area," Calum concluded.

"Yes, but after what they've done for the clan, we felt their lives were priority…."

Blair snapped out of it. He knew both Kobie and Jay would be grateful. "Thank you."

"We're going to try to get someone in the area to keep an eye out." Devin said, "from all accounts of those that were there. We don't think any more members are going to turn up back at the houses."

Blair glanced to Calum briefly, "how many were in the graves?"

"Six, including Damar," Shepard said in a hollow tone.

Blair nodded. That meant there were no more left. He could only hope that the six that were taken were still alive. "I will let them know." He didn't know how only knew it was his place. "Is there any way to identify exactly who?"

"We're working on it," Shepard stated, "we recovered some clan documentation from Damar's and are processing it."

Blair nodded again. "Please keep me up to date."

"Absolutely."

"If that's all, we need to go, the furniture will be delivered soon," Calum said quickly.

"We'll be in touch." The king hung up.

"Give us a direction, Dev," Calum said in a low tone.

"I'm working on it. Do you need me to find more bodies to send there to help?"

Calum looked at Blair.

Glancing at Ed, then Gage, Blair shook his head. "We're good for now, thanks."

"Okay. I'll talk to you later." The line went quiet.

Blair closed his eyes and clenched both fists.

"You good?" Gage said quietly.

Opening his eyes, Blair nodded and turned for the door. "I'll be better when my brother is dead." He growled out and then jogged toward his truck.

Chapter Twenty-Seven

Cale seemed to know that Blair wasn't in the mood for words and sat there silently on the drive back.

When Blair got out of the truck, Cale gave him a quick nod. "I'll go run the perimeter."

"Appreciate it." Blair headed for the house, pausing once he reached it to look at the sky. It matched his mood. Dark and churning. They were in for some kind of storm.

Blowing out a breath, he went inside and glanced around the kitchen. It was empty. Turning, he headed to go to Jay's room when Nichelle came down the stairs. "Have you seen Kobie?"

Nichelle grinned and pointed up, "she's up in the Alpha den." She motioned to the door. "Mika and I are going for a quick run."

"There's a storm coming in, try to get back before it hits."

"We will."

He took the stairs two at a time and then made fast work of the steps up to the attic. Kobie was up here alone. She stood in the middle of the room, looking at the window.

"Hi." The smile faded as she looked at him. "What's wrong?"

In two long strides, he reached her and pulled her against his chest. He held her, resting his face in her throat. Inhaling slowly, he assured his cat and himself that she was here and well.

"What's going on?" She didn't pull away, just wrapped her arms around his waist and let him stand there and breathe her in.

"In a minute." He straightened and cupped the back of her head. He'd intended a gentle but thorough kiss but felt starved for her. His kiss was rough and close to devouring her. She didn't pull back or even hesitate as she returned his heated kiss with just as much passion and need.

Blair's cat was quite happy with being this close, in fact, he wanted closer. Usually, in synch with his animal, Blair ended the kiss slowly. If he continued in his current mental state, he would end up going too far and he did not want their first time to be on a dusty, unfinished wood floor. Rubbing his cheek against hers, he slowed his breathing. "What are you doing up here?"

She returned the rub, a very cat-like gesture. "Trying to decide how you want this room decorated."

Lifting his head, he looked down at her lust-filled eyes. "I don't care, just as long as you're sharing it with me."

"I thought that was the plan…"

He kissed her mouth softly. "Then do it however you want it."

"Okay." She licked over her lips, making him want to kiss her again. "What happened?"

Blair straightened and stepped back. He needed to feel her near, so he settled by keeping his hand on her waist. "There's news." He brushed the hair back from her face. "I was going to share it with your brother…"

"Okay, I'll come."

He started for the steps and pulled her along with him.

"Is any of it good news?"

He shook his head and started down the steps, holding his hand over his head so he didn't have to release hers. "No."

"Wonderful." She followed him down the next flight of stairs, not once trying to reclaim her hand.

As they reached Jay's room, Blair's phone rang. He pulled it out and looked at it. It was Cooper. He frowned. "I'll be a minute." He reluctantly let go of her hand.

When she closed the door, he answered the phone. "Coop?"

"Last time I checked."

"What's…"

"Calum was saying you have had no time with your lady."

Blair rubbed his hand over his hair. "There's always the next urgent event…"

"Why don't you take her to the lookout," he paused, "after the storm passes. It's a good spot. No one can sneak up you there or bug you."

Blair nodded slowly. "Yeah. That's a good idea. Thanks, Coop."

"You almost lost it today, kid. You need to solidify this with your gal. It will make you stronger."

Blair looked at the door she'd closed. "I definitely need to do something."

Cooper chuckled, "just don't be an ass and you'll be fine."

Blair smirked. "Got it. Thanks."

"At least I'm doing something other than just sitting here. Advice is better than nothing." He hung up.

Blair looked at the phone. He'd have to remember to ask Shaelan how much longer Coop was to stay off his leg. He couldn't have done this long if it had been him. Tucking the phone back in his pocket, he went to share the not-good news with the twins.

He didn't even get the door closed before Kobie asked.

"So what is it?"

Blair shut it and turned to look at Jay. He was almost sitting up today. "How are you feeling?"

Jay rolled his eyes, "marvelous." He sighed, "sitting up is better than looking at the ceiling."

Blair leaned against the wall and crossed his arms. "You're

healing, that's what counts."

"I suppose." He looked at his sister. "Better talk before she lays into both of us." He grinned at the bored look Kobie gave him.

"It's all shit news." He wanted to be straight with them. "I don't even know which part to begin with."

"Wherever you want," Jay told him.

"All right. Your friend Fischer called Devin, Tomas' people are still hanging around the area hoping the women, or anyone, comes back." He waited while they exchanged a quick look. "They wondered if they should go to their cabin for a while and wait it out. Dev's dad agreed they should."

"Okay, that's good, keeps them out of it from now on," Jay whispered.

"Yeah, but it also means we don't have anyone keeping an eye out for them, so they're going to send someone to be in that area."

"Do they think any more of the men will come back?" Kobie asked quietly.

Blair blew out a breath. "As far as we know, the only surviving ones were taken. Six, wasn't it?"

Jay nodded his head slowly.

"They found the site where they ambushed you and," he looked at Kobie, "fresh graves."

She put her hand over her mouth.

"How many?" Jay asked.

"Six," Blair said without hesitation.

"If, uh," Jay looked at his sister, "any of them have any marks or distinguishing features, we could probably identify them."

Kobie nodded but said nothing.

"I'll let Devin know that." He wanted to go to Kobie but knew she probably needed space for a minute. "It will also let us know who was taken captive."

Jay nodded. "To know who we're looking for."

"Yeah." Blair rubbed his hand over his hair. "There's another thing."

Kobie raised her eyebrows as if to say how can there be.

"It seems my brother, *Lindon* wants one thing in particular." He had to take a moment to keep his anger under control. "He's desperately trying to get his hands on the black cat."

Jay's expression hardened.

"He wants me?" Kobie stood up. "Why?"

"To take control of what's left of the clan," Blair said in a lethal hiss.

"Shit," Jay mumbled. "That's why they keep coming."

Blair nodded. "We're going to have to tighten security." He pushed away from the wall and started toward Kobie. "At this point, they'll take whoever they could get their hands on and use them as bait for you." He stopped in front of her and gave her a look that told her no one, on this earth or elsewhere would touch her.

"Kobie told me about the team going to rescue people?"

Blair pulled Kobie against his side and kept his arm around her before he looked at her brother. "That's right. The Alliance is sending someone to do weapons training with us and hopefully, once Jesse is back we'll be going to get people out and back to their clans."

"Weapons training?" Kobie looked up at him.

Blair nodded, "it won't always be a situation where claws and teeth can be used."

"She's crazy good with a spear," Jay said, a note of pride in his voice.

Blair looked down at her. "Yeah, I figured that when she caught fish with a stick."

"It was bigger than a stick." She informed him.

"So, if you're both going with this team, where does that leave the clan?"

Blair cleared his throat and looked away from Kobie. "I've asked Cale to join the clan, and he agreed. I'm hoping Robbie is healed enough to shift before we have to go, but even if he's not, the guys from Ed's clan are going to keep a watch over here."

All of them turned to look at the door when there were

many voices all of a sudden.

"I'll go see what's going on." Kobie gave Blair a squeeze and then left.

Jay looked at the door she'd left open and then back to Blair. "How's," he motioned to the door, "that going?"

"Well, if we can ever get five minutes without some sort of urgent happening, it would be much better."

Jay chuckled softly, then held his ribs.

"She agreed that we're going to be sharing the top floor of the house together…"

"Did she say when?"

Blair shook his head.

"She'll drag this out for months if you don't change her mind."

Blair had already figured that out.

"If you're going off on stealth missions together, you need to be solid with each other." Jay said quietly, "have that mate's bond and way of communicating or it's going to get crazy."

"I know…"

"But I want to go to school."

They both stopped and looked at the door, at the upset tone Daisie was using.

"I'll go see what now," Blair said, shaking his head.

"You're doing great if that helps," Jay told him before he stepped out.

"It does. I think." Blair gave him a nod and went out to the kitchen.

Beth was there with piles of boxes and bags on the table. Blair took a quick inventory. Laptops and tablets, it looked like.

"Oh, Blair." Beth motioned to the items. "I have everything set up for the girls to do the online school."

Blair gave her a questioning look.

"Oh, for heaven's sake, I told Shep to get you on the mail list so you got notices," she pulled out her phone and started tapping the screen impatiently, "I mean he is the damn King, he could bypass the ceremony and such and get you on the Alpha email updates." She held her phone out to him. "It was sent out a few days ago.”

Blair took the phone and started reading the email. Cortney and Kobie were beside him, reading along with him. “So, until we’ve put a stop to Tomas, we’re not sending any kids to regular schools?” He let the women finish reading before handing her back her phone.

“That’s right. We have many teachers in the clans, so they’ve been working to get some online classes set up.” She motioned to the girls, “it would be different ones, of course, being the age range…”

“I was considering College,” Annamarie said quietly.

Beth nodded, “The clans are paying for distance learning at the college level for now.”

“I guess that works.”

“I had co-op this year for my final year,” Nichelle said quickly. “If I don’t do that, I won’t graduate.”

Beth nodded again, “there’s a conference meeting taking place for that this week.” She gave her a soft look. “We will figure everything out.”

“I want to go to school and see other kids.” Daisie visibly pouted.

Blair inhaled deeply and then released it as he squatted down to look at her face to face, “tell you what, you do what Beth and your mom say and get started on this online stuff and I’ll talk to Bruce and see if he’s up for a house guest at the farm.”

“Are there kids there?” She crossed her arms over her chest.

Blair nodded, “three girls around your age and two boys.” He smirked when she scrunched up her nose at the mention of the boys. “Just as long as your mom agrees.” He glanced at Cortney, who nodded.

Daisie chewed on her lip for a few seconds and then nodded. “Okay.” She held out her hand to him, “I’ll do my work.”

Blair shook her hand and then winked at her. He stood up. “Same goes for the rest of you girls, there are a lot of young people at Bruce’s farm, but if you go, you may have to help with chores."

"Are there boys there?" Kasia asked quietly.

"Some." Blair grinned at Torrey, who rolled her eyes at her daughters' questions.

"I wouldn't mind helping," Nichelle shrugged, "it's better than having nothing to do."

"All right, I'll talk to Bruce and see if he agrees with one or two visitors at a time." He pointed to the table, "but all of you have to buckle down and make this work until we have a better arrangement." All the girls nodded.

"I thought to get them out of the house, they could come over and work at our place during their course times," Beth suggested.

Blair gave her a quick look. She was asking, not telling. "If that's what you'd like, I don't see a problem with it." He glanced at Torrey, then to Cortney before seeking Kobie's approval. She gave him a soft look and a slight nod of her head. "Okay, set up a schedule and make sure all those involved know their times." He looked at the table again. "And what do I owe you for all of this?"

"Nothing." Beth grinned. "The Alliance is paying for the equipment." She nodded. "We need our future to be educated."

Blair nodded. A horn honked outside interrupting him.

"Furniture's here." Cale stuck his head inside the door. "And the storm is almost on us."

"Jake still here?"

Cale nodded.

"Grab him." Blair exhaled again and looked at the women all watching him. "I don't know who does what best, but we're also going to need someone to keep the clan books, keep up with grocery lists, and all that."

Mika smiled, "I'll do the clan books."

"Done." He grinned.

She nodded, "I'm going for a run." She grinned and wiggled her eyebrows, "I love running in storms."

"Uh, pass." Nichelle said with a smirk, "I don't think my

cat likes water.”

Beth’s smile was so wide he wondered if something was wrong with her. “I have some more bags in the car, a few TVs, and stuff.”

Blair knew the Alliance wasn’t paying for televisions.

“They will hook up the internet and cable tomorrow morning.” Beth continued.

There were several loud cheers in the room.

Blair went over and dropped a kiss on the top of her head. “Have I told you lately how amazing you are?”

She shook her head. “No, you’ve been too busy being pretty amazing yourself.”

“Thanks, Beth.” He cleared the lump out of his throat and then glanced to Kobie, “you want to direct what goes where?”

She nodded, a soft-hearted smile on her face.

Chapter Twenty-Eight

With furniture placed, dinner in the works, Blair stood and looked out the living room window at the rain coming down. Mika hadn't returned. Both Torrey and Kobie had assured him that was normal, and she was fine. He only knew of one other cat that loved runs in the rain, Gage, but he'd never worried about him like this.

"You're going to give yourself wrinkles." Kobie came up beside him.

"That obvious, huh?" He glanced down at her before looking through the rain-streaked glass again.

"It's not a bad thing that you care."

"No? I'd just like—" he stopped and looked down at her. At some point, she'd pulled her hair up into that tight ponytail she wore too often. He debated for a second on pulling it free to watch her hair surround her face again. "After dinner, once the storm has passed, I'd like to take you to the lookout."

"Where's the lookout?"

At least she hadn't said no. "Off to the one side of Ed's property, it drops off over the river, the view goes on for miles and miles…"

"I'd like that." She glanced over her shoulder, "think we can

222

sneak out without being followed or before something else happens?"

Blair grinned, "I like your style. Sneaking out it is." He reached over to pull her closer as Cale burst into the room.

"Mika just came back, says there's a scent she can't place."

"A person or shifter?"

Cale shrugged, "she used the word peculiar, like chemical."

"Shit." He started for the door, then stopped and lifted Kobie's chin. "To be continued." He kissed her hard on the mouth and released her.

"Jake and Noah are still here."

Blair nodded, "Get them, Calum too."

Cale nodded and lit out of the room at a run.

"Can I come?"

Blair paused in the doorway. "I need you to stay here."

She looked like she was going to object.

"I have no idea what we're going to find, but I trust you to get the girls to safety if needed." He held her look and waited for her to say something.

"Okay. I'll get the run packs ready in case we need them."

He nodded. "Toss a backpack in my truck, if you have to, you haul the whole group over to Ed's in my truck."

She glanced at Jay's room.

"Call Gage and tell him what's happening. If we're not back in forty-five minutes you get the girls out."

She nodded again and then came over and kissed him quickly. "You better come back. We have a date."

Blair grinned, "I won't miss it."

Calum came running into the room, he tossed Blair's pack at him. "Let's go." He glanced at Kobie.

"Go." She said, "we've got it here."

Kobie called for the girls to come downstairs. She stood at the window and watched as the men left. The white tiger and black jag were side by side, followed by two large orange tigers.

"What's happening?" Torrey asked, walking into the room.

"I picked up some kind of strange scent out there." Mika

came from the kitchen, water dripping off her.

"Like what?" Torrey glanced at Cortney as she came down the stairs.

"I'm not sure, like chemical, strange."

"Who went to look?" Cortney wrapped her arms around her waist.

"Blair, Calum, Noah, and Jake," Kobie said quietly, turning from the window.

"Kobie."

Everyone turned to look toward Jay's room.

Kobie went and opened the door and peeked in.

Jay motioned to the wheelchair, he had yet to be in. "Get me in that. If you have to run, it will be easier to load me up in a chair."

She gnawed on her lip, then nodded. "Okay." Looking back out the door, she motioned to Torrey and Cortney, "help me get Jay up and into the chair." They both jolted and came toward her. Kobie glanced at Mika, "get the packs ready and a backpack, toss them all in Blair's truck."

Mika nodded and ran up the stairs.

Jay only sounded like he was going to scream a few times as they got him upright, bent, and into the chair. He was pale but insisted he was all right.

"Oh," Shaelan came into the room, "I was just coming to do that."

Kobie motioned to the chair, "I have to call Gage, maybe you could make sure we didn't do too much damage."

Shaelan nodded. "Did Blair give us a time limit?"

"Forty-five minutes."

"Okay, I'll get a go-bag ready for Jay, his meds, and things."

Kobie pulled out her phone and went to the kitchen. She kept going and opened the door and stood in it. Before she dialed, she inhaled slowly, trying to see if she could pick up what Mika had scented. With the heavy rain, there were too many smells out there. Dialing Gage, she held the phone to her ear and waited.

"Hello."

"Hi, Gage, it's Kobie."

"Hey, what's up?"

Kobie glanced in the direction the men had gone. "Mika picked up a strange, possibly chemical smell on a run…"

"Do you need us over there?" His jovial tone was gone.

"I'm not sure. Blair, Calum, and two of your guys went out to look."

"Okay, Gary and I are heading over. You have packs ready?"

She nodded and then remembered she was on the phone. "We're working on it. Blair said if they're not back in forty-five minutes to go over to your place."

"We have more security over here now." He spoke to someone quietly. "We'll be there in five."

"Okay, thank you." She hung up and noted the time. It had only been eight minutes. Blowing out a breath, she tucked the phone in her pocket and looked to the back again. The rain stopped so suddenly it was silent.

The evening sun made everything sparkle in its bright light. Kobie gnawed on her lip where she stood in the middle of the yard, watching the trees. She heard a vehicle and knew it was most likely Gage and Gary racing here.

Walking past the house, she inhaled slowly now, without the rain. She couldn't even smell the men out there. What could make a chemical smell? Chemicals, clearly, but what kind and what were they for?

She heard a truck door slamming and then turned. It wasn't Gage, it was Beth. She gave Kobie a half-hearted smile. "I thought I'd pick up the young ones and take them over to our house."

Kobie breathed a quick sigh. Not having to worry about them was welcome right now. "Take Annamarie and Nichelle as well."

"Will do." She paused at the door. "My boys will find it." She gave her a look of encouragement and then went inside.

Shaelan came out and toward her. "I have everything Jay

could need ready."

Kobie nodded and looked back toward the trees.

The fifteen-minute mark passed, and then a half-hour. Kobie was having to work hard to not go find them herself. Each time she considered it, she remembered Blair was trusting her to look after the others. She smiled, even if it was to herself. None of the other males in her life had ever given her that kind of trust. Ever.

"How long now?" Shaelan was standing in the doorway.

Kobie glanced at her phone she clutched in her hand. "Almost forty."

"I'll go get everyone ready," Cortney said softly.

Kobie nodded but didn't look away from the direction Blair would come when he got back.

"Kobie."

She glanced over at Gage and the urgent look he was giving her. She nodded, "I know. Just a few more minutes." She took a few steps, so she was away from the others and took a deep breath. Closing her eyes, she filtered through the scents. Her eyes popped open. "I can smell them." She said loud enough the others would hear her.

Gage was beside her now and took a long breath. He looked over at Gary, "she's right, they're close but something is…"

"Not right." She finished for him and rushed toward the trees.

Before she could reach the trees, Calum as his cat came running out. He bound past her and right to Shaelan and then turned around and ran back again.

"Get everyone in the house," Gage called out and took off jogging in that direction.

Shaelan ran alongside Kobie.

Kobie's heart was hammering in her chest. Blair had to be all right. The others too, but if anything happened to Blair…

Out of the trees came Blair and Noah, in undone jeans and bare feet. Between them, they half carried, half dragged Jake. They tied a shirt around his waist and his head hung down.

They both stopped and lowered Jake toward the ground where he started throwing up violently.

Shaelan stopped and looked at Gage. "Run back, grab water, and…" she looked at Jake again, "milk."

Gage didn't question her, just turned and ran back.

Kobie reached them and quickly assessed that Blair was intact, then dropped to her knees beside Shaelan to where they gently set Jake.

"I don't know what it is, but he stuck his face right into it and then started heaving."

Gage was back and holding out what Shaelan had asked for.

She leaned down and inhaled close to Jake's face. Lifting her head, she turned his face and looked at it. "It's not a contact. He had to have inhaled it." She was murmuring to herself. Leaning down again, she opened his mouth and looked in it. "He didn't ingest any of it. Let's get him in a steamy shower. Sweat it out of him until I know more." She opened the bottle of water and poured it on the ground, then turned to her mate, who was still on four paws. "I need a sample. When you find it," Calum came over to her, she put the empty bottle in his run pack, "shift, cover your mouth and nose and bring back as much as you can."

He nudged her with his head. Then looked at Blair.

Blair motioned to the trees. "The fewer of us out there, the better."

Calum needed no more words; he took off into the trees.

Gage watched Noah and Gary lift, Jake, up and start toward the house. Shaelan was right behind them. "Is it a spill or something the rain-washed on the lot?"

Blair shook his head. "No. We did the outside perimeter first. This was in the middle of the bush." Blair grabbed Kobie's hand as he passed her. "It was done purposely. My guess is they planned to grab someone when they were too sick to do anything about it."

"Fuck." Gage growled. "I'll call Dev. We need people here that are trained to deal with this shit."

Blair nodded. "How the hell are they getting on the

property without us knowing?"

Kobie moved closer to him. Her cat wasn't happy how upset he was. "In the morning when things have dried up a bit, I'd like to go look around the outside of the property." She motioned with her hand, "on the other side of the fence." Blair gave her a look of doubt. She shrugged, "I spent half my life figuring out ways around the permitted areas," she gave him a hesitant look, "maybe I can figure out what Devin's team missed."

Blair looked over at Gage, who was handing Jake off to Gary to be carried through the door. "Okay. Calum and I will come with you and see if we can figure it out." Blair looked at the trees. "Until someone comes that can clean it up, runs will have to be on Ed's land."

Kobie nodded. "Beth came and got the girls when I called Gage."

"Good. I don't want them to see Jake like this."

He squeezed her hand. "I thought Gage was going to load me into the truck." She confessed.

Blair smirked, "you were waiting until the last second, huh?"

"Yes. I knew you'd be back."

"We ran dragging Jake between us, afraid to breathe the air." He squeezed her hand. "I'm glad you waited. Three naked half-naked men with a big black jag in the back of the truck tearing down the road could have presented a problem if we'd had to get over to Ed's."

She couldn't help smile at that description. "I guess we cancel our date?"

"To be determined." He answered, then lifted their hands and kissed the back of hers. "Shae will tell us more when she knows."

Kobie nodded and continued the walk bedside him in silence. Her cat still wasn't happy that Blair had placed himself at risk, but she wasn't about to voice that out loud.

Chapter Twenty-Nine

"Are you sure it's okay?" Kobie looked back down the lane when they got out of the truck.

"You heard Jake, he said to get out of his face." Blair shrugged.

She bit her lip. "He sounded more like himself."

He walked around to the front of the truck and held out his hand. "He was much more polite once you came in."

She placed her hand in his and smiled at him. "Do you think Shaelan will figure out what it was?"

"She was on some video call with a few doctors or science people when I was checking in with Calum. I didn't understand a thing any of them were saying, but my guess is she'll know by morning."

Blair stopped and looked down at her. "Let's just take some time and pretend we have nothing else to worry about, okay?"

"Okay." She smiled at him, "it's going to be dark soon, do you know the way in the dark?"

He knew she was teasing him. Both of them could see just as well in the dark as they could in the light. "With my eyes closed." He told her, holding his hand over his heart.

"We wouldn't want to get lost." She said with a smirk.

"Wouldn't we?" He glanced around them. She laughed softly. "I have the best hunter and tracker with me. I'm confident she could find our way back."

"The best?"

Blair nodded, "you beat Cal. I never could."

"I don't think that counts. He was more focused on finding the men on the property."

"So were you, but you still did it." She said nothing. "This is nice." He motioned around them. "Out here, alone, the quiet—do you realize since the second we met we've been running or dealing with one crisis after the other?"

She nodded. "I could do with some boredom for a short while."

Chuckling, he pulled on her hand so she was closer, and he could put his arm around her. They were almost at the cliff edge.

"It's beautiful here." She stopped and looked around. "Even in the low light, the last of the sun's rays show us miles of nature."

"I love living in this area."

"I think I'm going to as well," she sighed, "as soon as we resolve a few issues."

"We'll deal with it." He pointed to the flat rocks. "They should be dry enough to sit on."

When they sat down, he was content watching her look around. He tried to think of something, anything to say. He'd never had an issue finding words before, ever. Probably because this was important, more so than anything had ever been before.

"This is nice." She grinned. "No noise, no bright lights. Thank you for thinking of it."

He opened his mouth, then paused before he lied. "It was Cooper's suggestion. I've been losing my mind trying to find five minutes to have you to myself..."

She put her hand over his mouth. "I don't care who thought of it. Thank you."

She sat there looking at him. He again couldn't think of

anything to say. As awkward went this was at the top of the scale. "What are you thinking?"

Kobie held his look for a moment, then looked away, "there's so much I'm not sure how to separate it."

"Pick one." He observed her as she lifted her chin and looked at the sky. *Beautiful.*

"I'm worried about my brother," she glanced at him for a second, "that if it ends up he can't shift ever again..."

"Has the prognosis changed?"

She shook her head, "no, not that they've said, but..."

"Then don't worry about it." He reached over and brushed the hair off her shoulder so he could see her face. "There's enough to worry about right now. I don't think you need to look for more things."

Amusement lit her face briefly, "that's true." She took a deep breath and blew it out in a steady, quiet way. "I'm not sure how I feel about the weapons training," her eyes connected with his as she spoke. "I'm assuming guns, and I honestly don't know if I could shoot someone."

He didn't want to dismiss her worry, but he knew there was something deeper bothering her. "I'm hoping you're not in a position to need to, but," he searched her face for a moment, "if it came down to you or them, I'd like to think you'd be able to at least incapacitate them."

Her eyes widened, "again, that's a good point. I guess we'll have to see what's involved."

"I'm pretty sure our king and Cal had tracking in mind for you." He shrugged, "we can ask for more details..."

"Do you it's something that can be decided in advance?" She licked her lips in a nervous tell. "I feel like it may be something we plan out, but then have to adjust as we go."

"Most likely. Are you having second thoughts about going?" As much as he had confidence in her ability to handle herself, he wouldn't have been disappointed if she decided not to be involved.

She shook her head without hesitation. "No. I want to help. I heard Calum talking to Jay about how long this has been happening, of how many have they taken—Calum's own mother?"

"I'm not sure if he could prove it, but yeah, there's a lot of missing or dead loved ones because of Tomas…"

"Then I'm still in." She gave her head a nod. "My mother is one of the missing." She glanced down as she spoke. "I keep hoping I'll find her someday." She cleared her throat quietly. "Jay said we need to figure everything out before we go—for the sake of the clan."

This may be the only opening he'd get. "For us as well. We can't just keep talking about it without ever discussing it." He smirked, "we're going to be sharing the *Alpha den*," he rolled his eyes at that description, "but we haven't talked about what that involves since the day you told me you hadn't decided."

"I know you're the right man to lead the clan."

That wasn't quite what he was looking for. "I appreciate you feel that way. I still have my doubts." He watched as she looked everywhere but at him again, "for that to happen, my mate, from the Alpha family, has to actually *be* my mate."

"I know." She whispered.

She'd answered too quickly as if she was annoyed with the whole thing. "What's the problem, Kobie. You said you hadn't decided. I accepted that, but earlier you're talking about our shared room, so there's another issue you need to share."

"It's just," she turned to look at him, her eyes searching his face, looking for something, "it's probably stupid."

"If it's bothering you, I don't think it's stupid. It means it's something we need to address."

Kobie inhaled slowly, "okay."

Blair sat there, allowing her the time to gather her thoughts and say them. A pained look went through her eyes. He placed a finger under her chin. "Just say it."

"Okay, when we spoke about Kelsey and Layna," she held up her hand when he went to speak, "I don't blame you for spending time with Layna. I get that, I do. I mean, I'm not a virgin or…"

He put his thumb over her lips. "Maybe don't say things

like that. I understand needs, but my cat is barely holding on where you're concerned and I'd rather not have to go kill someone."

She nodded. "Sorry. Okay, you said you loved Kelsey. I didn't understand how recently you were talking about until I spoke with Jake," she shrugged, "we barely know each other..."

Blair would be having a discussion with Jake, later. He touched her mouth again, so she'd stop. She was getting more upset by saying it. "What I feel for you is not what I felt for her. I..."

"Blair, I know most women want pretty words and all the right words—I just want the truth. What you feel. I'm not like other women."

He smirked, "I know you're not, and I'm glad you aren't."

Now she sat there giving him that look, one that was 'well I'm waiting, impress me,' or close to it. He nodded slowly, "I think what you're afraid of is—if I could love Kelsey one week and then—want you more than my next breath, that I'll change my mind again."

"Something like that." She heaved a deep sigh.

What was he missing?

"I don't want *just* that." She glanced down at her hands. "That we're just mates."

Blair wanted to grin but suppressed it. "You don't want the pretty words, but you want more than our animals being mated?"

"I told you it was stupid. I feel like a confused child."

"No, it's not stupid. I have my own worries about this."

"You do?"

He scoffed softly, "yeah."

"Like what?"

Clasping his hands, he rubbed them together while he thought of how to say it. "I keep hearing I'm supposed to be an Alpha, a leader, but I don't know the first thing about any of that. I'm not a leader. I've followed instructions my whole life..."

"But you are." She smirked, "while the rest of us are

shocked or bumbling around trying to figure out what next, you're already doing it or telling others what to do," she held up her hand, "and not in a bad way." She gave him a soft look, "all of the women are obsessed with you if you didn't know." The humor left her face, "they probably think I'm crazy for not already being mated to you."

"I don't care what others think. Okay, I do, but not in the same way it matters to me what you think. I don't want to let you down. I don't want to fail *you.*"

"You've already treated me with more respect and consideration than anyone in my whole life. I don't care if something doesn't go as planned, just as long as you treat me with respect and don't push me aside just because I'm a woman."

"I would never do that. To any women, most definitely never to you."

"And that's one reason you are the leader this clan needs."

"You seem to be doing a better job of assuring me than I am you..."

"I just need to know this is more, Blair, more than our cats found their happily ever after."

He grinned at that expression. "You haven't heard long-time mates with each other—this ain't no fairy tale."

"You know what I mean."

He nodded his head several times while trying to figure out how to explain it to her. "I didn't know we were mates, you made sure of that, but still I was bordering on being obsessed with you. How fast you were, how agile, your tracking and directions are crazy good, how you looked out for everyone else before yourself," he held her gaze, "I won't give you the usual flattery and go on and on about how fucking gorgeous you are but know that I see that too." He slipped off the rock and got on his knees in front of her, touching her cheek, so she'd continue to look at him, "I know you don't want to be mated just because your cat tells you to, hell if that was all it took we would have marked each other long before we reached here, all I'm asking is give me a chance, give us a chance." He watched her lick her lips and momentarily forgot what he was going to say, "no more of this kissing me quickly and walking away to avoid me for the rest of the day. Never mind your cat," he cringed, "I know she can hear me, but never mind the nudges and prompting you to seek me out. Go with what *you* feel, what *you* want." He brushed his thumb over her cheek, "we can talk about your concerns or worries as much as you want, any time you want, just *please*, give this a chance, Kobie, let me in, just a little. I promise you will not regret it." He searched her eyes as she looked at him. He had no idea what she was thinking.

"I know you meant every word, but you're so damn charming. I feel like I've just been blindsided."

His lips quirked as he suppressed a grin. "I'm not trying to charm you, babe, I'm laying it out here just asking for a chance to be your everything, anything you need."

She held her breath for a second, blinked, and looked at him differently. "Coming from your lips, that's not even a line, is it?"

He shook his head slowly.

"Okay. I'll stop running the other way every time I think about it." She reached up and placed her hand over his against her cheek. "It's just a lot, Blair, really. I never thought I'd ever *have* a mate, so I have to rethink everything I ever thought."

"You don't have to change who you are to be my mate. That's not how it works." He frowned, "or that's not how it's going to work with me. I honestly have no idea how it works with other mated couples." He blew out a breath. "I know there will be times you want to beat me, but I will *always* listen to you."

"Are other Alpha couples like that?"

"From what I've seen, Beth may agree with Ed in front of people, but she puts all her cards on the table as soon as they're out of sight."

"I can see her doing that."

He leaned back from her and lowered their hands, keeping hers enclosed in his own. "Is that why you're having trouble with this? Not that we're mates, but that as soon as we're mated, we're in charge of the clan?"

"Some of it. Aren't you?"

"Honestly, I have no idea what I'm doing with suddenly being an Alpha. I *know* that when I have your input and know you're with me, it's easier."

She grinned, "you have all the pretty right words without even trying."

"It's how I feel..."

"I know. I just needed to point that out." She grasped his other hand and sat there studying him. "I suppose," she lifted her shoulders and let them drop, "it wouldn't be a real hardship being your mate."

Blair grinned, "yeah, not too hard to look at?"

She shook her head, with a slight smirk, "you're charming, sweet..."

"Sweet?"

Kobie grinned, "you know you are. The way you handle Daisie," she glanced down at their hands, "it's touching."

"Mmm," Blair leaned forward so their faces were closer, "there might be a few other perks too."

Her eyes locked on his, a heated look was now in them. "You think so?" She whispered.

"I do." Turning his head, he brushed his lips over hers lightly. Once, twice. He caught the slight hitch in her breath and reached up to put his hand behind her head as he kissed her completely. When she responded and opened her mouth to his exploration, he grasped her by the waist and stood with her long enough to sit down and have her straddle him. He broke the kiss, "I think about kissing you a thousand times a day." He crushed her mouth with his own, needing her taste to fill his whole body.

Kobie held his head tight and slid forward so their bodies were fit together.

Blair growled in the back of his throat and grasped a handful of her hair. Tearing his mouth from hers, he gently leaned her back and nipped along her jaw with his teeth. "Your taste sets my insides on fire." Biting her throat, he licked it after. "Your scent calms me but energizes me at the same time." Softly, he bit her again, then sucked the skin into his mouth. "I could spend a day just tasting every inch of you." He tugged the shoulder of her shirt down so he could nip her shoulder.

Grasping his hair not so gently, she jerked his head back up so she could bite his jaw. "I feel the same way." She lowered her mouth to his neck and dragged her teeth over his skin. "I've never felt like this before, not even during my cycle."

Blair growled a deep guttural sound and clutched her hips, rocking her into his painfully hard erection. Her mouth continued to move over his throat and his cat went crazy inside him, feeling her teeth that close to where she'd eventually claim him as her own. "You're killing me." He hissed out but made no move to stop her. He heard his shirt rip as she exposed more skin. Sharp teeth bit into his shoulder and he threw his head back, rejoicing in the pain. His mate was a little hellcat.

Without warning, a deluge of water hit him in the face. Kobie gasped and lifted her mouth from his. The storm had returned. He'd been so lost in her he hadn't even sensed it.

Panting to catch her breath, she snuggled her face into his chest. "I didn't even know it was going to rain."

Blair held her against him and looked up. "It's moving fast and going to get worse." He blew out a breath and then wiped the water from his eyes. "As much as I don't want to, we need to get back."

Kobie nodded, "yeah, after the last storm, I'm worried…"

He stood up, holding her tight. "They're nearby and will take advantage of the storm again."

She nodded and slowly slid down him. When she stood in front of him, she looked up at him and gave a little shiver. "That's a new kind of cold shower."

Blair bared his teeth at her. "We're not discussing how even nature is tossing up roadblocks lately."

Kobie grinned and tried to fix his shirt. "I wrecked your shirt."

"Thirty more seconds and you would have wrecked my

control too." Wrapping his arm around her, he pulled her along as they hurried back to the truck.

"Avoiding you seems like the safer option now."

Blair stopped abruptly and looked down at her. "Don't even…"

Kobie smiled, "I was kidding."

"Killing me." He mumbled and then grabbed her hand and jogged along the path.

Chapter Thirty

Jake was perfectly fine in the morning like it hadn't happened. His anger was proof it happened and everyone was more tense than normal. Maybe tense was going to be the new vibe in the clan. She hoped not. Happier times were definitely welcome to invade the tension and paranoia.

The ground squished with each step as she walked. She turned and glanced down at the rock-covered area they'd just climbed. Blair and Calum were giving her lots of space and not following right now on her heels. She waited until they were closer before she spoke. "With all the rain, yesterday and last night, there's not going to be any scents to track." She adjusted her run pack, so it was riding along her hip.

Calum nodded.

Blair looked down the incline to the fenced area. "Think if a cat took a running leap, they'd clear it?"

She turned to look at the fence and examined the space between where she stood and the metal wiring. "I know I couldn't."

"I couldn't even make that leap," Calum said quietly.

Blair scoffed, "then no one can." He grinned.

Calum gave him a bored look and then turned to her. "What

are you looking for?"

Kobie started walking again, her eyes on the ground. "I'll know it when I see it." Neither of the men commented, or to her surprise, questioned her. She wasn't lying. She had no idea what she was looking for, but they had to figure out how they were getting on the property. Kobie wanted a safe place to run, to teach the young shifters how to track, and more. Glancing behind her, she looked at Blair to see he was watching her. He gave her a heated look and her insides responded. She felt her cheeks flush and looked back in front of her. He was distracting. It wasn't a bad thing necessarily, but she needed to focus.

Their talk last night had made her feel more at peace with everything. Any other male and she would have said they were giving her a huge line of bull, but Blair, he meant every syllable he spoke. She not only felt more at ease but lucky. What she had done for fate to bring her a mate such as Blair, she didn't know. He was kind when needed. He was all Alpha but didn't flex it like a muscle to show off. Sweet, she smirked at his reaction to her using that word. He was though, a sweet man. She had a flash of him coming back to the camp after he'd dealt with those men that had taken Daisie. He wasn't afraid to do whatever was needed. She admired that.

Stopping, she turned and looked back to where she had just walked. Something was off. Moving over, she went down the slight incline and moved carefully along it. The men didn't ask or make a move, just stood there and let her do whatever it was she was doing.

It was slick from the rain, but—she moved down to the bottom and walked along slowly. Nodding her head slowly, she turned and looked up to where Blair stood. "There are dead patches."

He gave her a questioning look and came down the slope to stand beside her. "Dead patches?"

Pointing to the rocks along the top, "that would have washed away with the rain, but look," she motioned to the path down the slope and ahead of them, "see the patches that are brown."

Calum was beside them now. "There's no reason for them to be here, they get plenty of sun and rain."

"Exactly." She grinned and started walking again, faster this time, "rubbing alcohol sprayed directly on grass will do that." Kobie leaned down and reached toward the ground, "if it's sprayed this close and not misted to cover more area," she nodded.

"Son of a bitch." Calum walked by her and then along the fence.

Blair smiled down at her and took her hand to catch up to him. Lifting it, he kissed the back of it and winked at her.

Kobie inhaled. She felt pride that she'd been able to figure this out.

Calum stopped and looked in both directions and then down at his feet. "This whole spot is dead."

Kobie pulled her hand from Blairs and went and squatted down beside the fence. "It's trampled too. Someone stood here for quite a while."

"Like they were waiting for someone else to come back." Blair turned and looked on the other side of the fence. "If someone boosted them over the fence so it wouldn't set off any alarms," he looked along the fence, "how would they get out again?"

"There's no way they could, one maybe, but what of the one that boosted them back over? How do they get out?"

Kobie went closer to the fence and looked at the area on the other side. There were no trees to leap from, not since that last time that mistake had already been corrected. No rocks. "What if they didn't come out here?" She turned to see both men look at her. "Three or more people would be noticed, or someone would trip an alarm in error, but one…"

"Could walk out the front gate in the commotion and no one would notice," Calum said.

Blair swore softly and looked down at the browned area again. "They camped out here for a while."

"Like they were waiting for the one inside to bring whoever

they incapacitated from the chemicals," Calum said in a venomous tone. Clenching his jaw, he pulled out his phone and walked a few feet in the other direction.

Kobie looked at him for a moment, then turned to Blair, "So someone else was on the land when you guys went out to check?"

Blair nodded, "most likely. Probably hoping a solo runner would fall ill and be easy to take."

"Mika." Kobie covered her mouth, "it could have been Mika."

Blair nodded, grinding his teeth together for a moment. "She was smart and ran fast and furious back to the house."

"Oh my god, it could have been Nichelle." She hugged her waist, feeling ill at the thought.

Blair wrapped his arm around her and pulled her close. He pulled his phone out and tapped the screen, using his arm around her neck and not releasing her. Dropping a kiss on top of her head, he blew out a breath. "Gage. I need all the guys here as soon as you can manage."

Kobie leaned her head against his chest so she could listen to his heart beating. She was trying to stay calm. To act like the Alpha mate she was. They didn't freak out, they stayed calm and did what needed doing. She blew out a breath.

"Kobie figured out how they got on the land and as far as we can figure one, of them was still on it when we went out looking…" Blair made a sound of disgust, "yeah, or worse." He took a deep breath and exhaled. "I want to sweep the entire property, especially with Robbie and Niles coming back tonight." He hugged her tighter with his other arm. "He's talking to Devin now." Kobie glanced to see the expression on Calum's face wasn't pleasant at all. "Yeah, I'm sure he will." He cleared his throat, "I'll help you get caught up in the shop tomorrow." He relaxed slightly. "I appreciate it." He hung up and tucked the phone back in his pocket.

Kobie looked up at him. "What do we tell everyone?"

Blair looked down at her, then leaned down and kissed her softly on the mouth. "The truth. If everyone is aware and on the lookout, it's better."

Calum came back over.

"What does Devin say?" Blair asked.

"A lot of words I won't repeat in mixed company." He gave his head a shake. "He's sending a team this way."

Blair stiffened.

"We don't have a choice, Blair. There's going to be three injured males here and not enough bodies to keep watch over everyone and every inch of this land." He pointed, "Ed's place will be patrolled as well. We're not taking chances."

Blair huffed out a breath, "yeah." He swore quietly, "can we get cameras or something set up around the outside of the fence?" He motioned in the direction we'd come, "if we end up with a few dozen shifters that can't safely shift and run, things are going to get ugly."

"I already asked." Calum started walking, "he's sending that too."

Kobie was glad he didn't move away from her but started following with his arm draped over her shoulders.

"I don't care if we have a camera every five feet and have to patrol every hour until we get these bastards…" He blew out a breath and squeezed her against him.

"I'll work out a schedule once I see who Dev sends."

Kobie leaned into Blair. If she let go of him, she was afraid she would panic. Her clan deserved a new start, not this.

"We'll deal with it, babe." Blair leaned down and looked at her face.

Kobie nodded, believing what he said.

"They were on the land when I was out there?" Mika grasped her head between her hands and stood there like that, looking at Blair.

"We're pretty sure they were." He answered honestly.

"Holy shit," Mika whispered and paced away a few feet before stopping and looking down at the ground.

"The Alliance is sending a security team here to help."

Calum offered.

Cale looked at Blair, "what do you need me to do, chief?"

Blair gave him an amused look at the nickname, "work with Calum to set up a schedule for patrols." He glanced to Ed for as he spoke, "no one goes for a run alone." Turning, he watched to see that Mika had heard. She was nodding.

"I have more phones at the house, I think everyone should have one," Beth said, looking from Blair to Kobie.

"That's a good idea," Kobie answered.

"I get a phone?" Daisie asked.

Blair sought Kobie's gaze before he answered, she gave a quick nod. Looking down at the excited-looking child, he held up his hand, "for *emergency* calls only."

Daisie nodded. "I see *a lot* from the trees." She nodded again.

Ed gave his mate a serious look. "You take one of the men on any more shopping outings."

Beth bobbed her head, making no comment.

"How long is this going to go on?" Torrey said in a quiet tone. She held up her hand, "I'm not whining, don't misunderstand, but why are they still trying to get to us?"

Blair connected with Calum's look before he looked down at Kobie.

"They probably aren't happy I lived," Jay said loudly from the doorway, where he sat in his wheelchair.

"You think they're after you?" Cortney hugged Daisie against her front.

"They left one of the Alpha family males alive," Jay told her but was looking at Kobie, then to Blair as he spoke.

"Then we should send them an announcement," Nichelle said in a snarky tone. She motioned to Blair, "tell them we have a new Alpha, and it sucks to be them."

Blair couldn't help chuckling quietly. He loved her attitude. "I'm sure that would do it." He grinned at her.

"It's not a bad idea." Cooper mused in a hushed tone. Everyone turned to look at him. He smirked, "not an announcement, but let the word get out."

Gage glanced at Ed, "have the Alliance announce it?"

"You think they have eyes and ears on the inside?" Ed frowned.

"We've suspected they have some way of knowing things." Calum crossed his arms over his chest and looked down at the ground. "Maybe not a spy on the inside, but they're tapped in somehow."

"I'll talk to Shep about it." Ed turned and looked at Blair, a questioning look on his face. "An official ceremony usually means like shifter clans Alpha's or seconds come to welcome the new clan Alpha."

Blair resisted glaring at Ed, he knew he was asking when that was going to be. They'd come a long way last night, but he knew Kobie wasn't ready to go there yet. "Make it a coming soon announcement." He said in a low voice.

Ed smirked, "I'll talk it out with Shep."

Chancing a glance at Kobie, he knew she understood what Ed had been driving at. She gave him a steady look, neither upset nor happy and he honestly didn't know what exactly that meant.

"I'll go get those phones." She looked at Ed and didn't move until he nodded.

"I'll come with you." Noah stepped around Annamarie.

Beth looked surprised but said nothing.

Kasia came over and hugged Blair's waist tight. She looked up at him. "I know you'll keep us safe, Blair."

Blair touched the top of her curly head and winked at her. "You know it." He looked at Kobie to see her giving him a soft smile.

Kasia turned and held out her hand to Daisie. "We stick together, okay?"

Daisie took her hand and nodded.

"Gage, Kelsey, and I will try to get the repairs in the shop done today," Ed said.

Blair rubbed his hand over his hair, his gaze connecting with Kelsey as he did. She smiled at him and gave him an abrupt nod to say 'you've got this'. He returned the smile and watched her walk away with Gage. When he looked down at Kobie, she was watching him. He went over what had just transpired and hoped it didn't look like anything other than a friend backing up a friend. She smiled slowly and stretched up and kissed his mouth, lingering for a moment. "I'm going to work on our room." She dropped back down on her heels and gave him a questioning look, "I'm thinking a nice little sitting area for two in front of the window."

Blair ran his hand down over her hair. "That sounds perfect." He smiled, "somewhere quiet to start the day."

She laughed softly, "like that will *ever* happen." She started walking to the house, Cortney falling into step with her.

He stood there, with hands-on hips, and watched as most of the others wandered in different directions. Blowing out a breath, he tried to take stock and figure out what next. Then he noticed both Cale and Calum standing there, smiling at him. He frowned.

"Run?" Cale asked.

Blair grinned, "yes. Please."

"We need to sweep the whole property," Calum said and turned to Jake and Gary. "You two stay here and keep watch around the house."

Gary nodded.

"What time is backup arriving?" Jake asked, looking around the yard.

"This afternoon," Calum told him. "Devin messaged when we got back, they can only round up five."

"Five helps," Jake said. "We have two vast properties to patrol."

Blair rubbed his hand over his head and looked over at Ed, where he spoke to Jay and Cooper. "Have you called Bruce?"

Ed nodded, "last night, told him to stay vigilant."

"Okay." Blair blew out a breath.

"All clans have stepped up security," Ed told him.

"I know, I just worry," Blair said quietly and then bent down and picked up his run pack. "You staying here until we get back?"

Ed smiled, "yes. I'm waiting on a call back from Shep, so I should have news when you get back."

Blair gave him a half-smile and then caught up to Calum and Cale. "Where's Shaelan?"

Calum snorted, "sleeping. I insisted. She was up all night on video calls with doctors and chemists." He gave Blair an unamused look, "she's unhappy she doesn't haven't her library with her."

Blair smirked. "You might have to invest in a van."

Calum scowled at him, "never say that where she can hear you, or I'll be hauling a library and equipment with me everywhere."

Blair shrugged, "I'll take your car off your hands."

Calum stopped a hard look on his face. "I don't think your clan of women will all fit in it." He pulled his shirt over his head and dropped it on the ground.

Blair knelt down and undid his boots, all while pondering the truth in that. His days of roaming around were over. He looked down at the ground and he stood up. Pulling the shirt over his head, he stuffed it into his pack.

"Jeeze, what happened there?"

Blair blinked and looked to see Cale looking at his shoulder. He'd forgotten about Kobie's bite. He grinned. "Love bite." He said and glanced at Calum. From the look on his face, he got it. Cale however, looked terrified.

"Pass," Cale muttered.

Calum chuckled as he stuffed his jeans into the pack, then his phone. "You say that now…"

Blair looked at the angry-looking bite and wished it wouldn't heal when he shifted. Huffing out a breath, he decided he'd have to ask Kobie for a replacement later when he could grab a minute with her.

Chapter Thirty-One

Blair stood with Calum and Shaelan as the clan members were reunited with their returning men. He honestly didn't know if he should be front and center or just stay out of the way, so he'd elected the latter.

Kobie was standing with Jay, who had insisted he be in the chair, and wheeled around to the driveway when they arrived. Blair had to hand it to him. He was one tough son of a bitch. How painful it had been to get in the chair showed clearly on his face.

He turned back to see Daisie talking fast to her father. Robbie was nothing like he'd pictured. He was tall, as most tiger shifter males were, but the strawberry blonde hair had surprised Blair. It had never occurred to him that Daisie got her looks from her father. Whatever his daughter had just said to him had the man look over at Blair. He studied him for a moment and then looked back down at his child.

Blair watched as he moved a few feet. The cane illustrated just how bad his hip was, he also seemed to be favoring his other shoulder, but that could be from the large bandage that went from his jaw to beneath his shirt. He'd have to talk to Shaelan later when things settled down. "Think he can do the stairs?" He said quietly.

"It will help with rebuilding the muscles," Shaelan answered without looking at him.

Blair exchanged a look with Calum, his expression mirrored what he was thinking, that it wasn't really an answer to his question of *if* he could do the stairs.

When he looked back over, Daisie was practically dragging her injured father toward him. He glanced to Cortney, who was looking nowhere but up at her mate. Robbie moved slow but didn't falter in his step. He kept glancing down at his daughter, the expression of a parent's love plain to see.

Blair didn't want to see him have to come to him and started to take a step when Calum put his hand on his arm and gave him a look telling him to stay there.

"You're the Alpha." He said so quietly, even with Blair's hearing he barely caught it.

Inhaling, Blair blew it out and stood there. It felt wrong, but he knew that if anyone could steer him in the right direction with this new status it would be Calum. He spent more time around leaders and the king than any other shifter Blair knew of.

Robbie stopped about five feet in front of Blair and stood there.

"Blair," Daisie bounded over to him, barely able to contain her excitement. "This is my dad." She bounced back over to her father, almost dancing. "I told him how you got us and I almost fell and you saved Kobie and let me ride when I was *really* tired." She hardly took a breath, "and stopped Nichelle from drowning and I have a phone." She waved the phone around.

Blair couldn't help smile at her for a second and then sobered and looked at her father.

"I'll have Cort tell me all of that again, later." He touched the top of Daisie's head for a second and then looked back to Blair. "I owe you a huge debt." He inclined his head, "thank you for looking out for them."

Blair wanted to wave it off, but didn't, "they're an amazing group." He said earnestly.

Robbie nodded his head slowly. He looked tired.

"You should rest after the trip," Shaelan said quickly. "I want to check the dressings once you're inside."

Robbie looked over at Jay and Kobie and paused. "I just want to speak to Jay, then I'm all for some rest." He gave Blair a slight nod and began moving slowly toward Jay.

Blair looked over to see the expression on Jay's face. The last time these two men had seen each other, many had died, including their Alpha.

"I'm going over to lend a hand with Niles," Shaelan said softly.

Turning, he watched as Cale, the driver, and two other men helped to lift the reclined chair out of the van.

"Fuck." Calum said under his breath.

Blair blew out a breath, having no words to describe how seeing the state Niles was in made him feel. The fact the three men were alive and here was a miracle. He couldn't even imagine what they'd gone through. He looked to see Nichelle stood out of the way, her hand over her mouth. Not caring if it was breaking some sort of Alpha protocol, he strode toward her with long strides.

The other women were standing out of the way with Kasia. Mika made eye contact with Blair and looked quickly at Nichelle. She looked relieved he was coming over. Later, when the young shifter wasn't close to a breakdown, he'd have to find out why none of the others had stepped forward to offer her assurance and comfort.

Reaching her, he put his arm around her shoulder. "It's going to be rough for a bit, but," he leaned down so she'd look at him, "he's here." He added quietly. She nodded her fist almost in her mouth. Blair looked over her head toward where Kobie stood, she had an odd expression on her face too. What was going on? He sent her a quick look to let her know he'd be asking later.

"Where's Jay?" The man in the chair growled out quietly.

"You can see him in a minute," Shaelan told him without

hesitation. "This one dressing has blood on it." She nodded to the men and motioned to the house, "get him inside, please so I can look at it."

Blair stepped over, almost having to drag Nichelle with him. The man was large, with coal-black hair. At first, he wrote off the hard expression in his eyes to the amount of pain he was in, then realized as those dark eyes looked at his niece that it wasn't pain at all, it was personality.

"Why do you have your arm around my niece?" The man growled out.

Blair raised one eyebrow and glanced over at Calum who now stood looking unhappy beside Shaelan. Keeping his expression neutral, Blair stepped over closer, "she's just a bit overwhelmed to see you again."

The man snorted in disbelief. He didn't even look *at* her. "I need to see Jay." He said again, glancing at the driver.

The man looked at Blair, then to Calum.

"You are going to be in the same room as Jay, so you can catch up all you like." Shaelan motioned with her hand to take him inside.

Blair gave Nichelle's shoulder a quick squeeze. "Maybe you can keep Daisie out of the way while Shaelan checks them over?"

Nichelle nodded her head again.

When he went to step away, she hugged him tight. "I'm glad you're here." She released him and went quickly toward where Daisie was.

Blair rubbed a hand over his hair and turned to Calum. "The hell was that?"

Calum shook his head, "I'm not sure, but we need to find out a few things I'm thinking about this clan prior to the events that brought them here."

Blair nodded and looked around at everyone. He didn't feel right asking any of the other women. Turning, he looked back to Kobie, tilting his head to the side in hopes that she'd get what he was asking. She held up her hand, telling him just a minute.

When Blair looked back to the other women, they weren't there anymore, they were going in the house. "I feel like someone forgot to mention something." He mused.

Calum patted him on the shoulder and gave him an abrupt nod. "I'm going to make sure Shaelan isn't alone with that asshole. I'll be right back."

Blair stood there, looking around for a moment. Two of the new guards, he needed to find out names, were still out checking the property. He pulled his phone out and checked to see a message from Gage telling him their patrol was clear. Stuffing it back in his pocket, he blew out a breath, he was still going to hold everyone to taking turns running on Ed's property. He clenched his jaw and looked around the yard. He still didn't know how they had gotten off the land, but until he did, he wasn't taking any chances.

"I was hoping he'd be mellower on his return."

Kobie was right beside him. "So that's not a one-off?"

She crossed her arms over her chest and shook her head. "No. He's been like that as long as I can remember." She chewed the inside of her cheek for a second. "His wife died a long time ago, then his sister, Nichelle's mom, disappeared about five years ago. He's eternally pissed off."

Blair digested that for a second.

Calum came back. "Did he ever challenge your father?" he asked without preamble.

Kobie opened her mouth, then closed it and shrugged, "not that I'm aware of, but they kept a lot from me."

Calum turned to see Jay was still sitting there talking to Robbie. "My gut tells me he has." He motioned toward her brother. "Let's go ask."

Blair caught Kobie's hand as she went to walk away. Lifting their hands, he placed a soft kiss across her knuckles. Despite the new arrivals, he still wanted her to be clear about where they left off. "Want to go for a run after dinner?"

She glanced up at him.

"At Ed's." He clarified.

She smiled. "Yes."

Gage rubbed a hand over his jaw and looked over at Calum. "So he challenged the rightful Alpha and was still part of the clan?"

Calum shrugged and crossed his arms over his chest. "They postponed resolution until they returned."

Cale sat in the solo chair outside the little building he'd claimed as his own. "What happens now? The challenged Alpha didn't return."

"I don't know. This is a question for Devin or his father." Calum said quietly.

"Did the women know?" Gage asked.

Blair shook his head, "Kobie had no idea. I don't think the men of the clan shared a lot with them." He looked up the lane toward the house. "The mated ones may have known."

"It's not like he's in any shape to challenge Blair right now," Cale said getting up.

Calum nodded. "The tension it's going to cause is more the issue right now."

Blair snorted, "yeah cuz it's bad enough they survive and manage to get back to the clan and find out some guy took over in their absence."

Gage grinned at him and then gave Calum a look. "You haven't taken over yet…"

Blair glared at him, "don't start."

"Oh, come on, you rode me hard for years about Kelsey, I'm due some payback." Gage looked at Calum again.

Cal lifted his hands in defeat, "I'm not getting involved." He walked by Blair. "He was a dick to me too after Shae."

"You guys are no fun," Gage stated.

Blair glanced to Gage, then quickly followed Calum. "Any suggestions?"

Calum didn't even hesitate. "Put him in his place, quickly, but with respect."

"Sure. And I do that how?"

Gage and Cale caught up with them.

"No idea." Calum glanced behind them briefly. "I'm going to find my mate so we can go for a run."

"Here or Ed's?" Gage asked.

Calum was silent for a moment. "Ed's. I want to do a run here when we get back."

"I'll go with you." Cale piped up. "When you get back."

Blair looked down at the ground. He needed to talk to Kobie about this, to see if she had any ideas on how to put Niles in his place without pissing him off more. He blinked. Was that even possible? The man was filled with so much rage it oozed from his every pore. Blair didn't blame him, losing his wife then sister, he would be pissed off too, but he had Nichelle and should be put her first now.

"Don't burst anything important while you're thinking, there," Gage said with a grin.

Blair blew out a breath. "I'll try." He stopped and looked around. "I'd just like one day where I didn't have to figure out how the hell to do something."

Gage smacked him on the shoulder. "You need to spend more time in the shop."

Blair nodded. "I plan on it as soon as this tidal wave of issues is gone."

Calum stopped and pulled out his phone. He answered it, then frowned. "Mari?" He looked surprised. "Well, no, Devin can't do…" He opened his mouth, then snapped it shut, "you can't just stab everyone with the fork, Marilyn." He nodded, "I know. I will tell Shae to call you later and then we'll get to the bottom of it." He grinned, "no. I'm sure you'd make a wonderful great-aunt, but that's Shea's call." He opened his mouth and then looked down at his phone.

Gage chuckled. "We need to get that fork away from her."

Calum sighed, "it seems Dev's been ducking her calls."

"Who gave her a phone? She wants to use the fork on him?" Gage grinned.

Calum nodded, "yeah. I better go fill Shae in."

Blair looked at Gage after Cal walked away. "Who is Mari?"

Gage laughed, "I hope you get to meet her soon. It's

Shaelan's aunt and probably the scariest woman I've ever met—in a fun sort of way."

Blair opened his mouth, then closed it having no idea what to say to that.

"He doesn't look happy." Cale motioned to the house.

Blair looked to see Robbie standing there. Alone, looking back at him with a hard expression on his face.

"I'm going to say he's been filled in," Calum stated quietly.

"I'll go grab you a beer." Cale jogged toward the house.

"Make it two," Blair told him before he was inside.

Chapter Thirty-Two

Blair waited until Robbie got down into the chair and shifted around a few times to find a position to sit in with the least amount of pain. He should have thought about asking him to sit in the large wooden deck chairs. "If it would be easier we could go sit in the house." He hadn't sat on the new furniture in the living room yet, but it looked comfortable.

Robbie shook his head, "no this is fine, now that I'm down." He leaned to the side, resting an elbow on the chair for more support. "I honestly never knew how many parts of the body were affected when the muscles on your side are injured." He gave Blair a quick look. "I wanted to be out of earshot to talk."

Blair offered one of the beers, then hesitated, "are you allowed to drink? I don't know if you're on any medication."

Robbie held out his hand. "As long as we don't tell that dark-haired one, I think I'll be fine."

Blair grinned, "Shaelan knows her stuff." He leaned over and handed him the bottle, then opened his own. "She's been trained to be the healer for her clan."

"Jags?" Robbie asked.

Nodding, Blair glanced around, there was no one nearby.

"Yeah, she's Calum's mate. He works for the Alliance a lot."

"Cortney told me about the trip here." He took a small drink, nodded, and took another one. "I appreciate all you did to get them here."

"It was a little more hectic than I'd have preferred…"

"Thank you. For getting my daughter back." He gave him a serious look.

Blair only nodded to that, having no idea what an appropriate reply would be.

"She thinks your superman by the way."

Blair grinned, "she's energetic." Her father smirked at his description. "But a pretty great kid."

"She is." He looked at the bottle for a moment. "I wasn't sure if I was going to get back to her."

"I'm glad you did." Blair motioned in a circle with his bottle, "when you're rested and feel up to it, I'd like more details."

Robbie took another drink. "Yeah, I figured you might." He glanced at the house, "Jay filled in a lot of blanks for me." He cleared his throat, "you're going after them? Well, not just our clan members but all?"

Blair inhaled a deep breath and blew out slowly. "I am. Kobie, Calum as well and one of the guys from Ed's too, he was actually one of their captives for fifteen years."

"Shit," Robbie whispered. "You've got balls, kid."

"I don't know about that." Blair sat forward, "how much did Jay share?"

Robbie gave him his full attention. "The trip, how he got back, all the things that have happened along the way." He looked over at the house, "that you're going to be our new Alpha as soon as Kobie stops avoiding it."

Blair bobbed his head a few times. "I wasn't raised with my blood clan," He swirled the bottle and watched the liquid against the tinted glass. "I came to Ed and Beth when I was two." He took a quick drink, "my father was overthrown, killed and well, long story, short, by my older brother," he sought the other man's gaze, "whom I've never met or even knew existed until recently," he'd needed to clarify that first, "was part of the crew that ambushed you guys." Blair watched his face as it registered, "so it's not that I've got balls for this, it's more of feeling obligated to right a wrong that's been going on far too long."

Robbie was silent for several moments before he looked at him again. He looked at the bottle in his hand and then took a drink. "I may have drunk the same Kool-Aid the girls have."

Blair wasn't sure what he was talking about.

Robbie smiled, "I see why they're all on team Blair. Between what everyone has told me and what you've shared, I agree with Jay." He tipped the bottle toward him, "I couldn't understand why Jay was willing to hand over his right to you, but with you and Kobie at the head of our clan, I think we'll heal and prosper."

Blair ran about six things through his head, looking for the right one before he spoke. "You backing me up means a lot to me." He took a deep breath and then turned when he sensed someone coming toward them. Kobie was walking toward him slowly. He looked back at Robbie. "Stay here for a moment, please. I'll be right back." He got up and jogged to meet her halfway.

She searched his face. "Everything okay?"

Blair dropped a kiss on her mouth quickly. "Yes." He straightened and then looked down at her. "What would you say to Robbie and Cortney being the second family?" He frowned, "I don't know what the other family was like, but…"

"I think that's a perfect idea." She smiled up at him.

He felt relief with her approval. He smiled. "Great. Can you grab Cortney and Cale if he's still in there, I'd like a quick discussion with them."

"What about Daisie?" She looked at the house, "she's had her nose pressed up against the window the whole time her superman and father have been talking."

Blair snorted softly and looked at the house, sure enough, there was Daisie looking out the window. He pointed to her and motioned for her to come here. Her eyes widened, and then she vanished from his sight.

"I'll be right back," Kobie said softly, then rubbed her hand on his chest.

Daisie got to him before he got back to his chair. "Am I in trouble? I wasn't spying, I just wanted to see when you were done talking because mom said the men needed to talk."

Blair sat down and grinned. "You are not in trouble."

"Okay." She turned to her father, "Blair is going to take me to Bruce's for my lessons some time. They have animals there, but no dogs because they'd be scared." She nodded, "but there are other kids, so it will be like I'm in school, but I'm not..."

Robbie watched every word she said, but he looked exhausted.

"Daisie."

She looked at Blair. "Your dad just had a long trip, and he's tired, maybe tell him the rest tomorrow."

Daisie nodded and then went over and kissed her dad's cheek and hugged him carefully. Robbie closed his eyes and leaned his head against hers.

"Should you be drinking?"

Blair turned to see Kobie and Cortney standing there with Cale.

"One beer won't hurt," Robbie said, giving Blair a quick side glance.

Kobie came over and sat on the arm of the chair, resting her hand on his shoulder.

Cale gave Blair a questioning look.

"Have you met Cale?" Blair asked Robbie.

He nodded, "briefly, yes."

"I've asked him to transfer to this clan, and he's agreed." He smirked, "I'm still waiting on the how that works part, but we need the help." He added.

Robbie closed his eyes briefly. "Yes, we do." He looked at Cale. "Welcome."

Cale inclined his head to him.

"I," Blair looked at Kobie, "we wanted to talk to all of you together before the dinner mayhem begins..."

"We're having spaghetti." Daisie blurted out. "I like

spaghetti.”

Cortney sat down by her mate's feet and tugged on her daughter's hand, so she'd sit too. "Let Blair finish." She said with quiet patience.

Daisie sat down and then stared at Blair.

"I want Cale to have an active roll in the clan," he motioned to Robbie, "most especially while you're healing."

Robbie looked to agree with that.

"Once you are back to full strength, we," he glanced at Kobie again to receive a soft look for including her, "would like you to be the second family of the clan."

Robbie looked surprised, he glanced down at his wife, who looked equally shocked.

"You don't have to answer right this second," Kobie said, "but please think about it."

"We will." Robbie glanced at him and then back to Cortney.

"We're honored." Cortney said slowly, "surprised, but honored."

"I want things to be different for the clan." Blair said slowly, "nothing crazy, but little things," he put his hand on Kobie's knee, "like including the women more." He looked over at Robbie, "they went through hell and didn't complain once. They did the clan proudly."

Robbie touched the top of Cortney's head. "I'm sure they were a force to be reckoned with."

Blair grinned, "and then some." He looked at Cale. "Do you agree with all this?"

Cale nodded and then smiled, "I'm all for good changes."

Robbie looked at Cortney again, she nodded even though they hadn't spoken a word. "I don't believe a lot of thought will be required, we accept your offer and will strive to not make you regret it."

Blair raised his near-empty bottle to him and then took the last drink.

"Does that make me a princess?" Daisie asked.

Everyone grinned.

"Close." Blair winked at her.

"Can I tell everyone?" She looked excited.

Kobie nodded, "yes, go."

Daisie shrieked and jumped up and ran into the house.

"Think she'll know what she's even saying?" Cortney asked.

"Probably not," Robbie answered.

"Before she comes racing back, I have one other thing," he waited until Robbie was looking at him, "about Niles—"

Robbie downed the rest of his beer and then nodded slowly. "Damar should have put him in his place years ago."

"This has been ongoing?" Blair frowned.

"Five, six years." Robbie motioned to the house. "He challenged everything the Alpha said."

Blair sat there looking at the ground for a moment, then glanced up at Kobie. "He's welcome to stay, but he's going to have to drop the attitude." He scowled and looked at Robbie, "he didn't even speak to Nichelle."

"She had her first shift," Cortney told him.

His eyebrows went up. "She's always been beyond her years in every other way."

"She jumped in the river," Kobie said with a smirk.

"Oh," Robbie shook his head, "actually that isn't surprising now that I think about it."

"She was fantastic," Blair said as he thought about it. "Fast."

Robbie looked at Kobie, "Kobie fast?"

"Close," Kobie admitted.

"Damn. Good for her." He sobered, and gave Blair a questioning look, "If Niles can't comply, is she still clan?"

"Absolutely." Blair didn't need to think about it. "She's clan. Always." He nodded.

"All right." Robbie took a deep breath and then exhaled. "Piece of advice?"

Blair met his look.

"Deal with Niles now, don't let him have time to come up with more bullshit."

Blair looked to Cale, who shrugged, and then to Kobie, she gave him a patient look, letting him know this was his call. He nodded slowly, "Okay, I'll talk to Shae and see if he's stable enough from the trip."

"I've got your back, chief," Cale said, standing straighter.

"I'll go see where dinner stands." Cortney got up. She leaned over and looked into her mate's eyes for a moment and then kissed him softly. "No more drinking." She whispered.

Robbie smirked and watched her walk away. When she went in the house, he turned to Blair, "give me a hand up, there's no way I can get out of this chair without pulling a stitch."

Blair got to his feet quickly, "you should have said something."

"Not in front of my mate. I would have sat here all night if needed." His chuckle was short-lived as he grimaced when Blair pulled him up to his feet.

Blair motioned to the house. "Go rest. We'll be in shortly."

"I'll go talk to Shae?" Kobie asked him.

"Yeah," he started to nod, "wait," reaching over, he pulled her closer and kissed her. "Okay, now go."

Kobie smiled up at him. "We still going for a run tonight?"

"Absolutely."

When she went into the house, he turned to Cale. "And if Niles doesn't comply," he made quote marks in the air, "what then? I send a broken man where?"

Cale lifted his hands up, "not my job."

Blair rubbed a hand on his hair, "think there's a dummy guide to this Alpha thing?"

Cale laughed, "probably not."

Blair sighed and shook his head. "Okay, I'm going to check with," he motioned to the small building they'd set up for security, "I don't know his name and then I'll be in." He turned and walked toward the building. "One step forward." They had a second family, "maybe two." Robbie had accepted him. He scowled, "three back." Talking to Niles was going to suck no matter what he said, he just knew it.

Chapter Thirty-Three

Jay's room was considerably smaller now with another bed in it. Blair stood in the doorway and watched as Shaelan changed the one bandage on Niles' side. He winced for the man that showed no pain when she poked around it and checked stitches, or whatever she was doing. He took the time to study the man. His eyes seemed dead; no emotion reflected in them at all.

Robbie sat in the chair beside Jay's bed, leaning on his cane and looking ready to fall over, but he'd insisted he was in the room for the discussion.

Kobie sat on the bed beside her brother. She too wanted to be here.

The way Jay silently observed everyone else here told Blair he knew what was happening.

Calum and Cale stood in the open door to the patio, mirrored stances of arms crossed and legs braced apart. The only difference was Calum tracked every move Shaelan made with his eyes. There was no way she would be near Niles without someone else around. Blair felt sorry for the man in the bed if he did something to upset Shae.

Shaelan taped the fresh dressing and then stepped back. She

glanced at Blair and gave him a brief nod.

Blair stepped out of Niles' blind spot and closer to the bed, so the man could look at him without having to move. "How are you doing?" He was going to try to do this nicely, respectfully as Calum had said. Regardless of what had happened, this man had gone through hell to get back here.

"I'll be fine." Niles barely glanced at him. "A few broken bones, they'll heal."

Blair gave a slight shrug. He wasn't a stranger to pain, clearly. "I thought I'd come and introduce myself now that you're settled." He waited until he looked at him, which he finally did, but it wasn't a friendly hello, pleased to meet you kind of look. It was loathsome. "I'm Blair Elden, I…"

"I know who you are." Niles looked around the room. "All I've heard is Blair this and that since I got in this bed."

"Have you spoken to Nichelle?" There was no way to read any of this man's expressions, Blair decided. "Did she tell you she had her first shift?"

Niles finally made eye contact with him. "Yeah. Said you saved her." His look hardened even more. "An unmated male shouldn't be around my niece."

Blair nodded. "I agree with that." He glanced briefly at Kobie, "but you're wrong, I have a mate."

Niles looked at him again, or more specifically Blair's neck. "I don't see any mate's mark."

Blair crossed his arms, "I didn't say I was mated, I said I *have* a mate."

"Where is she? Does she know you're around all this clan's women?"

"She does," Kobie answered.

It took a lot of restraint to not grin at the expression on Niles's face as he looked at Kobie. He looked back to Blair, "your mate is part of the Alpha family? What do you think that will get you?"

Blair shrugged, "a beautiful mate."

"He's from an Alpha family too." Jay piped up.

If Niles could have shrugged with his broken collarbone, he

probably would have, judging by the expression on his face. "Still doesn't get you anything in this clan."

"Actually, it does," Kobie told him, standing up and coming over and weaving her fingers into Blairs. "Jay has passed his place as the next in line as Alpha."

Blair watched carefully and knew the moment Niles put the pieces together. His dark eyes connected with Blair's again.

"*You're* going to be the new Alpha of the clan?" The older man glared at him.

"I am."

Niles snorted in disdain. "That's not how it works. If the Alpha family has no more males, the second family assumes leadership—whereas they're all dead now, the oldest family in the clan takes their place." His gaze narrowed. "That would be *my* family."

Pieces clicked together for Blair. Why this man was so jaded. At some point in history, his family had probably lost the role of leadership in the clan. "That may be how it works in most cases…"

"In *all* cases." Niles corrected.

"Unless the king of the shifters has given his blessing," Jay told him in a tone that dared him to speak against the King.

Niles looked at Jay for a moment and then at Robbie. "And you're okay with this?" He jerked his chin toward Blair.

Robbie nodded slowly, "I am." Robbie stood slowly, not without a painful expression. "I completely support his leadership as Alpha of this clan."

Niles looked back to Jay, "your father and I…"

"Anything that was agreed to by Damar is no longer valid." Robbie leaned harder on his cane, "Blair is going to take the clan in a new direction and I…"

Niles flicked his hand toward Robbie, "I don't care for a new *direction*, my niece and I will be leaving…"

"Nichelle isn't going anywhere," Blair stated. "In fact, her care is no longer your responsibility." He released Kobie's hand and went over and leaned on the bed, so he was sure that Niles had to look at him and nowhere else. "What you have to decide is if you want to be a contributing member of the clan—if that's not something you can do, then absolutely, we'll arrange for you to recover elsewhere."

"You can't just come across the clan and decide you're in charge, you little punk," he spat, "that's not for anyone outside the clan to decide…"

"The clan decided." Kobie stepped back into Niles' view, "all surviving members, except you, chose Blair as our new Alpha."

Shaelan came over and put a needle into the IV line and then adjusted it. Stepping back, she stood beside Calum.

"I'll give you a few days to think about it," Blair stated with a small nod. "We'll talk about it when you have."

"Do the right thing, Niles, don't leave Nichelle with no blood family," Robbie said quietly.

"I don't…" Niles blinked; his eyes looked heavy. "I…" he closed his eyes.

"He'll nap for a few hours," Shaelan said and then dropped the empty needle into the wastebasket. "I'm hungry. Who's for dinner?" She smiled at Calum.

Blair rubbed his jaw and looked down at the man in the bed. Shaelan had put him to sleep to end the conversation.

"Hopefully he thinks about it."

Blair glanced at Cale. "I'll stay out of his way for a few days and see if he does." He looked at Shaelan, "letting him be awake some of the time would help that."

She shrugged, "he's toxic, and I heard enough."

Grinning, Blair shook his head at the enamored expression on Calum's face as he looked at his mate. "I guess it's dinner time then."

"I'm starving. The drama around here builds up an appetite." Cale strode across the room and out the door.

Nichelle was standing in the living room when they went out. Her eyes were huge. "Do we get to stay?" She looked from Kobie to Blair.

Blair sighed and went over to her. "Regardless of what your

uncle decides, you are part of this clan." He bent his knees, so he was looking at her face to face. "Do you understand?"

She nodded her head, her eyes tearing up. "Thank you." She wiped at her face when a tear rolled down it. "I'm glad he's alive, but…"

Kobie hugged her. "We know." She leaned back and looked at her. "This will always be home, this clan, okay?"

Nichelle heaved a loud sigh. "Okay." She looked up at Blair. "I'm so glad you're here." She looked at him for a moment more and then turned to go out to the kitchen.

Blair wrapped his arm around Kobie and pulled her against his chest. "So, what did I do? Taking her out of his care?" He rested his cheek on the top of her head.

"It's okay, she's been looking after herself for years. We just nudged her in the right direction most of the time." She squeezed his waist.

"She's a great kid."

Kobie looked up at him. "She is, I was thinking of training to track and hunt."

Blair kissed her on the forehead. "I think you should." He grinned and turned to walk them both to the kitchen. "We could train all the women to kick ass in the tracking at Alliance gatherings."

Kobie laughed, "you'd like that, wouldn't you? Blair, the Alpha of the clan of female hunters."

Blair pretended to think about that for a second. "I think I would like that."

"Sign me up," Mika said with a smirk as they stood in the door talking about it.

"Me too," Shae said.

Calum gave her an odd look.

"What?" She shrugged, "I know I'm not a tiger, but I didn't even know I was shifter until I met you so," she motioned to the women in the room, "I think they could catch me up faster."

Calum made a low growling sound. "I do not need to be outdone by my mate." He tugged on her hand so she'd come to him, "Especially if Kobie trains you." He shook his head. "I'd go from unbeatable to the laughing..."

Blair held up his hand. "Almost unbeatable," he motioned to Kobie, then grinned at Cal, "almost."

Calum sighed, "so when do we eat?"

Chapter Thirty-Four

Blair tugged on Kobie's hand. "They'll all be here when we get back." He pulled her toward the truck and opened the door. She climbed in. He put one foot in and then caught the look Calum was giving him as he spoke on the phone. "See, now I have to go see what's wrong now."

Kobie laughed. "We can still go for a run after you do."

Blair gave her a blank look. "We were leaving almost an hour ago, woman." He huffed out a breath and leaned on the open door as Calum was walking toward them.

Calum tucked the phone into the pocket of his jeans and leaned against the hood of the truck. "That was Jesse."

"Is he on his way back?"

Calum shook his head. "Not yet. He's having a real hard time tracking down some of those clans."

"Is he finding them though?" Blair tossed the keys on the seat and stepped around the door.

"Few. He said some are gone without a trace. Addresses listed are vacated or the people there are not shifters and have no idea."

"Shit." Blair rolled his neck. "So, how many more does he have to do?"

"I think he said three more, or two, the signal wasn't the greatest." Calum ran his hand over his jaw. "He said if we don't hear from him for a few days to come to find him."

"Why is that?"

Calum grinned. "He's heading into an area that's not really fond of outsiders."

"Great," Blair said sarcastically.

Calum nodded, "I'm sure he'll be fine. I filled him in on life here and he said he was glad he was away for all of it."

"I'm sure there will always be something happening here," he looked at Kobie sitting in the truck, "speaking of, I'm going for a run before I bite people."

Cal grinned. "I'm going to check around here."

Blair backed up a step. "Take Cale with you." He looked around and didn't see him. "Kind of let me know…"

"I'll put him through the gauntlet and let you know."

Blair saluted him. "Appreciate it."

Blair cut across the rocks. He'd be able to catch her as she ran through the thicker brush this way. He knew every tree, rock, and weed in the area, had spent years running it—and yet, he was still having to work to keep her in his sights. His mate was amazing. Although, it didn't help that his cat was completely besotted with the sexy black she-cat that was running circles around them right now. Twice he'd almost caught her and his animal half had all but put on the brakes. His cat liked the chase. He liked that their as yet unclaimed mate was happy. Blair did as well, but he had his pride and needed to at least keep that intact, as Kobie more than demonstrated that her smaller, lighter female cat was more agile in the uneven terrain.

Slowing at the top, he caught sight of her racing along the bottom. Now his cat was on board as the reserve speed he knew he was capable of kicked in. Ten more feet and he could jump down there and be in front of her.

Why did he feel the need to do this? Blair had no idea, but

he was doing it despite any logical reasoning.

Five feet, they were stride for stride now.

Using all the strength in his back legs, he leaped.

Kobie knew he was up there. She knew that he thought he had her. As usual, her cat and she were in synch. She slowed just a fraction and prepared to submit.

Never in her life had she ever had that thought, but now she did. It was Blair and if anyone had earned that, deserved her loyalty and complete devotion, it was him.

A few more feet. She couldn't just hand it to him.

He'd looked to her for input, he'd included her, allowed her to speak freely. Blair had let her be herself completely and it dawned on her earlier, what her cat had been trying to convey to her all along.

Blair was her Alpha, her mate, her partner in this life.

She heard pebbles bouncing off the rock and slowed even more. She was handing him the catch now and didn't seem to mind at all.

The shadow of him jumping down blocked out the light of the moon for a split second. She slid to a stop and the large sexy white cat, their incredible mate, landed in front of them, almost nose to nose with her.

Kobie let out a playful prusten, almost a whisper. Blair gave a gentle chuff in response. She backed up a few feet, her tail twitching, and lowered the front of her body in a submissive pose.

Blair's cat eyes never left her own as he moved closer, an inch at a time.

Kobie's cat went completely silent inside her, giving her the cue that this next part was all hers and she would comply with whatever her human half decided. She had never shifted in full view of anyone before, her stomach knotted, but she did, a foot from him. When she felt the damp ground under her hands, she pushed up onto her knees and watched Blair. His beautiful cat eyes were locked on hers. If he was surprised, she couldn't tell.

Sitting, Kobie leaned back until she lay on the cool earth. Neither of them had worn their packs tonight, and she was glad for it now, she wanted nothing between them. Straightening her legs, she opened her arms at her sides and watched as he moved with caution to stand over her. A rough, warm lick was placed over the cat tattoo on her abdomen as he moved up her body. Her heart was racing as she looked up into the eyes of a cat, the eyes of her man.

Without warning, he closed his eyes, and now above her was Blair's face, his human eyes. He held his body just close enough she could feel the heat of his skin, without touching. Her breath hitched in her throat as he looked at her mouth and slowly lowered his lips to hers. Just their lips touched, no other part. Kobie felt like she was going to climb out of her skin with the need that coursed through her.

The kiss was gentle, coaxing, a sweet tasting of each other's mouth. Lifting her arms slowly, she touched either side of his face and pulled him closer so she could deepen the kiss. A deep noise rumbled in his chest and her cat stirred enough to fill Kobie with intense anticipation. Her cat stayed there, just below the surface, waiting, wanting.

Kobie moved her mouth from his and kissed along his jaw. Her sex clenched as she could feel his hard need resting just against her stomach, but he made no move to rub against her. Laying her head back on the ground, she continued to hold his face. She was breathing heavier now, just looking up at him. He held himself above her, his muscles steady. Licking her lips, Kobie reached for her voice, "Blair Elden," she licked her lips again and looked into his heavy lust-filled eyes, "I accept you as my mate." Her voice was barely audible, but she knew he had when his expression changed.

In a fast move, she found herself laying on top of his naked body. She could barely force the air into her lungs, and she looked down at him when he dropped his hands away from her completely and placed them at his sides.

Her cat gave her a gentle nudge, knowing well enough that Kobie was scared, nervous, and surprisingly the happiest she'd ever been. Placing her hands on his chest, she lowered her face closer to his. He licked his lips and then clenched his jaw as he fought to keep his hands off her. Pushing her nose into his neck, she inhaled slowly and took his scent into her body. She groaned softly as it moved through her. This was her home, this was where she was meant to be, with Blair. Licking over his skin, she heard him blow out a harsh breath, fighting to control himself. For the briefest of a second, she considered drawing it out, then her cat's teeth filled her mouth and she bit into that sweet spot where his neck and shoulder met.

Blair growled deep in his throat, his hands clamped around her hips like a vice. She didn't want to release her bite. She loved the taste of his blood in her mouth. When he shifted her and lowered her quickly onto his body, she was forced to open her mouth and gasp as he filled her. He held her there, his eyes holding her own as fiercely as his hands were her body.

She wanted to move, squirmed as much as his grip would allow. Using inner muscles, she squeezed him and made him groan out loud. Her eyes looked at the blood on his skin, her mark she'd placed on him, and her need grew. "Blair…" she pleaded.

Blair inhaled slowly, his pupils changing as he did. "You won't regret it, ever." Flipping them again, she found herself flat on her back beneath him. He thrust into her, hard as his teeth bit into her flesh.

She cried out as the intense pleasure filled every pore of her body. He didn't release his hold on her neck as he continued to move in a slow rhythm. It was so gentle until their bodies connected. With each stroke, he made sure she understood she was his. Kobie was so overwhelmed by the sensations, she had no choice, but to wrap her legs around him and hold on tight as he took her higher than she'd ever imagined.

He lifted his head, and she felt bereft that his mouth wasn't on her, his teeth claiming her. When he crushed her mouth with his, she could taste her own blood. Combined with his and moaned. Blair lifted his head and watched her as he continued to move into her, sending her closer to the edge.

With one hand he reached under her and lifted her hips higher, making it so she couldn't move with him.

Seconds later she cried out and shattered beneath him. Her body convulsed so intensely it robbed her of her breath. Opening her eyes, she looked up at the moon shining down upon them and a slow smile formed on her lips. This was right.

Before she could catch her breath, he withdrew and flipped her onto her stomach. Lifting her by the hips, he pulled her body up into his and pushed into her again. A deep guttural moan came out of her mouth when his sharp teeth bit into his mark again.

Moans and cries of pleasure echoed in her ears and she knew they were coming from her, but couldn't have stopped them if she tried. Blair kept going until she crashed over the peak twice more before he let himself go and stiffened over her.

Her whole body was a pulse as he lowered them to their sides, their bodies still connected in the most primal way they could be. She could feel his hot breath against her hair as he struggled as much as her to remind his body how to breathe. "I don't have the strength to move." She gasped, then inhaled through her nose, trying to bring oxygen into her system.

"Mmm," he rubbed her nose into her hair, "too damp out to sleep here." He whispered.

She nodded but couldn't catch her breath enough to speak.

"Long-run back." He leaned up and kissed her cheek. "You ran us to the edge of the property, you little hellion." He chuckled.

She licked her lips, trying to moisten them. "Maybe I wanted to be far enough away no one would hear." Her whole body flushed as he stirred inside her.

"Babe, you were screaming." He pulled out of her and rolled her to lie on her back. "*Everyone* heard." The look of male pride displayed clearly in his eyes.

Her cheeks heated. "Think we could soundproof the Alpha den?"

Blair grinned and leaned down to kiss her bruised lips

gently. "I think we should look into that."

Kobie touched his rough cheek, "I think you might have to carry me back."

Shaking his head, he shifted to his knees and looked down at her. "Not a chance. I'm going to have to hunt down a few rabbits and other critters just to rebuild the strength to get back."

Kobie inhaled slowly, then pointed to their left. "Rabbits den over there."

"Fucking amazing." He growled quietly and leaned over her to give her a hard kiss. "I herd; you take them down?"

She accepted his hand to pull her up to sit. "Deal. But we can't eat any black ones."

He raised an eyebrow at her, "for real?"

She nodded, "Yeah, my cat is opposed to it." She shrugged and then shifted without drawing another breath.

"I love you, Kobie." He said to her just before he shifted.

Her cat was so energized it shocked her as she bumped up against Blair's and then, without pause, the chase was on.

Chapter Thirty-Five

Blair grinned at her as he got out of the truck. "At least it was Coop sitting there by the truck." Her cheeks flushed as she accepted his hand and let him pull her across the seats to get out. "Would have been much worse if it had been Gage standing there."

"I suppose." She stood in front of him and rubbed her hand over his chest.

He didn't know why, but he loved when she did that. Searching her eyes, he glanced at her neck. His mark was swollen and very plain to see. How their bodies knew not to heal those when they shifted, he had no idea but was glad that it was bold and visible and announced to all that she was his. Forever, only his.

"Stop it." She hissed.

He chuckled, "I can't help it." Pulling her close, he kissed her hard on the mouth. Like a stamp that said 'mine.'

"Do you think it carried it over here?" She gave him a hesitant look.

Shrugging, he was just about to say he doubted it until he spotted Calum leaning against his small room. He was trying hard not to grin and failing badly. "That can't be good." He motioned with his head to the other man. "He's waiting at my door."

Kobie gave him an assuring look. "Whatever it is, we'll handle it."

Calum wiped the smirk off his face before they reached him. Blair caught the slight movement as he looked at his throat and then at Kobie's.

Blair hoped the warning look he was giving was also noted.

"Good run?" Calum asked without in a serious tone.

"Yeah." Blair put his arm around Kobie and hugged her against him. "What's going on now?"

Calum straightened away from the wall. "Jesse is at his last stop," he smirked, "and not happy about the location at all." He pulled out his phone and tapped the screen, then held it out to them.

Blair looked at the picture and smiled. It was a forest, thick growth, full of trees and Blair doubted the inner part ever saw daylight. "Damn, that's going to be some hard work to get in there."

Nodding, Calum tucked his phone back in his pocket.

Blowing out a quiet breath, he studied him. "You didn't wait here just to show me that."

Calum shook his head, then crossed his arms over his chest. "No. I didn't." He glanced at the house briefly before continuing. "Niles is awake," he shrugged, "still grumpy as fuck, but not being stupid—yet."

Blair nodded. He still believed there may be hope for the man. "And?" He knew there had to be more. Calum was tense and for that to show it had to be something big.

"Spoke to Shep tonight too." He inhaled a sharp breath through his nose. "A team watching some of the locations spotted your brother." He waved a hand toward the makeshift guard shack, "the pics are in there."

Blair's spine stiffened, "spotted him somewhere or do they know where he lives?"

"Where he lives."

Blair dropped his arm away from Kobie and put both hands

on top of his head. He felt the heat of his blood pulse through his veins, filled with fury and retribution.

"I requested *our* team be the ones to take down that location," Calum said in an even tone.

Blair nodded and dropped his hands away. "Good. Yeah." Putting his hands on his hips, he looked down at the ground, trying to focus through the vivid images of revenge.

"Slow down, Blair, we're not going there until Jesse is back, we do some surveillance, and," Calum paused until Blair looked at him again, "you guys get your training in."

Blair frowned, "how long with that be? He could be somewhere else by then."

"They're going to track his every move." Calum straightened and pointed at him. "You need to pull it together and get things in order here before you go rushing off on some suicide mission."

Blair clenched his jaw and nodded. "Fine."

Calum looked at Kobie, gave her a quick nod, and then walked away.

"Hey," Kobie was right in his face now, her hand on his chest, "we'll get him. Together, when the time is right." She held his look as she rubbed her hand in a slow circle on his chest.

Blair blew out a breath and then wrapped his arms around her and squeezed her tight. "It consumes me, babe, the feelings of righting all he's done."

Her warm arms moved around his waist. "I know." She nuzzled her face into him, "and you will. Right all of his wrongs and stop him." She leaned back and looked up at him. "But not now." Her look softened. "Right now, you and I are going to go have a hot shower and get some rest."

"Together?" He still couldn't believe she was his, that he was hers.

"Always." She smiled and then backed toward the door of his room.

Blair nodded and let her pull him along with her. "Always."

KEEP READING FOR AN EXCERPT OF

SOLACE

Animal Senses Book 5

Jacqueline Paige

Chapter One

Jesse pulled the van in and looked at the path that led into the trees. It was so overgrown; he could barely make out the trail. There was no way he was driving on *that*. He groaned, which meant he was going to have to walk it. He was so tired of this back country-middle-of-hell's forest area—

"One more, then I'm hopping back over the border and going home." He mumbled as he put the van in park. It wasn't unusual for him to talk out loud to himself, he spent a lot of time on the road alone. Grabbing the phone, he sighed. If a forty percent complete house and a small trailer could be called home. He'd had every intention of finishing it and enjoying that beautiful space he'd bought near his clan—and the Tomas organization had ramped up their chaos in his world.

Opening his window, he snapped a picture of the unforgiving dense growth and typed out a message to Calum. He hadn't talked to him for a few days, so he figured he'd better get in touch, so the big man didn't send out a search party.

He read the message. *Lost in hell. Your kind of fun. After this one I'm coming back.* Nodding he hit send.

He should probably report to Devin too. Jesse liked that he was dealing with him most of the time now instead of his father. Devin didn't care how much he swore, he didn't have to be political or be afraid of crossing some hierarchy rule. He had the greatest respect for the king of all shifters—but didn't envy the job the man had to do.

His phone beeped. Opening the message from Calum he grinned. *Be careful not to hurt your delicate pads on the undergrowth.* No reply was needed for that, he decided.

He pulled the van in as far as he dared. Shutting it off, he leaned back and looked at himself in the mirror. He looked rough, with good reason, he hadn't stopped to rest much in the past week. His hair had taken on a new style of its own, not that it lay down and behaved normally. His eyes were bloodshot, which only made the pale green look even paler. If he found this clan, they were going to take one look at him and pass on any offers of assistance because he looked like a wretch.

Getting out, he stretched. The amount of driving he'd been doing lately couldn't be good for a body. His cat ached to get out and run. Looking up the mountain, he debated on going for a quick run, then changed his mind. The last thing he needed was to run onto another clan's territory. Five years ago, he would have without much thought. Now, with everything he knew about the shifter world, not a chance.

Things were messed up. Really messed up. If he hadn't been with Devin and the others when they'd gone to find Calum, he never would have believed the bizarre events that had been going on. Bizarre was a nicer way of saying 'fucked up shit'. The fact that clans had lost touch with the Alliance over the years wasn't shocking. There hadn't always been internet and cellphones—but after the last few months, of looking for those clans he was ready to admit shit was getting real—and not in a good way. Entire clans were gone, without a trace and the only way that could happen was if Tomas had found them. Jesse thought of it as a failure on several levels, the Alliance and the clans themselves. He knew if it were his clan they would have packed up and gone to find the Alliance or even the next closest clan.

Opening the door, he looked in his cooler and found he only had two energy drinks. Should shifters drink these things? No. Most shifters didn't have to drive the entire length of provinces and states constantly either. Ducking his head, he checked out the 'trail' again. Yeah, he was drinking one of these. Grabbing it, he closed the cooler and took a long drink. Setting the can on top, he brought up his contact list on his phone and hit Devin's name.

"Jesse. Where are you now?"

He grinned, he *really* liked how Devin always got to the point quickly. "I'm at the last location on my list."

"Is anyone there?"

Leaning against the door, he twisted the can back and forth on top of the cooler. "I don't know yet, it's a long walk to get up there."

"Middle of a bush?"

Jesse nodded his head slowly, "yeah, on top of a mountain I'm guessing."

"I'm jealous," Devin said in a quiet tone.

"Don't be. I have to do it on two feet."

"Oh, well, not as envious now." He cleared his throat. "I talked to Dad about the last location."

Jesse gave the bottom of his jaw a vigorous rub. A shave was long overdue. "What was the decision?" His last stop had in fact found a long-lost clan of lynx shifters, unfortunately, due to isolation and no communication the clan had more or less died off. There had been six almost geriatric shifters remaining.

"He's going to offer to move them to live among another lynx clan."

Jesse shrugged, "elder knowledge is always welcome."

"That's his take too."

"You know we need to start getting like clans together more or there's going to be a lot going extinct."

"Easier said than done with that Tomas lunatic lurking around every corner." There was a low growl in his voice.

Jesse understood why, Devin's mate had been engaged to

Aiden Tomas, without ever knowing what he was all about. Then again at that point, she hadn't even known about shifters. He didn't know how that was possible when you were one, but this year had been enlightening in so for many, himself included.

"What kind are you looking for now?" Devin mumbled something, "I have so many papers on this desk now I can't find anything."

Jesse swallowed the laugh, not wanting to offend the future leader, who was still adjusting to going from being in hiding to the most active in the Alliance. "*My* kind." He grinned.

"That's good, I saw bears on the list," there were papers rustling, "wherever it is and was worried if we should send like or at least similar-sized Alliance reps to look."

Jesse took another quick sip. "That's a thought." He'd never actually seen a bear shifter after they'd shifted and was sure he could go without ever having to, never mind walking into their area and saying 'hey, Alliance sent me, sorry we lost you' to a clan of much larger shifters than himself.

"How long do you figure you'll be?"

Picking up the can, he closed the door and walked to the front of the van. "Well, as long as this path leads to their area, and I don't have to go searching I should connect with them."

"Great. Dad wants you at Blair's when they're working on weapons training."

"Do we have definite locations now?" Jesse felt like he was out of the loop and that annoyed him. He'd seen the damage Aiden Tomas was doing to his kind and had vowed he would not stop until that organization was stopped.

"We have several. Including the location of Blair's brother."

"Oh shit," Jesse smirked. "I'll get back as soon as I can so we can start coming up with a plan. Is Calum sticking around Blair's for now?"

"Yeah, he's refusing to go anywhere until they figure out how Tomas' people got on the property and basically walked off."

"What?" He'd missed a lot in a few days. "Put a leash on

him and Blair, until I get there."

Devin chuckled, "Blair is newly mated, so he's distracted enough."

"He's one brave SOB. Taking on a whole clan of women." Jesse set the drink on the hood of the van and went over and opened the door, reaching in he grabbed his run pack.

There were voices in the background. "Call me once you've found that clan's area and let me know what you find, and Jesse?"

"Yeah?"

"Try to find some that don't need canes, it will be easier for them to walk down the mountain."

Jesse sighed, "let's hope I do."

Devin hung up without notice. Looking at the phone, he checked for any messages. There was none, that was rare, but he'd take it. Stuffing the phone into his pack, he put it over his head and flipped it to his back so he wouldn't get hung up on any branches as he walked. He debated if he should grab the handgun under his seat and add it to the pack. Shrugging it off, he decided not. That was for moments when he couldn't shift and haul ass.

He realized he hadn't asked if a decision had been made about moving smaller clans. Half of the clan reps were for it though, and he agreed with them. Moving clans that were less than twenty to either another clan of the same likeness or closer to any clan would make security easier seemed like a solid plan. When he'd spoken to Zain earlier, inquiring about how the rest of the clan co-ordinating team were doing, the news hadn't been promising. Clans were disappearing and Jesse was willing to bet Tomas was responsible for all of it.

Downing the rest of the drink, he tossed the can in the van and closed the door. Inhaling slowly, he started up the rough trail. This was going to be a long walk.

About Jacqueline Paige

I am a multi-published author of 'all things paranormal'. My book list proves this is my niche with my stories of witches, ghosts, psychics, shifters, and more now on the shelves. My current genres are paranormal romance, paranormal fantasy, and paranormal romantic suspense.
My books are available in many formats around the globe, including book/reading apps. Since adding them during the pandemic, my books have had over a million reads and my 'to be written' list is growing longer each day. I can't write fast enough.

I began my writing career in 2006 (as a joke) and my first book was published in 2009. I haven't stopped since then. I am an avid reader and will read 'anything with words', whether it's a novel, article, or even every sign I pass.

I live in Ontario, Canada in a small town that's part of the popular Georgian Triangle area. Even though I can see the mountains, I do not ski.

When I'm not in one of my writing worlds, I spend time with my grand-monsters. I have nine of them (so far) and I look forward to corrupting them in the years to come.
Jacqueline also writes under the pseudonym of J. Risk

Jacqueline loves to hear from her readers, you can find her at

http://jacquelinepaige.com/

Author note:

Did you enjoy reading one of my books?

If so, PLEASE help spread the word on social media. You can help by sharing on Facebook, tweet about it, post something on Instagram, Pinterest. Posting a review on your favorite book sites go a long way to help authors. With your help in keeping my books "out there", I can continue writing to keep those stories coming.

Writing and promoting can be very time consuming. I love talking to readers, but the hours spent on keeping so many social media outlets current can become overwhelming and time for writing pays the price. If you can take a few minutes to help, that would be awesome. Thank you!

www.ingramcontent.com/pod-product-compliance
Lightning Source LLC
Chambersburg PA
CBHW032219050726
47591CB00001B/192